THE LEGEND OF THE BAWDSEY BOYS

The Legend Of The Bawdsey Boys

J.D. MISSEN

This is a work of fiction. Names, characters, places, and incidents either are the product of the author's imagination or are used fictitiously.

Published 2025 by Carrot Press
Book cover and image design by Carrot Publishing

ISBN: 978-1-917767-002 (paperback)
ISBN: 978-1-917767-019 (ebook)

In memory of all those who have given their lives
for the freedom of others.

Other Books By The Author

Fiction
Confessions From A Fractured Mind

Detective Inspector Morgan Mystery Series
Secrets From A Misty River
The Evil Within Us All

Poetry
Love, Death and Madness

Children's
The Little Spider
The Little Mole

Prologue

I have never known darkness like it; a thick wall of impenetrable gloom that despite the brightness of the full moon reflecting on the North Sea, barely allows me to see well enough to put one foot in front of another. The sound of my heavy boots sinking into shingle tells me that I am no longer on the soft salty sand but have reached the bank of stones that separate the shoreline from the rock face. I pause to catch my breath, which is still laboured from my earlier exertion and watch as each ghostly exhalation floats away into the darkness then disappears. It is chilly despite the intense heat of the day and even though sweat is pouring down the small of my back, I cannot stop shivering. The beach is so eerily quiet that I am almost afraid to keep going but I must, for this is not the time to lose courage, not after what I have just done. Fleetingly I allow my mind to slip back to what has just passed and my heart thuds faster at the recollection. How did it all go so wrong?

A soft noise coming from somewhere behind stirs me from my thoughts. Someone else is here, treading lightly over the sand dunes of Shingle Street. I am no longer alone. Squinting to see more clearly through the gloom, I spot a large crop of beach grass close to the base of the cliff. Stealthily I traverse the shingle then crouch down behind the foliage. Only a few feet away, the shadow passes by the place where I was standing only moments ago. The figure stops and looks around, as if searching for something they have lost. They are looking for me. I desperately want to stay here, hiding behind the tall grasses until the dan-

ger passes but I cannot, however much I wish to. It will soon be dawn and I need to finish what I have started.

I wait for the shadow to move past me, then I double back on myself and creep onwards towards the pillbox. Hurriedly I lay out the explosives, placing them equidistance from each other at the bottom of the cliff then reel out the wire until I am a safe distance away. There is no time to lose, I must do this quickly before the shadow returns. Before they discover what I have done. I push down hard on the handle and wait for the explosion to deafen me, just as I have been taught will happen, all those months ago when I was assigned extra training that the others were not given.

For a moment nothing happens and I run through my mind the actions I have just taken, checking that I correctly followed all the steps. Then my fleeting doubt is replaced by a deafening sound that rips through the tiny hamlet that until now has been as silent as the dead. The force of the blast shatters the fragile sandstone surface of the cliff face, triggering a rockfall that rains down onto the concrete pillbox below, burying everything in its path. Hiding what I have done.

When the shuddering blast finally abates, silence once more fills the void that has been left behind and I am paralysed by the enormity of what has just happened. I cannot move from the sand dune that I am crouching behind, my body is frozen, as is my mind. Then through the quietness, I hear a familiar noise becoming louder. It is the sound of boots crunching over the coastal pebbles. The shadow is returning, no doubt attracted by the noise of the fireball ripping through the blackened skies. The footsteps are drawing closer to me now. Time is running out.

~ One ~

Detective Inspector James Morgan has always loved intense hot summer days and balmy evenings, sitting in the garden with a cold beer or walking along the beach just as the sun is setting. It is his favourite time of the year and always puts him in a jovial mood, well, usually. Today however is an exception, today is not a good day for the Suffolk detective.

On this particular summers' day, Detective Inspector Morgan and Detective Constable Fallow are being sent on a team-building course at Bawdsey Hall. Not everyone in the Serious Crime team gets to go on this course, particularly given the constraints of Deben Quay Police Forces' meagre training budget that seems to be diminishing every year. This course is only reserved for those officers who Chief Superintendent Bennett has decided are in sore need of learning how to work as part of a team.

A wall of hot air hits Morgan as he steps down from the minibus, landing both feet onto the gravel driveway that sweeps up towards the red brick building, which dominates the small hamlet of Bawdsey. Morgan sighs theatrically as he looks up at the imposing building, which he recalls from school history lessons was used for radar development in the Second World War. It is not his fault that his line manager and closest friend DCI Tom Cook is unable to tell when he is joking. It is also not his fault that the youngest member of the squad, who also happens to be Chief Superintendent Bennett's nephew, cannot take a bit of ribbing by his teammates. And it is definitely not his fault that his wife is now not speaking to him, having had to give up their long-awaited holiday to Italy, so that he can attend the three-day course. Morgan does not know who is to blame for this situation but it is certainly not him and he has already decided before even stepping foot in the building that it will be a complete and utter waste of his time.

The sound of footsteps crunching across gravel diverts Morgans attention from his thoughts of the holiday that DCI Tom Cook and his wife are now enjoying instead of him and Celia. The detective stops gazing up at the imposing building and instead looks across the driveway to see a tall, slender woman striding towards him with a hand outstretched to shake his.

'Hallo, I'm Jane Stokes, pleased to meet you.'

'DI Morgan,' Morgan says gruffly, still peeved at the thought of having to spend the next three days with the one member of his team that he really cannot stand.

Jane Stokes smiles knowingly at Morgan, instantly recognising the detective's ambivalence at being forced to attend the course. 'Welcome to Bawdsey Hall. I hope you enjoy your stay here, I'm sure you'll find the course to be very interesting. It does also help being in such a beautiful environment, the sea is just the other side of the house and the River Deben that separates Bawdsey from Felixstowe, is only a few feet away. It's a great place to learn.'

Morgan manages to produce a tight-lipped smile then looks over the woman's shoulder at the vista beyond. He can just make out the glint of the tidal river behind a crop of rocks that separates the garden from the small strip of man-made beach.

The sound of a minibus door being slammed shut prompts the detective to turn his attention away from the river and back to the driveway again. Morgan tries to suppress a chuckle as he watches Fallow struggling over the pea-shingle with a large suitcase in tow. Morgan of course has very sensibly only brought with him a roll bag and cannot imagine why the younger detective has felt the need to bring so much with him on a work outing.

'Do you need a hand with that?' Morgan asks, feeling the need to appear chivalrous in front of Jane Stokes, who is the administrator and event coordinator for Bawdsey Hall.

'I'm ok thanks,' Fallow replies, dragging the suitcase behind him, which leaves a thin trail in the stones.

'Welcome to Bawdsey Hall,' Jane Stokes calls out to Fallow as he approaches.

'Thank you. It's a beautiful building, I'm looking forward to finding out more about the history of it.'

'Ah well you've come to the right place then,' Jane Stokes replies. 'There's lots of information about the building and surrounding area inside the house. We also have a small museum that's open to the public over the summer months.'

'Excellent,' Fallow replies, a broad smile replacing the earlier scowl.

Morgan rolls his eyes in annoyance at the younger officer's enthusiasm, then picks up his bag and saunters past Fallow to reach the front door first. Morgan holds the heavy oak door open for Jane Stokes to pass through then allows it to shut with a heavy clang.

'I think we forgot about your colleague,' Jane Stokes says, smiling at Morgan, instantly understanding why the two detectives have been assigned to the course.

'Oh yes, I'll get the door for Fallow,' Morgan mutters as he pads across the tiled hallway to open the door for the younger officer, who is now pulling the heavy suitcase up the stone steps.

'Right, now you're both here, I need to ask you to sign a set of rules that must be followed during your stay here.'

'You're joking?' Morgan snorts.

'No, I'm not. Not only are you staying in a valuable, historic house that's right next to a sea with strong currents but you're taking part in this course because your line manager thinks you need help with working as part of a team. So no, I'm not joking,' Jane responds.

Morgan bristles but does not reply. Even though he has only just arrived, he already seems to have managed to upset the course coordinator.

'Am I late?' A voice says from the entrance porch. The trio have been so focused on their conversation that they have not noticed the arrival of another course attendee. 'DC Max Foster,' the man says, smiling at Fallow, Morgan and Jane Stokes in turn.

'Welcome to Bawdsey Hall,' Jane Stokes beams.

Morgan rolls his eyes again, the administrator clearly says the same thing to everyone. 'Where can we put our bags?'

'I'll just get the keys for the rooms. You've all got separate rooms so no need to fight over which bed you have.'

'That's really funny,' says Max Foster, throwing his head back and laughing loudly. 'I'm going to like it here.'

'I'm DC Fallow,' Fallow says, stretching his hand out to shake Foster's.

'Nice to meet you mate. So, why'd you get sent here then? What you done that's so bad?' Fosters guffaws.

'Nothing,' Fallow responds meekly, looking at Morgan who has one foot on the bottom step of the ornate staircase, waiting to go up it.

'Oh, right mate, I get yer,' Foster says, following Fallow's gaze.

'Right then, let's get you all settled in,' Jane Stokes says, breaking the uncomfortable silence. 'Follow me everyone.'

Jane sashays past Morgan to walk up the staircase first, her slender hand caressing the oak banister that has been lovingly polished for over a hundred years. She elegantly makes her way across the landing and unlocks the door furthest from the stairs.

'Detective Inspector Morgan, you're in this one,' Jane says, handing a key to Morgan.

Morgan steps inside the room, which would have been the master bedroom when the house was a family home. The room is dominated by an enormous bay window that looks out over the North Sea and a smaller window with a view of the River Deben that meanders its way to the town of Deben Quay, where both Morgan and Fallow live.

'DC Fallow, you're in here,' Jane says, opening the door to the room next to Morgan's. 'There are interconnecting doors between the two rooms but they're locked and the key's been lost, so no opportunity for secret midnight feasts I'm afraid.'

'Not much chance of that,' Morgan grumbles to himself, though loud enough for everyone else to hear.

'Last of all is DC Foster of course,' Jane says, unlocking the door to a small room at the top of the stairs.

'Looks great thanks,' Foster replies, craning his neck into the room. He strides through the doorway and throws his small suitcase onto the single bed, then moves across the room to gaze out of the window that overlooks the tidal river.

'Well, I'll leave you all to settle in and will see you all again downstairs in the dining room later. Dinner will be at 7pm.

'When does the training start?' Fallow asks, still standing on the landing holding onto his suitcase.

'9 AM tomorrow morning,' Jane says warmly. 'So, you can all relax this evening and get to know each other. There are some books laid out in the sitting room about the house and its role in the second world war, if you're interested.'

Fallow smiles at Jane Stokes then waits politely for her to leave before heading towards the room that has been allocated to him. He stands on the landing for a moment to drink in the ornate architrave, picture rails and deep skirting boards that caress the historic building then steps inside his bedroom, shutting the door behind him.

Two

The dining room was once used as the Bawdsey family's formal drawing room and would have been reserved only for use by the most revered guests. The large room is located at the back of the building, overlooking the small man-made beach that nestles up to one side of the River Deben.

One wall of the room is almost entirely filled with photographs and maps of Bawdsey Hall and its' surrounding area, providing a very thorough history of the place since it was built over a hundred years ago. In the centre of the wall are a plethora of black and white photographs depicting groups of soldiers and airmen, along with the women who were billeted to the Hall in the Second World War. Fallow, who is engrossed in reading the information printed on rectangular white labels underneath each of the photographs, does not notice when Morgan sidles up to stand next to him.

For a moment Morgan studies Fallow, trying to work out exactly what it is about the young man that irks him. Perhaps it is the way that he got this job so easily, whereas Morgan has had to struggle through school and police exams without the patronage of Chief Superintendent Bennett. Or perhaps it's the officers' never-ending diligence and enthusiasm, which is so different from his own attitude. Morgan lets out a quiet sigh, wondering if perhaps DCI Cook is right and that he has been too harsh on the lad. After all, it can't be easy having Bennett as an uncle or being so different from the other officers.

'Anyone fancy a drink?' Foster says cheerfully as he strides into the room holding a bottle of Merlot and three glasses.

'Where did you get that?' Morgan asks, deciding that perhaps this evening is not going to be as bad as he imagined.

'There's a bar over there,' chuckles Foster, setting the bottle down onto the table next to Morgan. 'Fallow, do you want a glass?'

Fallow turns around, realising it seems for the first time that he is no longer on his own. 'Thanks, just a small one.'

Morgan raises an eyebrow, he has never known Fallow to drink alcohol before. Perhaps the lad is feeling out of place, Morgan deduces as he picks up one of the now filled glasses. 'Thanks. Sorry I've forgotten your name.'

'It's Max.'

'Cheers then Max, let's have a toast to a pleasant evening and getting through this bloody course as quickly and as painlessly as possible,' Morgan says, raising his glass.

'Sounds good to me mate. So why have you two been forced to come on this course?' Foster asks, taking a sip of the fruity liquid.

'Apparently we need to learn how to work better as a team.' Morgan grimaces before gulping down half of his wine.

'What about yourself?' Fallow asks, picking up the one remaining filled glass from the table.

Foster chuckles, 'Mate, you know how it is. If you're different they don't like you, it's as simple as that. See this face here, it's different. You know it, I know it. The face doesn't fit and they don't like you, it's as simple as that.'

'Yes, I understand that one all too well,' Fallow responds, looking sideways at Morgan, who has just finished emptying the rest of the contents of his glass down his throat.

'Any more wine left?' Morgan asks, placing his now empty glass down onto the table.

'Just a bit mate, might want to save it for dinner though,' Foster says diplomatically. The tension between Fallow and Morgan is obvious and he does not want to get stuck in the middle, if it all kicks off after one too many drinks.

'Dinner's ready,' Jane Stokes announces, standing in the doorway to the kitchen, which is located on the other side of the bar. 'I'll take you all to your table. I see that DC Foster has already managed to find his way to the bar.'

Foster smirks then picks up the almost empty wine bottle to take to the table.

'Please follow me,' Jane says, looking back at her entourage to ensure that they are following her.

The three detectives follow Jane across the room towards the French doors that look out onto a veranda. Two of the tables are already occupied by other course attendees who they have yet to meet. Morgan sits down at one of the unoccupied tables nearest to the bar, with Fallow and Foster following closely behind. Morgan picks up the almost empty bottle of wine and is just about to ask his host if they can have another one, when a tall man walks into the room.

'Ah Bobby, would you like to join these gentlemen?' Jane suggests, turning to look at the three detectives. 'This is Bobby Chalnor, who's taking the training course.'

'It's nice to meet you all, I hope you're settling in well. We're going to have a busy three days so make the most of relaxing this evening.'

Morgan waves the empty bottle of Merlot in front of Jane Stokes. 'Any chance of another glass of wine then, seeing as we'll be so busy after tonight?'

'Yes of course,' Jane says, taking the empty bottle from Morgans outstretched hand. She leaves the men to talk amongst themselves whilst she retrieves another bottle from the bar and places it onto the centre of the table. 'I hope you've all had the chance to read through the training notes that were emailed to you?'

An instant hush falls across the room that rapidly falls into an uncomfortable silence. 'I'm guessing that's a "no" then,' Jane says, rolling her eyes.

The chatter resumes at the two tables closest to the French doors, which are fully open to allow in a gentle breeze that tussles the net curtains pushed back into the corners of the room. On the other side of the door is a small veranda, which overlooks a neat lawn and beyond that, the river glints as it is bathed in light from the setting sun. Morgan strides over to the occupied tables to take a closer look at the view through the door. The occupants of the table nearest to him, turn to look at the stranger with unveiled curiosity.

'Hallo, I'm Detective Inspector James Morgan. Are you all here for the training course?'

'We certainly are,' replies the woman sitting closest to the French doors. 'I seem to be the only person here though who has actually read the course notes in advance. I do hope that it won't disadvantage the rest of you.'

'I'm sure it won't,' Morgan says smoothly, trying to read the name badge on the woman's thin blue cardigan.

'Camilla Fields,' the woman informs, as if reading Morgan's thoughts. She stretches her hand out to shake Morgan's.

'Nice to meet you all,' Morgan replies. 'If you'll excuse me though I have a nice bottle of red that is awaiting my attention.'

The occupants of the two tables resume their conversations as Morgan returns to his seat, where he discovers that Fallow has ordered a bottle of tap water and that Foster and Bobby Chalnor have each acquired a pint of Suffolk ale.

'Might as well make the most of sampling the local produce,' Foster says cheekily as he sips the golden liquid.

Fallow pours water out into each of the four empty glasses on the table then sits back down with a heavy sigh. It is clearly going to be a long evening and not one that he is likely to enjoy.

'So, what's the plan for tomorrow?' Morgan asks, looking at the bowl of soup that has just been placed in front of him.

'The idea is to get you all to work as a team, so you'll all be put into groups, then you'll be set a task to solve,' Bobby Chalnor explains.

'Sounds interesting,' Fallow says in earnest.

'Thrilling,' Morgan mumbles as he picks up a bread roll then uses his knife to scoop up some butter from a ceramic dish in the centre of the table.

'I'm sure you'll all enjoy it,' Bobby Chalnor assures before taking a mouthful of the thin spring vegetable soup. 'As it happens, the task is based on something that occurred here a long time ago, well, allegedly. It'll be your job to find out what really happened.'

'How will we do that?' Foster asks, putting his spoon down into the now empty soup bowl.

'You'll do what you normally do when you investigate if a crime has been committed,' Bobby replies smoothly.

'But how? If it was a long time ago, there won't be anyone to interview?' Fallow asks, a confused look spreading across his face.

'Ah well that's where you're wrong, there's plenty of evidence and in any case, it just so happens that several members of staff here at Bawdsey Hall are descendants of people who were here at the time of the alleged incident and stories often get passed on down through the generations.'

'So, we'll be working together to solve a mystery?' asks Fallow.

'Sure, that's right. As I said earlier, it will be an interesting task,' Bobby replies. 'If you want to know more about it then you can either wait until tomorrow morning or read through the course notes that Jane emailed to you. I'd like to finish eating my meal in peace now, if you don't mind.'

Morgan tilts his head to one side. This is not what he was expecting, the task actually sounds as if it might be interesting. Of course, it won't make up for the fact that he should be sitting in a café in Italy with his wife testing out the local produce but perhaps it might be a little less onerous than he had imagined.

The main course of roast beef arrives and is eaten ravenously by all, followed by a raspberry cheesecake and filter coffee that is accompanied by small chocolates that were made in nearby Orford.

'I think I'll take my coffee onto the veranda,' Morgan says, glancing in the direction of the open door.

'Good idea,' Bobby Chalnor says, pushing back his chair. 'If anyone wants to get a head start on the course though, then I'd recommend taking a look at that wall display, there's a lot of information on there.'

Foster immediately stands up and strides across the room to look at the photographs that Fallow was looking at earlier. Bobby Chalnor quickly joins the detective, eager to share his enthusiasm of the Hall's history.

A few minutes later, Bobby Chalnor returns to the table, 'I'm going to get an early night, so I'll see you all tomorrow morning.'

'Good night,' says Fallow. 'I'm going to do the same soon.'

Morgan looks at Foster, who has also returned to the table. 'What about you Max?'

'I think I'll get an early night as well,' Foster replies, looking at the people on the other tables, who are still engrossed in conversation and seemingly unaware that some of their fellow attendees have already finished eating.

'Well, good night,' Morgan says, picking up his coffee and padding across the room towards the French doors. He steps out into the garden where a number of tables and chairs have been set out and finds one that is still warm from the setting sun. Morgan sits down, legs stretched out towards the river, which is as calm as a millpond and looks almost inviting despite its' murky greyness.

As the sun finally sinks down behind the row of poplar trees that line the edge of the estate, Morgan begins to feel a little more relaxed about the days to come. It is such a beautiful setting that he is certain his time here will be pleasant despite his initial reluctance. At this point in time, Morgan has no idea how wrong he is.

~ Three ~

It is not often that Morgan goes for an early morning walk but the quiet ambience and scenic vista seem to be calling to him as soon as he is awoken by the sun filtering through the venetian blinds.

The building is quiet except for the clattering of plates being washed up in the kitchen and the whir of the extractor fan over the hob where eggs and bacon are being fried ready to be kept warm for the course attendees' breakfast. Morgan creeps through the hallway as if not wanting to awaken anyone else, then pads through what used to be the servant's quarters, where he knows there is a side door that leads out into the garden. He pushes open the partially glazed door and is immediately greeted by a delicate overture from the blackbirds in the conifers and poplars at the edge of the estate, accompanied by the soft cawing of seagulls as they dive over the nearby rocks.

Despite the early hour, it is already warm and Morgan is glad he had the foresight to leave his jumper back in his bedroom. His trainers sink into soft earth, which quickly gives way to sand as he reaches the thin strip of beach that was made for the family who once occupied the Hall.

The sand is pristine, with any footprints that might have been made during the previous day now washed away. Morgan's own footsteps leave a fresh trail behind him as he traverses the shoreline to reach a cluster of rocks at the water's edge. The detective perches on one of the larger rocks that is covered in green algae and bladder-wrack then gazes into the shallow pool below, containing a starfish and two crabs that have been left behind by the previous night's receding tide.

Morgan jumps down onto the lower rocky ledge to take a closer look at the rockpool and immediately sees something lying on the sand between the rocks that should not be there. Carefully he manoeuvres towards the edge of a narrow ledge, then crouches down to take a closer look at the object; it is a pair of men's brogues.

'That's odd,' Morgan says aloud to himself with only the nearby gulls to hear his words. He reaches down to pick up the dark brown shoes then turns them over in his hands, looking at them as if somehow they might reveal to him the mystery of how they got to be there. Morgan is still pondering on the mystery when he hears the sound of a bell ringing from the Hall, announcing that it is time for breakfast.

Morgan leaps down onto the sand and heads straight towards the dining room. It is only when he reaches the building that the detective realises he is still holding the shoes. Morgan stops to put the shoes down on the floor of the veranda then squeezes through the French doors to avoid needing to push them further ajar.

'Good morning Detective Inspector. Did you have a restful night?' Jane asks as she is strides into the dining room carrying a silver-plated coffee jug.

'I did thank you, the sound of the sea is very relaxing,' Morgan says smoothly.

'That's good to hear. I shall go and find Maisie and see if breakfast is ready to be served,' Jane replies, marching across the room towards the door on the other side of the bar that leads into the kitchen.

In the distance, Morgan can hear the soothing sound of waves crashing onto the beach, which reminds him of the rocks that he has just left. In his haste to eat breakfast, Morgan has momentarily forgotten about the shoes. He begins to step towards the kitchen to find Jane to ask her about them, when Foster comes into the room.

'Morgan, you're up bright and early,' Foster says cheerfully, pulling out a chair at the table close to where Morgan is standing. 'Looking forward to the course today?'

'Not really, are you?'

'Same here but it's got to be done, so we just have to get on with it.'

'True. I went for a walk on the beach this morning and saw something a bit odd,' Morgan begins to say.

'Oh right. Hold that thought, it looks like the food's being brought out. I could murder a coffee.'

'Didn't you sleep very well?'

'Not too bad, the bed was a tad lumpy and it was a bit stuffy in my room but I guess that's what happens when you get the smallest one.'

Morgan inwardly grimaces but does not respond to the detective's grumble, reluctant to be drawn into a conversation that involves moaning about room sizes. After all, it is only right that he, as the more senior officer in the group, has the better room.

'I was telling you about what I found this morning,' Morgan continues.

'Yeah right, look there's the coffee coming out. Do you want me to get you one?'

'Sure, thanks.'

'Well, it looks as if the others are starting to filter in now,' Jane says, walking over to the table. 'Please do help yourself to food, there's toast and a wide range of cooked food.'

'Thanks Jane. I'm a bit worried about something I found on the beach this morning.'

'Ok well why don't you come and find me after breakfast. Look there's Detective Constable Fallow, he looks as if he could do with someone to sit with,' Jane says smoothly before ushering the quieter officer to sit at the table with Morgan and Foster.

Morgan smiles thinly at Fallow then walks over to the long table that has been set out near the bar and is laden with a range of food and cold drinks. He can imagine very well how his wife Celia would feel about what is on offer but as she's not here to chastise him, Morgan piles up his plate with greasy bacon, fried eggs and black pudding. He also picks up a small glass of orange juice to appease the slight feeling of guilt that is nagging at him.

Fallow has collected a bowl of cereal accompanied by a large glass of milk and is already half-way through consuming them by the time Morgan returns to the table with his plate of fried food.

'Well, now we are all here, I'll tell you what will be happening today,' Jane says, standing in the centre of the room to address all the course attendees who have now gathered in the dining room.

'Excuse me,' Fallow interjects.

'Yes, DC Fallow, what can I help you with?' Jane asks in a clipped tone, clearly irked at the interruption.

'Mr Chalnor isn't here,' Fallow says, looking around the room to make sure that he has not missed him.

Jane also looks around the room, 'you're right, has anyone seen Mr Chalnor this morning?'

There is a low murmur from the attendees, indicating that no one has seen the course trainer.

Suddenly Morgan has an awful thought, 'I was trying to say earlier, I found a pair of shoes on the beach this morning.'

Jane turns to stare at Morgan, her cheeks draining of colour. 'Ok let's not panic, DI Morgan please could you go and check Bobby's room, its number 2, just down the corridor in the servant's quarters. DC's Fallow and Foster, perhaps you could both go down to the beach area and take a look?'

The sound of three chairs scraping on the floor as they are pushed back, cuts through the tense quietness. Everyone else in the room watches transfixed as the detective's spring into action. They all know that if someone is missing and a pair of shoes have been found near the water's edge then there is a real need to be very concerned.

It does not take long for Morgan to locate Bobby Chalnor's room, which is on the ground floor at the back of the building. The servant's quarters are a stark contrast to the more ornate and sumptuous rooms that the course attendees are staying in but are still considered to be far more luxurious than they were in the days when they were occupied by servants.

Morgan tries the handle of the second door that he reaches. The door is unlocked and the detective peers inside the shadowy room, immediately noticing Bobby Chalnors' laptop left open on the narrow bed and an empty glass on the bedside table. A brown leather suitcase that is propped open in the corner of the room, is half-filled with neatly folded clothes. A glass containing a toothbrush and toothpaste occupies one corner of the small desk underneath the window as if awaiting use by its owner. Wherever Bobby Chalnor has disappeared to, it looks as if he planned on returning.

The detective steps across the threshold into the room. He switches on the laptop and his efforts are immediately rewarded when the home screen appears with a prompt for a password. As most people use something obvious that they can remember for their passwords, Morgan tries a few words that he thinks could work but none of them do. He places the laptop back onto the bed and continues to look around the small room.

With a cursory search of the sparsely filled room completed, Morgan returns to the dining room to find that it is now almost empty of its previous occupants. He spots Camilla Fields still seated at the table closest to the doors that lead out into the garden. The regally sat woman is muttering loudly at her perceived ineptitude of the other course attendees, who are searching around the beach and rocky outcrop for any sign of Bobby Chalnor.

Morgan strides across the room to stand next to the elderly woman. 'Any news?' he asks, grateful for the opportunity to benefit from the slightly cooler air that is wafting in through the open door.

'Those fools won't find him.'

'What makes you think that?'

'It's obvious,' Camilla retorts. 'If he's ended up in the water then he'll be long gone, taken far out to sea by last night's high tide and if he's not in the water then there would've been footprints on the beach leading away from the shoes and back towards the Hall. Of course, those idiots have now left their own footprints all over the beach so there's no way of knowing which ones might have been Bobby Chalnors.'

'You're right, though my footprints will also be there and in any case, we need to begin somewhere and the rocks are the obvious place to start,' Morgan responds diplomatically.

Camilla snorts loudly, placing both hands firmly on her knees. 'So, what's the plan of action?'

'I'll organise a search further along the beach towards Shingle Street and also around the Felixstowe peninsula. In the meantime, we need to talk to everyone whose here, staff, guests, everyone.'

'And find out any possible reason for Mr Chalnor going missing of course,' Camilla muses, still looking out towards the beach where Foster and Fallow are standing alongside some of the other course attendees.

'Mrs Fields, perhaps you'd like to assist me in finding out who has been at Bawdsey Hall during the past 24 hours?'

'Yes of course, I'll go and find a notebook and pen then we can get started straight away.'

Morgan watches as Mrs Fields glides across the dining room towards the conference room, where the room has already been set out for today's training session. He wonders what it is that the woman does as a job, she seems to be remarkably astute and could be an excellent asset in finding out what has happened to Bobby Chalnor.

'Are you ready Detective Inspector?' Camilla shouts from the other room.

'Yes ok, I'll go and round up the guests then ask Fallow and Foster to find all the staff. Jane should have a guest list and of course employee records that we can cross check against.'

Morgan steps outside into the warm air, realising for the first time how cold it is in the house. He strides over to the rocky outcrop where he found the pair of shoes earlier. The once quiet, calm ambience is now alive with nervous tension, everyone wondering the same thing – has Bobby Chalnor ended up in the grey, uninviting water and if he hasn't, then where has he gone?

'Have you found anything?' Morgan asks as he approaches Foster and Fallow, who are unsuccessfully trying to keep the other guests from further disturbing the beach.

'Nothing,' Foster replies glumly. They are all thinking the same thing - the course trainer must have ended up going into the water at some point during the night.

'Let's get everyone back in the house, we need to interview them all.'

Fallow strides over to the group who are still standing at the water's edge, peering into the murky water that Bobby Chalnor has seemingly ended up in. 'Please can everyone go back into the building, we need to ask you all some questions.'

One member of the group peels off and slopes back across the lawn to the house, the others meekly following behind.

'Foster, would you mind finding all the staff? I'm not sure how many there are but Jane should know who's here and where to find them,' Morgan instructs. He takes one last look at the grey water then turns around to stride back towards the building. As he walks, Morgan pulls out a mobile phone from his trouser pocket and calls Bawdsey Police Station.

~ Four ~

The tense quietness that descends across the conference room when Morgan appears is rapidly replaced by the course attendees resuming their excited chatter.

'Please quieten down,' Camilla Fields says, putting a finger to her lips to shush the rowdy group.

Morgan inwardly smiles, Camilla is clearly someone who has experience of gaining control over an audience and it is obvious that he could learn a lot from her. He takes the opportunity to study the stout woman, taking in her tweed skirt with matching handbag and the flat, lace up shoes that although smart, inform him that the wearer of them values comfort over style.

'Thank you, Mrs Fields,' Morgan says as he traverses the room to stand next to the whiteboard. 'Let's make a start, shall we?'

A low murmur resonates through the room, providing the group's affirmation that they are now ready to listen.

'So, as you all know, our course trainer Bobby Chalnor seems to have gone missing. I found a pair of brogues on the beach this morning, which we believe could be his but other than that there's no sign of him.'

'Did you find anything in his room?' asks Fallow, who is studiously sitting at the front of the room.

'It looks as if Mr Chalnor was intending on returning, his laptop and clothes are still there.'

'What about his phone?' enquires Foster, who is perching on a table near the window.

'No sign of it but I'd expect him to have it with him,' Morgan replies. 'When was the last time anyone saw Mr Chalnor?'

The group begin to talk amongst themselves, trying to work out who last saw the missing trainer.

'We all saw him in the dining room yesterday evening, did anyone see him after that?' Camilla asks, trying to gain the attention of the group again.

There is a vigorous shaking of heads amongst the group - no one else saw Mr Chalnor after dinner yesterday evening.

'Ok, well I've asked the local police force to come and help look along the coastline this morning and we also need to speak to you all individually.

'What about the staff?' Someone shouts from the back of the room.

'We'll be speaking to them as well....what's your name?'

'Baker, Murray Baker.'

'Ok thank you Mr Baker. Please can I ask everyone to give their names to Mrs Fields, who is going to take notes,' Morgan instructs, looking at Camilla to ensure she is in agreement of the task.

Camilla Fields nods at Morgan then takes a seat at the top table, giving the appearance of being very comfortable with taking charge. 'Thank you, Detective Inspector Morgan. Please could everyone form an orderly queue, I will be taking down your details then DC Fallow will question you all.'

'What are you going to be doing then DI Morgan?' A heckle comes from someone close to the window at the back of the room.

'I'll be coordinating the search of the beach area,' Morgan replies smoothly. 'DC Foster, please could you go and talk to the staff, Jane has a list of who they are and where you're likely to find them.'

'It's here,' Jane responds as she enters the room, holding out a sheet of paper for Morgan to take hold.

'Thank you, so now we all know what we're doing, so let's get on with it. The sooner we find Mr Chalnor, the better,' Morgan explains, stepping across the room towards the door that leads out into the hallway. He makes his way to the front door, where a group of local police officers are waiting for him.

'Right then, let's make a start,' Morgan instructs. 'I suggest we begin from the place where I found the shoes this morning and then make our way up the coast towards Shingle Street.'

A murmur of agreement echoes through the hallway, then the group of officers make their way down the wide steps that lead onto the driveway. They walk in silence around the perimeter of the house, observing everything that they pass then continue onwards to the rocky out-crop where Morgan found the shoes earlier that morning.

The sun is now much higher in the sky and is fiercely beating down on Morgan as he strides over the narrow strip of shingle and onto the beach. After checking that the other officers are still following him, he then turns towards the rock pool that has now dried up.

'This is where I found a pair of shoes this morning, just over there near that flat ledge,' Morgan explains, pointing towards one of the rocks.

'What time was that?' PC Steve Dodds asks as he peers over the top of a large boulder so that he can see the exact location where the shoes were found.

'It was about 6.30am.'

'When was the last time anyone saw Mr Chalnor?' PC Terry Smith says, looking out across the river towards Felixstowe.

'It was at dinner last night. He left the dining room to go to his room about 8.30pm,' Morgan replies.

'That's not good, he's been gone quite a while then,' PC Jim Mason declares, placing a foot on one of the larger rocks. The local officer tilts his head to one side and chews on his bottom lip as he stares at the plethora of small boats littered across the channel. 'Could the tide have taken him out that way?'

Morgan gazes thoughtfully at the tidal river and then at the foreboding North Sea beyond. 'The currents are very strong in the river just here according to the Hall's administrator, Jane Stokes. She thought that if Mr Chalnor did enter the water last night that he would've been take out to sea rather than across the river to Felixstowe. Ok, I think it's time we made a start on searching the area. I suggest we walk in a line one foot apart and sweep up the coast, that way we shouldn't miss anything. Let's get going before it gets any hotter than it already is.'

It takes a little over an hour for the four officers to walk up the coastline towards Shingle Street. Morgan is glad he had the foresight to bring bottles of water with them as they now seem to be in the midst of the long-awaited heatwave and it appears that there is nowhere to access any drinking water along the beach.

The group walk on in silence, accompanied by the crunching of heavy boots through dry shingle and the intermittent caws of seagulls that are heading inland to escape an incoming storm. Even Morgan, who is dressed in clothes fit for a training course rather than work, is perspiring heavily from the humidity that seems to be worsening with every hour that passes. He stops to sit down on one of the wooden groynes that pepper the beach then takes out the bottles of water from his rucksack.

'Here, have one,' Morgan says, passing a bottle to each of the officers, who are red faced from trudging through the low-lying sand that is still claggy from last night's high tide.

'What's that over there?' asks Mason, taking a break from greedily swigging down the much-needed water.

From where he is perched on an algae covered groyne, Morgan cannot see what it is the officer is looking at. He stands up and walks in the direction that PC Mason is pointing in and immediately notices there has been a recent landslip from the cliff that towers above the beach; a frequent occurrence on this coastline and one that is seemingly worsening because of climate change.

'I can't see anything other than a landslide,' Morgan grumbles as he peers at the top of the cliff, a hand cupped over his forehead to block out the worst of the suns glare.

'Down on the beach, just beneath where that landslip is, it looks like something concrete,' Smith says, walking over a stone bank towards the bottom of the cliff.

Morgan strides across the shingle to take a closer look at the object, which appears to be a mangle of concrete and rusty metal sticking out from the displaced sandstone. 'It looks like an old pillbox,' Morgan replies, squinting at the object to try to make sense of it.

'There were loads of them built on this stretch of the coast during the Second World War,' Smith informs as he sidles up next to Morgan. 'Most of them have gone into the sea now though. I don't remember this one being here before.'

'I can see footprints in the sand leading up to it,' Dodds exclaims, also shielding his eyes from the glaring sun.

'Are you sure?' Morgan asks, puzzled as to why he cannot see what the others are looking at. 'Anyway, it's a public beach, there's bound to be footsteps all over the place.'

'These are barefoot,' Dodds continues, making his way across the sand to take a closer look.

Morgan narrows his eyes to get a better view of the footprints that are almost hidden by the dense shadow being cast from the cliff face towering above them. As his eyes adjust to the low level of light at the bottom of the cliff, he finally spots a feint indentation in the sand, leading towards the pillbox.

'You're right, they're footprints though I can't imagine that Bobby Chalnor would have walked all this way from Bawdsey Hall with bare feet to look at an old pillbox,' Morgan chides with more than a hint of sarcasm.

'He might have if he knew what was in that pillbox,' Smith says quietly, his face no longer red from the morning's exertion but now with a pasty appearance.

'What's in there then?' Morgan responds impatiently, keen to resume walking again.

'You'd better come and look for yourself,' replies Dodds, who is kneeling down next to PC Smith to gain a better view of the inside of the concrete structure.

Morgan sighs loudly then strides over a sand dune that is peppered with beach grasses. He crouches down next to Dodds and Smith so that he too can peer into the dark chasm inside the pillbox.

It takes a moment for Morgan's vision to adjust to the change in light levels again. He blinks away the soreness in his eyes caused by the strong UV light reflecting off the sea and the minuscule grains of sand that keep being blown into his face by the North wind. Then he sees it, he sees what the other officers have already seen. Without taking his eyes off the pillbox, Morgan pulls his rucksack off from his shoulder and reaches inside it for his mobile phone.

~ Five ~

The sun is already high above Bawdsey Hall, nestled between the North Sea, the River Deben and the neighbouring Hollesley Farm estate, by the time Detective Constable Foster marches across the estate in search of the outbuildings that once housed the estates Suffolk Punch horses.

For someone who is used to the hustle and bustle of city life, Foster is finding the quietness of the countryside something of a novelty and not one he would wish to experience for too long. Still, even he has to admit that the gentle tweeting of the Linnets and Dunnet's that are busily nesting in a Hawthorn bush close to the workshop entrance, are a pleasing sound.

The entrance to the building seems far too grand for a workshop, decides Foster as he stares up at the structure, though he concedes that there is scant need for the buildings original purpose given that horses have long-since been replaced by heavy machinery. The London detective steps inside the barn and automatically gazes upwards to the green oak rafters that are supporting the cathedral-like gambrel roof. On the dusty floor below are several vintage vehicles covered with plastic tarpaulins to protect them from damage by the salty sea air. The coverings are sufficient to keep them in pristine condition until they are wheeled out each summer and duly presented at the local fair.

'Hallo, is anyone in here?' Foster asks, standing just inside the doorway where he can take advantage of the coolness of the building.

'I'm in the back,' a voice says.

Foster makes his way around a large wooden cart that was once used for transporting hay bales, to find a young woman dressed in greasy overalls and holding a wooden shaft. 'Hello, sorry to disturb you, I'm Detective Constable Foster.'

'Hi, I'm Britany, I'm doing an engineering apprenticeship at the local university. I've got a summer placement here so I can learn about vintage vehicles. Are you here for a training course?'

'I am but the trainer Bobby Chalnor has gone missing. Do you know him?'

'I've met him once or twice I think. When did he go missing?'

'We think it was sometime late yesterday evening or during the night. When did you last see him?'

'Not for a while, maybe last week? I don't go up to the house very often and he'd never come down here, he's not the type that likes to get dirty.'

'Ok thanks, do you know where the gardener's cottage is? Jane Stokes said that it's not far from here.'

'Sure, just follow the path at the back of the barn, it leads to a couple of cottages, the gardener's one is on the left.'

'Thanks, hope you learn lots from being here,' Foster says smoothly before stepping back out into the sunshine again.

Foster finds the path easily, though he might not have spotted it if he hadn't known about its location as it is partially hidden by a tangle of overgrown shrubs and weeds. At the end of the path there are two cottages that look as if they date from the 19th century and were doubtless once used by the plethora of staff who supported the Hall. Now staffing numbers have dwindled down to a kitchen hand, gardener and Jane Stokes, who oversees practically every part of running the building and its' grounds.

As Foster ambles along the path towards the front door of the cottage, he ponders as to why anyone would want to work in such an isolated place before concluding that perhaps the opportunity to live rent free in an historic building would be an attraction for some people. Not for him though, born and raised in London, surrounded by constant noise and the comforting knowledge that a neighbour is nearby, however unfriendly they might be.

As there is no doorbell on the cottage door, Foster raps loudly on the wooden door frame. The oak door is low and clearly not been built for someone as tall as Foster, who is 6 foot 2. The detective waits for a few moments to see if the door might open, though it appears to be un-occupied. When his meagre patience has depleted, Foster turns around to leave. As he does so, he catches sight of something in the corner of his vision, a movement in the adjoining cottage. Curious, Foster knocks on the door, which slowly opens to reveal behind it an elderly man, who looks to be about 90 years old.

'What do you want?'

'Sorry to disturb you Sir but I'm looking for the gardener. Do you happen to know where he is?'

'My grandson's not here, he's probably repairing the fence in the lower field, there's been a landslip there.'

'Thank you, I'm sorry again for disturbing you,' Foster says, retreating back up the path again.

Foster follows the path back to the barn then takes a left turn towards the lower field, close to the cliff edge that runs along the east perimeter of the estate. He immediately spots the landslip mentioned by the elderly man and a little further on, the broken fence that is now in the process of being fixed.

'Hello,' Foster shouts as he approaches someone who he assumes to be the estate gardener.

The man puts down the length of wood that he is using to fix the broken fence and strides towards the detective. 'Hello, are you looking for the Hall?'

'Actually, I'm looking for you. You are the gardener for Bawdsey Hall?'

'Gardener, carpenter, brick layer and anything else you can think of. I'm Reece by the way.'

'DC Foster. Have you worked here long?'

'Since I was a young lad, my grandad was the head gardener here, so I was brought up on the estate, know it like the back of my hand.'

'I imagine you must know it well and the people who work here. Do you know Mr Chalnor?'

'Not very well, he's not been here long.'

'What about the other staff?'

'Maisie who runs the kitchen has been here for years but that Jane Stokes has only been here a few months, she seems ok.'

Foster nods thoughtfully, 'have you heard that Mr Chalnor has gone missing?'

'Missing? What like disappeared?'

'It would seem so, he's not been seen since last night. When was the last time you saw him?'

'Let me have a think. Well, actually it was last night when I walked along the beach at sunset, which I do most nights.'

'Where was he?'

'Not far from the Hall, he was standing near the rocks looking out across the river, looking very thoughtful.'

'Did you see anyone else?'

'I don't think so, we get the odd bird watcher and kids looking for fossils on the beach but that's about it really.'

Thanks, well if you think of anything else, please let me know, I'm staying at the Hall.'

'Will do mate, I'll keep an eye out as well when I'm on the estate, see if there's anything out of place or different.'

'That's great thanks,' Foster says before turning back along the cliff path and walking at pace towards the Hall; the sun is becoming unbearably hot and he will be glad to get back into the coolness of the building again.

Foster finds most of the course attendees still in the conference room when he returns. The detective cranes his head into the room to check if Fallow is still there, then moves towards the dining room to find something cool to drink. He finds an industrial fridge behind the bar and helps himself to a fizzy drink, which he sips as he ambles around the perimeter of the room, looking at the photographs and drawings of the Hall that are on display. There is also an old map, which shows how the hamlet looked in the Second World War, accompanied by a blank and white photo of the beach, dotted with pillboxes, landmines and barbed wire fencing. At least a dozen of the photographs are of the people who were stationed at the Hall during the war as well as a group of local Home Guards who were tasked with patrolling the beaches. Foster reads the information card below one of the photos that informs him that the Hall was used for training radio operators at the start of the war. The corresponding photograph above the label shows a group of young WAAFs, who would have gone on to take part in vital communication work. Nearby is a picture of some US

Airforce airmen and their aircraft, who were stationed at nearby RAF Martlesham.

'Find anything of interest?' Jane Stokes asks as she walks brusquely into the dining room.

'I guess it's all kind of interesting,' Foster says wistfully. 'It must be great to work in such a place, all the history and all that?'

'Yes it is, I'm very fortunate,' Jane replies, looking at the photograph of the young women who trained at the Hall during the war. 'Any news on poor Mr Chalnor?'

'Not yet I'm afraid. We'll find him though, so try not to worry.'

Jane nods thoughtfully, her attention reverting back to the wall display. 'Was your grandad in the war?'

'He was but my Ma doesn't talk much about him, not sure why.'

'Both of my grandparents were stationed here during the war.'

'Well, that's a coincidence, you working here as well.'

'It certainly is. Why don't we go back and join the others, they might be wondering where we've got to.'

'Sure,' Foster says, swigging back the remnants of his drink before putting the empty bottle on the bar. 'I'm sure Fallow will want a break by now.'

'I'm sure he will, perhaps he should go out and get some fresh air, it can get very stuffy in this building.'

Foster takes one last glance at the photographs on the wall then follows the estate administrator back into the conference room.

~ Six ~

Harry Turner whistles quietly to himself as he trudges across the sand dunes, a short walk from the car park where Dr Bootle is still pulling on his protective overalls.

'Hallo Morgan, what have you got for us this time?' Harry asks as he approaches the pillbox where the detective is waiting.

'Well, I'm guessing they're pretty old judging by the state of them and it looks like they're wearing some sort of uniform.'

'Sounds interesting,' Harry exclaims, placing one hand on the top of the concrete structure to steady himself as he crouches down to look inside.

'SOCO are on their way with some shovels, though we might need something bigger than that looking at the amount of sand that's blocking up the doorway. It's amazing how no one's seen this before.'

'The local plods think it's been uncovered by the land slip. The pillbox is definitely from WW2 but what we don't know of course is if the people inside it are as old as that. I wonder how it ended up being covered up?' Morgan says wistfully, standing up straight to ease the cramp in his right leg.

'This whole beach was covered in landmines,' Dr Bootle explains loudly as he strides across the beach towards the pillbox. 'We need to be careful, the landslip could have uncovered all sorts, including munitions. Any luck finding your missing man?'

'Not yet, we were looking for him when we found this.'

'Right O', let's take a look then,' Dr Bootle says, kneeling down to peer inside the concrete structure.

Morgan watches as the aging pathologist takes a torch out from his bag then shines it into the dark void, the conical beam momentarily resting on each body in turn. As always, the detective is impressed at how spritely Dr Bootle is - all those rounds of golf he keeps playing must be keeping him fit, Morgan deduces. Perhaps he too should venture onto the golf course, he's starting to get a middle-aged spread and very much doubts he would be able to chase after the nimbler criminals.

'There's three of them, all wearing what looks to be army uniforms. Not my area of expertise though I'm afraid, I'll have to get someone from the local university in on this one,' Dr Bootle states.

'Do you think they date back to the Second World War?' Morgan asks, stepping back a little to allow Dr Bootle to move away from the pillbox.

'I would think so but as I just said, it's not my area of expertise,' Dr Bootle replies tersely. The pathologist turns to look at the incoming tide, which is bringing with it dark clouds that are menacingly rolling in overhead. 'Looks like we're in for a storm.'

'Yes it does. I'll wait for SOCO to retrieve the bodies then I'll head back to Bawdsey Hall and see if there's been any news on Mr Chalnor,' Morgan says, stepping out of the way of PC Smith who has been pushing stakes into the soft sand to fix a cordon around the pillbox.

'Right, well I'll leave you to it. Harry, have you seen enough?' Dr Bootle asks his assistant, who is diligently taking photos and making notes of the findings.

'I'm ready to go,' Harry says cheerfully, shoving his camera and notepad back into his bag.

Morgan watches as the two men make their way over the sand dunes then disappear from view at the exact time that a group of Scenes of Crime Officers arrive.

'It's just over there,' Morgan says, pointing the SOCO team in the direction of the pillbox.

The forensics team work quickly and efficiently, shovelling sand away from the doorway, creating mounds of silt and debris a short distance away from the pillbox. When the route into the building is clear, the officers begin to document and photograph the inside of the pillbox, following strict procedures to ensure they maintain the integrity of any findings. Morgan watches as one of the team crouches down then crawls into the pillbox, quickly followed by a second officer who is carrying a number of body bags.

A low rumble cuts through the tense atmosphere just as the last body is being hauled out of the pillbox. The body bags are then solemnly carried across the sand dunes to the awaiting private ambulance that will take them to Hemley Hospital. Morgan follows the sombre entourage, wondering how long it will take to do the post-mortems - it will not be as straight forward as it usually is given the age of the cadavers. As Morgan stands on the grass verge to watch the ambulance depart, a figure approaches from the other side of the car park.

'I thought I'd wait around in case you need a lift back to Bawdsey Hall,' PC Smith says as he strides across the roughly made surface.

'Thanks, much appreciated,' Morgan replies, looking up at the ever-darkening sky before following the local police officer back to the car that one of the local officers had dropped off earlier along with the stakes and cordon tape.

'I hope your Mr Chalnor has found somewhere to shelter, looks like the storm could be a fierce one,' Smith says, opening the door and clambering in behind the wheel.

'I wish I knew what's happened to him. Of course, we're all assuming the worst because of finding those shoes but really anything could've happened.'

'That's true, though I think if it was something benign, we would've heard by now,' Smith concludes before returning his attention to driving through the narrow road that is winding its way towards Bawdsey Hall.

Before Morgan can respond, his phone bleeps. He looks up to see that the car is now pulling into the gravel driveway of Bawdsey Hall, then he reaches down for his phone from the rucksack, which is lying in the footwell.

Tom

I heard what happened, do you need me to come back?

No don't worry, just enjoy your holiday

Cheers mate, Tom

Morgan sighs, as peeved as he is at missing the holiday, he is also glad that Tom has had the opportunity for a week away with his wife Sarah. With the kids packed off to their grandparents, it is the first time the couple have been able to spend some time alone since they became parents.

'Let me know if there's any news,' Smith says as Morgan opens the door and swings his long legs out of the car.

'Likewise. A search around Felixstowe Ferry was done this morning and the coastguard is going to keep an eye out along the coast there. Apparently the press are going to get onto it as well, get a bit of coverage on the story.'

'Sounds like you've got it all covered. If you need any more help though, just let me know, I only live in Alderton so can be back here again in no time.'

'Thanks, I'm not sure we can do too much more though at the moment. I'm going to have another look at his laptop and see if Fallow and Foster have got anywhere with interviewing the guests and staff. Thanks for the lift,' Morgan says as he slams the car door shut then strides off towards the house without looking back.

As Morgan approaches the front door, he sees a shadow in one of the ground floor rooms at the front of the house. He pushes open the heavy wooden door and steps inside the quiet building, which leaves him wondering where everyone else has gone. The door to the right of the hallway is slightly ajar. Curious to find out what it is that he just saw from the driveway, Morgan peers into the room and immediately catches sight of DC Foster rifling through a filing cabinet.

'What are you doing?'

'Oh my god, you scared me half to death,' Foster says, slamming shut the drawer he was just looking through.

'And you didn't answer my question,' Morgan replies sternly.

'I was just looking for information about the staff.'

'You should know by now that you can't just rifle through personal data without permission.'

'Well, I thought that seeing as it's an emergency, with Mr Chalnor going missing, that it would be ok. Anyway, I'm all done now so why don't we go and find the others, they're all still in the conference room drinking cups of tea.'

Morgan steps to one side to allow the detective through the doorway then follows him back out into the hallway, shutting the door to the office behind him. 'Did you speak to all the staff?'

'Yeah, they weren't much help really.'

'Who did you speak to?'

'Let me see, there was the woman in the kitchen who does the washing up, Maisie, then there was the gardener, Reece. His grandfather is living in one of the old cottages on the grounds. Apparently, he's been here since the war.'

'Anyone else?' Morgan asks, stopping just outside the door to the conference room.

'Oh yeah there's that Jane Stokes as well, she seems to do all the admin stuff and look after the building as well. She reckons that the electrics need sorting out as they keep tripping out but the owner won't spend any money on the place.'

'That sounds about right,' Morgan murmurs to himself before entering the conference room.

'Detective Inspector Morgan, you seem to have brought the bad weather back with you,' Camilla Fields says, just as there is a low rumble out at sea.

'How are things here? Any news?' Morgan asks.

'None I'm afraid. DC Fallow has gone for another walk along the beach just in case anything was missed earlier.

We've spoken to everyone here and were just waiting for you to return before we got some lunch sorted.'

'Lunch sounds good, thank you,' says Morgan, swinging his rucksack off his shoulder and placing it onto the floor next to the table that Camilla Fields is sitting behind.

Another rumble of thunder cuts through the quietness, this time slightly louder than the last one. 'That storm's getting closer, I think I'd better go and find Fallow,' Morgan says, moving across to the window and pulling apart two slats of the venetian blind to peer at the rapidly darkening sky.

'Good idea, I'll go and get some food sorted,' Camilla Fields replies smoothly as she pushes back her chair to gingerly stand up, having become stiff from sitting for so long.

Morgan makes his way through the hallway again and back onto the gravel driveway, then cuts across the neat lawn that leads him to the back of the building. The sound of the waves crashing against the shoreline becomes louder the closer he gets to the narrow strip of beach that separates Bawdsey Hall from the North Sea. Morgan stands at the water's edge and watches the waves lapping close to his feet, then turns to look south across the River Deben towards Felixstowe, where a flash of lightening breaks through the clouds with a shuddering crack.

'Did you find anything?' Fallow says, trudging across the shingle towards Morgan. 'Looks like we're in for a big storm.'

'That's why I came to find you, plus Mrs Fields is sorting out some food for us all as well.'

Even though Fallow is wearing light-weight trousers and a cotton shirt, the high humidity is taking its toll and he is sweating profusely by the time he reaches Morgans side. 'Has something happened? You were gone a long time.'

'We found three bodies in an old pillbox at Shingle Street,' Morgan replies, perching on a nearby rock.

'Three? Who are they, how did they die?'

'We don't know yet, Len Bootle's going to do the PM's though he said he'll need some help with this one as it looks like they could be from the Second World War.'

'How come they haven't been found before now?' Fallow asks, kicking at the sand beneath his trainers.

'The pillbox must have been covered up by sand, there's been a recent landslip from the cliff above it, which must have uncovered it again.'

'Any sign of Mr Chalnor?' Fallow asks hopefully, though already knowing the answer – if there had been, he would have heard about it by now.

Morgan does not answer, he does not need to. Instead, he looks out to sea to watch another fork of lightening split through the sky. They need to go back into the building soon, the storm looks like it could be a fierce one. He just hopes that wherever Bobby Chalnor is, he has somewhere to shelter.

~ Seven ~

The electrically charged atmosphere matches the tension that has fallen across the dining room as the guests await the return of the police officers. Another rumble of thunder rolls out, even louder than the last one, announcing that the storm is heading their way.

Morgan steps into the dining room and makes his way straight to the table, which has been laid out with sandwiches, jugs of water and fruit juice. As he is pouring out an orange juice into a small glass, the sound of a car engine, accompanied by tires crunching over the small stones, diverts him from his task. He places the glass down onto the table then marches out into the hallway, just in time to see Jane Stokes hurrying through the open front door.

'That was good timing,' Morgan says looking at the rain which has just started to pelt down onto the ground in front of the house. 'We've just started lunch.'

'Thanks for sorting it out. I've just been driving around the area to see if I can find Bobby.'

Morgan smiles sympathetically. Often when someone goes missing, their friends and relatives feel the need to do something proactive. 'There's some sandwiches and fruit, if you're hungry?'

'I'll just go and freshen up, I need a moment to myself,' Jane responds as she walks off towards the back of the house where the servant's quarters used to be.

Morgan waits until Jane Stokes has disappeared from view then returns to the dining room. Mrs Fields, having made the assumption that Morgan has been distracted by something important, has retrieved his orange juice from the buffet table and assembled a plate of sandwiches for the detective to consume on his return.

'Thank you, Mrs Fields,' Morgan says smoothly as he sits down at the table nearest to the French doors that overlook the garden.

'Please do call me Camilla. That storm looks like it could cause some trouble. I hope the house doesn't flood, it would be an awful shame to ruin such a beautiful building,' Camilla says, looking wistfully at the ominous dark clouds.

'It's also the last thing we need right now.'

'Oh, has something else happened?'

'Yes, we found some bodies in an old pillbox on the beach at Shingle Street. It looks as if they're very old but still a rather shocking find.'

'I can imagine, was it you who found them?'

Morgan nods, 'yes, along with the local officers I was with. We were searching for any sign of Mr Chalnor on the beach north of here.'

'Poor Mr Chalnor, I wonder what has happened to him. I was so looking forward to the course as well, it sounded like such an interesting case.'

'What case?' Morgan asks, having failed to read the introductory email containing the course notes.

'The one we were going to work on for our team building exercise.'

'I can't imagine that you need to go on one, you seem pretty good at teamwork.'

'Ah it's a course that all elected members go on, though most of them do it online. I chose to pay privately for this one as I thought it would be good for my learning'.

'I see. What's the case we were going to be working on?'

'It was to solve the mystery of the disappearance of three Home Guards.'

'Do you think that the task was based on a true story?'

'I believe it could be, apart from anything, Mr Chalnor mentioned something about it being based on a real story when we were at dinner. I've just been looking through the photographs on the display wall, there were a lot of young men who passed through this building at the start of the war and women as well of course.'

'What did they do here?'

'Amongst other things, radio operator training though that was moved elsewhere in 1941 as the area was considered vulnerable to being bombed. After that the work here focused on experiments, such as flame warfare and the infamous bouncing bombs.'

'So in the course task, these Home Guards who went missing, were they stationed at Bawdsey Hall?'

'Yes they were and all three of them disappeared one night in 1941.'

'That's strange, I could understand if one went Absent Without Leave but not three of them on the same night. I wonder what happened to them?'

'Well, that was the mystery for us to solve. Did they go AWOL, which it seems the locals thought, or did something else happen to them?'

'It's also rather interesting given that we just found three bodies in a WW2 pillbox,' Morgan murmurs, his mind beginning to whir.

'Yes it is. Quite a coincidence isn't it and I don't believe in coincidences.'

'Neither do I', says Morgan, stretching out a leg, which is beginning to ache. 'Oh, look there's Fallow and Foster.'

Morgan waves to the two detectives who have just come into the dining room. They both head straight to the coffee machine and retrieve a couple of cappuccinos before making their way to the table that Morgan and Camilla Fields are occupying. Just as they sit down, a large clap of thunder crashes overhead, startling Fallow so much that he nearly drops his cup of coffee.

'The storm's right over the building now, there's hardly any gap between thunder and lightning,' Fallow informs as he wipes up the dribble of coffee that has split down the side of the porcelain cup.

'Mrs Fields was just telling me about the task Mr Chalnor had set us to do for the course. Rather a coincidence, don't you think?' Morgan says, picking up a warm bread roll and smearing it thickly with butter.

'What do you mean?' asks Foster, matching Morgan's efforts in putting as much butter as possible on his roll.

'I wasn't the only one who didn't read the course notes then,' Morgan chuckles.

'I did, I just don't understand what you mean,' Foster continues, breaking off a chunk of the roll.

'The three bodies we found this morning at Shingle Street,' Morgan explains.

'I think you might have forgotten to update me on that one,' Foster says, putting the roll down. 'I'm going to get a bottle of wine, does anyone want a glass?'

'Bit early for me thanks,' Morgan replies, watching Foster carefully as he waltzes behind the bar and grabs a bottle of Chilean Shiraz.

'Rather an interesting reaction, don't you think?' Camilla says quietly to Morgan, as she watches Foster walk thoughtfully back across the room towards them.

'Yes it is,' Morgan replies softly.

Foster returns with a bottle and four glasses, ignoring Morgans previous protestation that he did not want to drink alcohol at this early hour. The senior detective is about to repeat his words when the lights suddenly go out.

'Damn, we've had another power cut,' Jane says as she walks across the room to flick the light switch on and off. 'It's fortunate it's still daylight, though knowing our luck it will still be off by morning.'

'Is this a regular occurrence?' asks Morgan, trying to recall when he last charged his mobile phone and laptop. Although the Wi-Fi will not now work, he could still access any documents that he has already downloaded.

'Unfortunately, yes. Bawdsey hamlet is not exactly on the priority list when it comes to upgrading the utilities and even if it was, the owner is not keen on spending any more money them they have to.'

'Do you have any lamps or torches?' Fallow asks, being practical as ever.

'We've got some hurricane lamps and candelabras, not ideal but better than nothing,' Jane admits as she returns to the table where the group are seated. 'It's likely that a power cable has gone down with this storm, who knows when it will be back up and running again.'

Foster sighs theatrically then tops up his glass of wine, which has already been emptied of its original contents. 'Maybe we should all go home? It's not like there will be a training course now.'

'Perhaps you're right,' Morgan says, looking around the room at the other course attendees who have all finished their sandwiches and are looking decidedly bored. 'Jane, I assume you have everyone's contact details?'

'Of course, they're all on my PC though, which I can't switch on with the power being out.'

'If it helps, I made a list of everyone's names earlier when DC Fallow talked to them about Mr Chalnor,' Camilla interjects, pulling a notebook out of her russet-coloured leather handbag.

'Right everyone, can I have your attention please,' Morgan says, pushing back his chair and standing up. 'Please can you give Mrs Fields your contact details then you are free to go home. I think it's safe to assume the course has been cancelled. I will be staying here to continue the search for Mr Chalnor.'

A low murmur is heard across the room, which is quickly replaced by one of grateful acceptance that at least they are able to go to somewhere with electricity.

'I'd like to stay if that's ok with you?' Foster asks, sipping more of the wine.

'Sure, that's fine, I could do with some help.'

Fallow coughs gently to interject, 'I'd like to stay as well, after all this is our jurisdiction and we have a missing person to find at the very least.'

'Thanks Fallow, I appreciate that. The question is what do we do next?'

'How about solving the mystery that Mr Chalnor set us?' Camilla suggests as she sits back down again having obtained the contact details of the course attendees.

'Do you think it could have some relevance to his disappearance?' Morgan asks.

'I don't know, I just know that there is something odd going on here and I want to find out what it is,' Camilla replies.

'I agree. Why don't we go through to the conference room and look at the course notes. Did anyone print them out?' Morgan asks.

'I did,' Fallow replies. 'I can't see what it could have to do with Mr Chalnor's disappearance though.'

'I don't see either but at the moment there's nothing else we can do but wait and I'm not a very patient person,' Morgan says before striding off towards the conference room.

'We need to find out the reason for Mr Chalnor's disappearance and it's possible it has something to do with his work,' Camilla explains to Fallow.

'I guess so,' Fallow admits.

'C'mon lad, this is the best training course I've ever been on, we get to solve a real mystery not just a made-up case,' Foster says cheerfully, slapping Fallow on the back.

'I bet you've been on a few courses,' Fallow murmurs quietly, just loud enough for Camilla Fields to hear, who smiles to herself.

'Ok let's go and find out what's happened to Mr Chalnor,' Camilla instructs as she pads across the floor towards the conference room, fully expecting the two detectives to follow closely behind.

~ Eight ~

Morgan spreads out the printed documents for the training course across the table. The first page outlines the purpose of the course, it's aims and objectives as well as the principles they all need to learn on how to work well as a team. Morgan snorts when he sees the last section, he knows how to be a good team player but he also cannot change his personality nor his lack of patience with certain members of the team who are in his opinion, not very well suited towards police work.

'It all looks pretty standard to me,' says Camilla, peering over Morgan's shoulder. 'They're a good set of notes, those principles for effective teamwork are spot on.'

'Remind me again why you bothered coming on this course? I believe it was to further your own learning?' Morgan says flippantly, wondering if perhaps the politician had another motive for being here.

'Yes it is and that's all I'm going to say on the matter. Now, let's take a look at the first task.'

Morgan pulls out the third sheet of paper, which details the task they were set and instructions on how they would go about it.

> Your task is to solve a mystery by working together as a team. The team who solves the mystery first by correctly identifying the perpetrator and their motive, will win a small prize that can be shared.

'This sounds interesting,' says Fallow, sitting down on a chair opposite Morgan and Camilla. He tries to peer at the piece of paper upside down but soon gives up as it becomes too onerous to read that way.

Morgan rolls his eyes, trust Fallow to think the task would have been interesting. He pulls out the next piece of paper and smooths down the sheet that has been crumpled up by the printer.

> In 1940, three local members of the Home Guards known as the 'The Bawdsey Boys', disappeared from Bawdsey. They were last seen on the evening of 25th August, when they left Bawdsey Hall for their routine nighttime patrol along the stretch of coastline up as far as Shingle Street. The mystery you need to solve is what happened to 'The Bawdsey Boys'.

'This is starting to sound oddly familiar,' Morgan says, looking at Camilla to see her reaction.

'Yes, it is rather a strange coincidence, almost as if this was all meant to happen,' Camilla replies softly, looking out of the window at the North Sea, whose grey waves have heightened with the incoming tide.

'What do you mean?' Foster pipes up, having been uncharacteristically quiet up until this moment.

'I don't know, just ignore me, I'm just a silly old woman.'

'I know what you're saying, it's all a bit weird, especially given Mr Chalnor's disappearance. Shall we carry on reading through the notes?'

'Yes, please do carry on Detective Inspector,' Camilla says, her attention returning to the room again. 'The storm seems to be passing over.'

'Yes, thank goodness,' Fallow says, shuddering.

'Oh my god, don't tell me you're scared of storms,' Foster bellows.

'There's nothing wrong with that,' Fallow responds quietly.

'Shall we carry on, it'll be getting dark by the time we've read through these papers,' Morgan says impatiently.

Just at that moment, Jane peers into the room. 'I thought you might all be in here, I just wanted to let you know that all of the other guests have now left.'

'Thanks Jane. I don't suppose you have any more lanterns?' Morgan asks.

'Sorry, no. I can go and ask Reece if he has any more candles though?'

'No, don't worry, it's still raining and we don't need them at the moment, maybe later.'

'Ok, well I'll leave you to your work. Maisie will do her best to rustle up some food for us all later, I'll let you know when it's ready.'

Morgan smiles at Jane then returns his focus to reading through the task set by Bobby Chalnor. 'Right, let's carry on then.'

> To solve the mystery, you will need to split into two groups, one group will look through the documents that are printed on the following pages, the other group will interview the staff in the Hall and the estate.

'Interesting, so the staff would have been prepped to answer questions then?' Fallow says.

'It would seem so,' Camilla replies, pulling the piece of paper towards her and squinting at the words on the page. 'What does it say to do next?'

Morgan pulls the paper towards him again and reads out aloud.

After your team has either analysed the documents or interviewed the witnesses, you will then swap tasks. But be warned, just as in real life, not all of the staff may be telling the truth and the stories told to each group may not be the same. Both teams will need to work together in order to solve the mystery.

'So, we're supposed to work together but the team that solves the mystery first would get a prize? That doesn't make sense,' Foster says, looking puzzled.

'Classic psychological tactics. How badly do you want to win? Would you do it at the expense of finding out the truth? Would you rather risk not solving the mystery rather than share the prize? Very clever,' Camilla says.

Morgan rolls his eyes, 'it's never straight forward is it, they're always testing us.'

'Indeed, perhaps this is all a test,' Camilla murmurs.

'What do you mean by that?' Foster asks.

'It seems a bit strange that the bodies of three people mysteriously turn up when we're supposed to be investigating what happened to three missing Home Guards,' Camilla snorts.

'Ok, I agree it's weird but I don't see how they could be linked, there's no way that anyone could have predicted a rockfall would uncover the pillbox,' Morgan says.

'Did you look at the photographs on the wall in the dining room?' Camilla asks, staring at Foster.

'Yeah I did, so what?'

'Did you see the group photos of the airmen who were stationed at RAF Martlesham?'

Foster nods slowly, his forehead creasing in puzzlement.

'And did you read the history of Bawdsey Hall on it's website before coming here?' Camilla says, starting to become slightly exasperated with the Londoner.

'Nope, I didn't but I guess that you did.'

'I did,' Fallow pipes up.

'Ah good, then perhaps you'd like to explain to DC Foster the significance of the photograph in the dining room?' Camilla says to Fallow.

'I assume you're referring to the one with the Canadian airman who was stationed here in August 1940?' Fallow replies.

'Yes, I am.'

'What's that got to do with Bobby Chalnor going missing?' Morgan asks, completely lost as to the point of the conversation.

'He's Canadian?' Fallow guesses.

'Well done, yes he is. I've always been rather good with accents and however well he tried to cover it up, it was rather obvious to me where Mr Chalnor originated,' Camilla explains.

'So let me get this straight. The trainer who has gone missing is Canadian and there was an airman here in 1940 who was also Canadian,' Morgan says, still utterly confused.

'Yes, that's correct,' Camilla replies. 'And the task set by Mr Chalnor was to investigate the disappearance of three Home Guards who went missing on the night of 25th August 1940.'

'You've lost me again, what's this all to do with Bobby Chalnor?' Morgan says.

'I would guess that the Canadian stationed here during the war is a relative of Mr Chalnor's and that for whatever reason, Mr Chalnor wanted us to find out the truth behind the disappearance of the 'Bawdsey Boys',' Camilla replies.

'So why has Bobby Chalnor disappeared?' Fallow says.

'Perhaps because someone else did not want the training course to go ahead, someone who did not want the truth to be uncovered,' Camilla says, nestling back into her chair.

'So, if we solve the mystery of what happened in August 1940, we may very well find out what has happened to Bobby Chalnor,' concludes Morgan.

Nine

There is something vaguely familiar about the dream, as if it has all happened before though he cannot remember how it will end. What Morgan does know though, as he fights to awaken, is that he does not want to find out what happens next and he is grateful when a low rumble of thunder is enough to stir the detective from the unsettling dream. Automatically Morgan reaches out to switch on the bedside table lamp, only remembering after the hollow click resonates through the room, that the power is still out.

There it is again, the sound he is now certain he heard in his sleep. In the distance, between the rumbles of thunder, is the sound of a dog barking. Fleetingly Morgan wonders if Fallow is awake and if he too has heard the incoming storm. He pushes himself up, pulls back the cotton sheet that is soaked in sweat, then swings his long legs over the side of the bed, his feet landing firmly onto the exposed floorboards. Reaching across the bed, Morgan peels back the corner of the curtains that are drawn shut across the bay window and peers into the darkness, trying to make sense of the myriad of shapes amongst the dense shadows.

A flash of lightening cracks across the sky, momentarily allowing the detective to see the river boats that are bobbing rhythmically against the incoming tide. It will not be long before the storm is overhead as a deep rumble is quickly followed by another the lightning strike. Another flash arcs across the sky, lighting up the figure who is standing on the beach looking up at the window where Morgan is still peering out. Beside the figure is the shadow of a dog who is barking nervously in the anticipatory atmosphere of the awaiting storm. Morgan draws back from the window then fumbles about on the bedside table for the small torch that he keeps on his keyring for emergencies. He uses the thin beam of light to locate a pair of jeans and a jumper. Once dressed, he pads across the room again to peer out of the window. Both the person and the dog have gone.

A loud noise coming from the other side of the wall makes Morgan jump though he quickly deduces it must be Fallow, falling out of bed. Morgan pushes down on the handle of the interconnecting door then remembers that the key for it has been lost. He kneels down and feels between the cracks in the floorboards beneath the door, almost immediately his fingers brush against cold metal. Using the torch to guide him, Morgan pulls off his suit jacket from the coat hanger then bends the pliable metal into a small metal hook. He dangles the altered coat-hanger down into the crack again and the makeshift hook makes contact with the loop handle of an old-fashioned key. Carefully Morgan pulls the object towards him then grabs hold of it as soon as it is within reach.

The key fits snuggly in the door lock, though a little stiff to turn, which is unsurprising given that it has not been used for many years. With a deep clunk that echoes in the stillness of the night, Morgan unlocks the door. He pulls the door towards him and pushes it against the wall then reaches across the void to unlock the second door that leads into Fallows room.

'Who's that?' Fallow whispers.

'It's me, Morgan.'

'What the hell are you doing scaring me half to death,' Fallow says from somewhere towards the rear of the dark room.

Morgan shuffles through the doorway and trips over an object that must have been wedged in the 'no man's land' between the two interconnecting doors. He crouches down and fumbles about with his hand, trying to locate the object. After a few moments, he makes contact with something that feels as if it could be a book.

'Are you still there?'

'Yes, hang on, I'm trying to pick something up.'

'What is it?' Fallow asks.

'I'm not sure, it feels like a book. Sorry if I gave you a scare, I heard you fall out of bed and I know you don't like storms so I thought I'd check on you.'

'You could've just knocked on the door like other people.'

'I know but I didn't want to wake everyone else. I saw someone on the beach earlier, they were looking right up at me.'

'Could you see who it was?'

'No, it was too dark.'

Just then a flash of lightning strikes the ground somewhere close to the Hall, which judders under the concentrated force of its energy.

'That sounded really close by,' Fallow shivers.

'Yeah it did but we're safe in here.'

'Unless the roof gets struck by lightning and catches fire,' Fallow replies gloomily.

Morgan ignores the comment, 'I wonder where Bobby Chalnor is and whether he's found shelter?'

'Apparently the gardener saw him the night he disappeared.'

'Did he indeed, who told you that?'

'Foster spoke to him when you were out. Apparently Reece often walks his dog along the beach at night and saw Mr Chalnor near the rocks, looking out across the water.'

'Ah so that was probably who I saw just now on the beach.'

'Probably, though it's a bit strange going out in this weather.'

'Yes,' says Morgan thoughtfully. 'I guess so, though some people actually like storms.'

A soft knock on the door interrupts the conversation. 'Who is it?' Morgan asks, forgetting that he is not in his own room.

'It's Camilla. Is that you DI Morgan?'

'Yes it is.'

'You might as well come in Mrs Fields, we seem to be having a party in here,' Fallow says uncharacteristically sarcastically.

The door tentatively opens to reveal the elderly woman holding a hurricane lamps that Jane had located for her the previous evening. 'I just wanted to check everything was ok, I heard a loud noise.'

'It was just Fallow falling out of bed,' Morgan responds facetiously.

'Ah well that's good. What's that in your hand?'

'A book, it was wedged between the interconnecting doors.'

'A book, how interesting.'

'He tripped over it,' says Fallow, getting back into bed and pulling the sheet up to his chin. 'Do you think I could go back to sleep now?'

'Of course, DI Morgan will see me safely back to my room,' Camilla replies.

Morgan tries to suppress a sigh, knowing full well that Camilla Fields does not need to be escorted back to her room and that she is very obviously engineering an op-portunity to speak to him alone. 'Goodnight then Fallow,' Morgan says as he closes the door behind him and follows Mrs Fields back to her room at the far end of the corridor.

'Could I please see that book?'

'Sure, do you think it's something significant?' Morgan asks as he passes the book over to Mrs Fields.

'There has to be a reason why it was hidden, so yes, I do think it's significant.'

'Are you sure you're in the right job? Perhaps you'd have been better suited to the police force.'

Camilla chuckles, 'Maybe, now let's take a look at that book.' Camilla passes the lamp over to Morgan so that she has a free hand to take hold of the book. She opens the front cover to reveal a handwritten scrawl on the first page:

Diary of Oswald Turner, 1940

'Well, this is an interesting find,' Camilla says smoothing out the page that has yellowed with age.

'Can you read any of the other pages in this light?'

'Not very well, especially with the storm clouds blocking the light from the moon.'

As if hearing that it is being spoken about, an enormous rumble of thunder fills the quiet building. Morgan waits with bated breath for footsteps that might indicate Fallow is awake again but the house remains quiet.

'I should leave you to sleep,' says Morgan, still standing in the doorway of Camilla's room.

'You may be right, I am feeling a little weary. Goodnight Detective,' Camilla says, closing her bedroom door.

Through the window above the staircase, Morgan can see that dawn is just beginning to break over the horizon, pink streaks zigzagging across the cloudy sky as the intense orange orb is beginning to rise above the North Sea. The light from the emerging daybreak is just enough to allow Morgan to see his way back to his bedroom without tripping over the large rug that covers the length of the corridor to protect the vintage carpet beneath.

Morgan feels for the door handle, his fingers connecting with the ornate brass knob, which he turns. For a moment he holds his breath as he remembers that this was not the door he left his room from earlier and it might be locked, but his fears are soon allayed as the door moves inwards. Morgan pads across the soft carpet, takes off his shoes and lies down on the bed, not bothering to change out of his clothes again. It will soon be morning and in case, the detective knows he will not sleep, too full of curiosity as to what is in the diary and why it appears to have been hidden between the interconnecting doors.

The detective must have fallen asleep though, for the next thing he is aware of is the bright sunlight streaming through the curtains, indicating that the storm has passed along with the night. Optimistically he tries the light switch on the bedside lamp but the power is still off. Morgan pulls on his shoes again then wanders downstairs into the dining room, hoping that the kitchen has a gas cooker and not electric so that they might have something cooked for breakfast.

'Good morning, Detective Inspector, did you sleep well despite the storm?' Jane asks as Morgan steps inside the dining room.

Morgan strides over to the table where Jane is seated, located in front of the French doors that lead out into the garden. 'Not too bad thanks. I don't suppose there's any breakfast is there?'

Jane laughs, 'Yes of course, I'll go and check to see if it's ready. It's fortunate that the kitchen still has the old larder cupboard, which keeps food cool even when the fridge is off.'

'Very lucky, I am a bit hungry.'

'So am I,' Foster says, marching into the room and sitting down at the table. 'Did you sleep through that storm?'

'Sort of, Fallow fell out of bed and it woke me up,' Morgan says, grimacing.

'Here he is now,' Foster exclaims just as Fallow walks into the room.

Fallow glares at Morgan, convinced that the pair of officers have been gossiping and no doubt laughing about him falling out of bed.

'And here's the final member of our merry band,' Foster says as Camilla moves purposefully across the room, clutching the diary in one hand.

'Good morning all. Fallow, please could you go through this book to see what's in it?' Camilla says, handing the book to Fallow.

'What's that then?' asks Foster.

'I literally tripped over it last night,' Morgan explains, wishing that Camilla had not mentioned it in front of Foster though without knowing why.

'Let's have a look then,' Foster says, snatching the book from Fallow. 'Oh it's a diary.'

'Yes we know, I tried to read through it last night but it was too dark to see with my poor eyesight. One of the downsides of growing old I'm afraid,' Camilla explains. 'I don't know about the rest of you but I'm famished.'

'Jane's just gone to sort out some food,' Morgan says, trying to peer over Foster's shoulder at the diary as he flicks through it.

'Hey, you guys should take a look at this, it looks pretty interesting,' Foster declares, waggling the book up in the air.

'We will do when we get the chance,' Morgan replies sarcastically.

'Here, listen to this,' Foster continues, ignoring the senior officer's comment. He places the book down flat on the table then randomly chooses a page to read.

July 1940
I've now been here for 4 months and have settled
into a routine now. N tells me what I need to know
then I make sure the information gets to the right
people. I don't know how long I'll need to do this for,
it's terrifying to think that I could be found out at
any moment and what will happen to me if I am.

'I wonder what he means by that,' Camilla murmurs, intrigued by the diary entry.

'Sounds to me as if he was doing something he shouldn't have,' Foster deduces, looking up from the book.

'You'd know all about that then,' Fallow says, undiplomatically.

'What the hell do you mean by that?' Foster spits, slamming a hand down on the table.

'Now come on, let's get back to working together, we need all the help we can get in solving the puzzle that Mr Chalnor has set us,' soothes Camilla, taking hold of the book again.

'You're right, why don't we get back to the task that Mr Chalnor set us,' Morgan says smoothly, trying to quell his irritation at Foster and Fallow's behaviour. Not for the first time, he is thankful for the calming presence of Camilla. He could easily imagine her in action at one of the parish council debates and has no doubt who would win.

'Let's get something to eat then have another look at the task. Oswald Turner's diary can wait until later,' Fallow concedes before walking over to the long table to collect some cereal, croissants and an orange juice that has been kept cool in the old pantry.

'Did you say Oswald Turner?' Foster asks, staring at the book that is now sitting on the table next to Camilla Fields.

'Yes, that's the name written at the front of the diary, why?' Morgan asks.

'No reason, just sounds familiar that's all,' Foster murmurs before he too makes his way towards the table laden with food.

'Interesting,' Camilla says quietly.

Morgan looks up, hoping that Camilla might continue verbalising her thoughts but she returns her focus to her breakfast and says no more on the matter.

~ Ten ~

The storm has long-since passed over by the time the power is switched back on at Bawdsey Hall. The group of three detectives and one parish councillor are so engrossed with discussing the task that Bobby Chalnor set before he disappeared, that they do not notice the lights flickering back into action until the afternoon shadows begin to fall across the papers they are working on.

'Excellent, we seem to have the power back again, which will make things much easier for us. So, who wants to be in which team?' Camilla says, trying to organise the detectives who are arguing over what they will each do.

'Well, I think given that this is a team-building exercise, Fallow and Foster should make up one team,' Morgan says, bracing himself for the imminent complaints.

'Great well we get to choose which task to do first then,' Foster snaps, picking up the piece of paper from the table that has the task written on it.

'Ok, what do you want to do first then?' Morgan asks evenly.

'We'll go and interview the staff,' Foster replies, without bothering to consult Fallow.

'Right, well that leaves me and Detective Inspector Morgan to look through the historical documents that Mr Chalnor collated for the exercise,' Camilla responds diplomatically.

'Let's get on with it then,' Morgan says, looking at his wristwatch. 'We'll meet back here around lunchtime.'

'That sounds like a good plan,' Camilla responds before walking off towards the conference room with a cup of black coffee in one hand and her handbag in the other, leaving Morgan the task of bringing the documents with him.

Camilla settles down at the top table again, which is seemingly more comfortable than the long tables set out in boardroom style ready for the training session.

'Which one would you like to start with?' Morgan asks, putting the papers onto the table. 'Do you want to take a look through these while I go and charge my phone?'

'Yes, ok. What about the diary?'

'It's at the bottom of that pile, we might get the opportunity to look at it again later.'

Foster and Fallow are already close to the front door by the time Morgan walks through the hallway towards the stairs. 'I hope you've got some suntan lotion,' Morgan teases, knowing full well that the pair will likely not be in the sun for long.

Morgan's sense of humour is clearly lost on the two detectives who turn around and walk out into the sunshine without saying a word. Morgan sighs loudly then trips up the oak staircase, taking two steps at a time.

Now that the electricity is back on, he can charge his mobile phone up and check up on Dr Bootle's progress with the postmortems. He also of course needs to phone Celia, who will by now have heard of the events and will be wondering where her husband is.

Half-an-hour later, the detective returns to the conference room, having collected a jug of coffee and a plate of pastries from the kitchen enroute. 'Sorry I took so long, I needed to catch up on some phone calls.'

'Perfectly understandable, after all you have an investigation to run. Have there been any sightings of Mr Chalnor?'

'Nothing confirmed, he seems to have just disappeared. Talking about disappearing people, has Jane Stokes reappeared since breakfast?'

'Not that I've seen. I'm a little concerned about her though I guess she must be worried about her colleague going missing.'

'I didn't think they knew each other that well?' Morgan says, pouring coffee out into two mugs and placing the plate of pastries onto the table between them.

'Oh yes well I suppose not, though being related must automatically give cause for concern even if they do hardly know each other,' Camilla replies, taking one of the pastries from the plate.

'They're related? How do you know that?'

'Mr Chalnor told me. He found out about Jane's existence through a family history website, it's the reason why he came to England. Did you not know?'

'No I didn't, this whole situation is becoming stranger by the minute.'

'Yes it is,' Camilla muses, sipping a little of her coffee. 'Now let's have a look through these documents.'

The storm has cleared the air a little, leaving a calm blue sky in its wake, replacing the tense humidity of the previous two days. It is still hot though and Fallow is glad of the cool shade afforded by the enormous lilacs and Hebes lining the narrow path that winds its' way through the garden. The sound of crickets hidden somewhere in the grass, reminds Fallow of the holiday he went on to Crete with his uncle, Chief Superintendent Bennett. It was meant to be an educational trip but the searing heat had made it difficult to do much other than laze about at the hotel, watching his uncle chatting to the other guests, seemingly more at ease with them than his own family.

The sun always seems to be much more enjoyable abroad, decides Fallow as he pushes aside an overgrown shrub that immediately pings back into place behind him. In front of him, Foster is striding off at pace. Fallow pauses for a moment and watches as the stout figure disappears from view. He is still unconvinced by Morgan's decision to look into a possible motive for Mr Chalnor's disappearance rather than allowing them to join the search party that is scouring the beach for any sign of the course trainer. Fallow sighs, then runs to catch up with Foster. Now is not the time to be questioning Morgan's decisions, even if he does not agree with it.

The first place to visit on the list compiled by Bobby Chalnor is the workshop. Unlike yesterday when Foster was last there, the workshop is empty, with no sign of either the apprentice Britany or the gardener Reece.

'Shall we go to the gardener's cottage?' Foster asks in a way that makes it clear it is more of a statement than a question.

Fallow smiles but does not respond, realising that one is not required. He follows Foster back down the narrow path that leads away from the workshop then into the wooded area again where the overhanging branches shield them from the full strength of the sun's powerful rays.

A few minutes later the detectives are standing in front of the two mirror-image cottages. Fallow pulls out a notebook and pen whilst Foster retrieves the sheet of paper written by Bobby Chalnor, which has a list of questions for them to ask the witnesses. A footnote at the bottom of the page states that they can also ask additional questions if they wish. Foster automatically takes the lead and raps loudly on the gardener's door. To their surprise the door immediately opens.

'Hello Reece, is this a good time to talk?' Foster asks, noting Reece's dishevelled appearance.

'Oh yeah ok, no problem,' Reece replies, pulling the door open wider and allowing the two men into the cosy cottage.

The cottage was clearly built for a much shorter generation and both detectives need to duck underneath the thick doorframe. Once inside the main part of the cottage though, the ceiling is high enough for them to stand up to full height.

Fallow looks around the small room that is used as both a living room and kitchen. 'Nice cottage, did it come with the job?'

'Yeah it did. My grandad lives in the one next door, I've been coming here since I was a toddler. Have you heard anything from Bobby yet?'

'No, that's why we're here. We're trying to find out why Mr Chalnor might have gone missing and thought we would go through the task he set us before he disappeared,' Foster explains.

'Do you think that's got something to do with it?' Reece says, creasing up his forehead as he tries to work out how the two might be connected.

'We don't know but at the moment we're exploring all possibilities,' Fallow explains.

'We also don't have anything else to go on at the moment,' Foster murmurs as he moves towards the squat window that looks out over a small courtyard garden at the rear of the property.

'Ah I see, well, why don't you both sit down and I'll put the kettle on. If I remember rightly from what Mr Chalnor said about the task, you need to ask me some questions.'

'Thanks, yes that's right, we have the list here,' Fallow says, sitting down at a pine table that has been squeezed in between a sofa and the enormous inglenook fireplace that takes up almost an entire wall.

'Ok, well ask away,' Reece declares, switching on the kettle before pulling three mugs out from a cupboard in the hand-made kitchen.

Fallow waits until the roar of the kettle has sufficiently diminished to be able to talk without shouting, then begins reading aloud the list of questions. 'Right then, so the first question is to ask what your role was during the war?' Fallow says, his forehead creasing in puzzlement.

Foster stares at Fallow and his obvious discomfort, it is clear that the detective has not understood the brief properly. 'All the staff are pretending that they were here during the war,' whispers Foster.

'Ah ok, that makes more sense. I don't see how this will help find Bobby Chalnor though,' Fallow replies glumly, the frown on his face deepening.

'Nor do I mate but what have we got to lose?'

'We were given a script of what to say to answer the questions. If it helps I can go and get it?' Reece explains as he sets the three mugs of tea down onto the table.

'Yes please,' Foster responds, picking up the mug nearest to him.

'I'm still confused,' Fallow says quietly as soon as Reece has disappeared upstairs to find the script.

'Me too but Mrs Fields thinks this will help and we haven't got any other ideas,' Foster replies, shrugging his shoulders.

Before Fallow can respond, Reece returns with the print-out that Bobby Chalnor gave to him a few days before he disappeared.

'Here we go. So, the first question is asking what I did in the war and the answer I'm supposed to give you is that I was a gardener,' Reece says, sitting back down at the table.

'Huh that's a coincidence,' Foster says.

'Yeah, especially when my grandad was a gardener here during the war,' Reece replies, picking up one of the mugs and spooning some sugar into it. He stirs the liquid thoughtfully before returning the wet spoon to the sugar jar.

'Ok, so what's the answer to the next question?' Fallow asks.

'Let me take a look,' Reece says, running a finger down the text on the print-out. 'Here it is – who else is at Bawdsey Hall in the summer of 1940?'

'What's the answer then?' Fallow asks as he picks up the mug of tea, inspects the stained vessel then replaces it back onto the table.

'There's a list of staff here who were working at the Hall and then those that were billeted to the Hall. Here, have a look for yourself,' Reece offers, placing the piece of paper onto the centre of the table so that all three of them can see it.

Staff
Maid – Molly Jaspar.
Kitchen Maid – Sarah Pearson.
Cook - Mrs Maggie Adams.
Gardener – Cedric Browne.
Housekeeper – Mrs Timmons.
Administrator - Esme Smart.

Other People at the Hall
Trainee radio operators – Meg Barron, Fanny Minter, Agnes Appleby, Eleanor Fulcher.
Radio operator instructors – Sargent Stanley Nicholls, Captain Oswald Turner (seconded from Royal Canadian Airforce).
Home Guards assigned to coastal patrol duty – William Foster, Frederick Longcroft, Harry Norman.

'Any relation to you then Foster?' Reece chuckles when he notices the same surname as the officer.

'Actually I think that might have been my grandad, he was billeted here.' Foster says slowly.

'Another coincidence then, this is all getting a bit strange,' Fallow replies, tilting his head to one side as he processes the information.

'Yes it is,' Foster agrees. 'I don't know why but I'm getting the feeling that we've all been set up.'

'What do you mean?' asks Reece before draining his mug of the sweetened liquid.

'I'm probably being daft, there just seems to be far too many coincidences here, what with those bodies being found at Shingle Street,' Foster replies, pulling across the document so that he can take a closer look at it.

'I heard about that, fair creeped me out thinking they'd been there all that time and no one knew about it. I used to play down that bit of the beach when I was a young nipper,' Reece grimaces at the thought of making sandcastles close to the place where the bodies were found.

'I don't know what to think about it all but I do think we should go back to the Hall now and find the others,' Fallow says, tipping out the contents of his mug into the sink then placing the empty vessel into the sink. He squeezes past the table then moves towards the front door.

Foster pushes his chair back to stand up, 'yeah I think you're right. We've got the answers to the questions anyway so we can look through them back at the Hall.'

'I'd better get back to repairing that fence,' Reece states, following the two detectives to the door. 'If there's anything else I can help with, let me know.'

'Thanks, we will,' Fallow replies as he makes his way back out into the glare of the late morning sun.

Foster waits until Reece has moved out of sight then strides up the path that leads to the Hall without waiting for Fallow. The short journey passes in silence as Foster mulls over all the strange coincidences that keep happening. This was not what he was expecting to happen when he agreed to go on the team-building course. The fact that his grandfather was stationed here at the Hall during the war is not a surprise to him but the name appearing on the occupants list like that has left him with a very uncomfortable feeling.

Eleven

Morgan and Camilla Fields have had an exhausting and somewhat fruitless morning pouring over the documents that were included in the course notes as part of the task set by Bobby Chalnor.

'So, let me get this straight in my mind, all we've learnt from two hours of scrutinising these documents is that there were a lot of people at the Hall during the war,' Morgan says with more than a little despondency.

'Correct. I'm really failing to see how any of these documents could help to solve the task we were set.'

'Or the case that we also have to solve in finding the missing trainer.'

'I still think there's a connection between the two,' Camilla says, shuffling the pile of papers into an orderly fashion and placing them next to the sheet of paper that contains the instructions on how to go about the task. 'What would you like to look at next, the photographs in the dining room or the diary?'

'I might be able to help you with the photos in the dining room,' Foster says, entering the room. He places the answer sheet from Reece Browne onto the centre of the table, 'one of the photos may well be of my grandad, Billy Foster.'

'He's mentioned on the answer sheet that the gardener gave us,' Fallow explains, slightly breathless from trying to keep up with Foster.

'Did you know that your grandfather was here during the war?' Camilla asks, picking up the answer sheet.

'Yes and I told Bobby Chalnor about it the night he disappeared.'

'Well, that's rather interesting and now your grandfather's name has appeared on the answer sheet,' Camilla says, narrowing her eyes as she skims through the text on the piece of paper from Reece Browne.

'What else do you know about your grandad being here during the war?' Morgan asks as he also reads through the answer sheet.

'Only that he went missing,' Foster admits.

'Did he go AWOL at the same time as two other soldiers by any chance?' Camilla asks.

'I don't know, no one in the family will talk about him. I tried to find out when I was a kid but they all closed ranks and wouldn't say anything about him.'

The sound of Morgan's phone ringing makes them all jump at the unexpected interruption to the quietness of the Hall.

'You should answer it,' Camilla says helpfully, pointing to the vibrating mobile phone that is about to fall off the table.

Morgan smiles at Camilla then picks up the phone. Automatically he walks over to the furthest corner of the room so that no one else can overhear his conversation.

'DI Morgan,' he says brusquely, not recognising the number.

'Morgan, I'm glad I caught you, it's PC Smith, we met the yesterday. A body's been found on the beach near Sizewell.'

'Any more info?'

'Only that it's male.'

'Ok I'd better come and take a look,' Morgan says, looking across the room at Jane Stokes who has just walked in.

'I thought you might say that, I'll pick you up in five.'

Morgan ends the call then pushes the phone into the back pocket of his trousers. 'I've got to go out for a while, why don't you all get some coffee then we can carry on with this when I get back.'

'Anything wrong?' Camilla asks, looking concerned.

'Nothing I can talk about at the moment, I'll catch up with you all when I get back,' Morgan replies, striding across the room. He collects two bottles of water from the bar in the dining room then makes his way out of the building so that he can warm up a little in the sun. It does not seem to matter how hot it is outside, the Hall always seems to be freezing cold.

The sound of a car engine alerts Morgan to PC Smith's arrival long before he catches sight of the car winding its way through the narrow roads that are lined with tall grasses, almost obscuring the view of anyone travelling along them. Morgan shields his eyes from the suns intense glare as he watches the vehicle come into the driveway then skid to a halt next to him, showering pea shingle across his shoes.

Morgan opens the passenger side door then stoops to get inside. 'I brought some water just in case we're there for a while,' Morgan says to Smith, who is wearing dark sunglasses to protect his eyes from the glare.

'Good thinking, there's not much around that area so we might need it.'

'Was anything found on the body?'

'No and it matches the description of your Mr Chalnor.'

Morgan breathes out slowly. These moments are always difficult – part of him hopes that the course trainer has been found and the other part of him hopes that it is not him - that Bobby Chalnor is still alive. Either way, they will soon find out.

Twenty minutes later, PC Smith pulls the car over onto the side of the road, half up on the grass verge so that it is not causing an obstruction. 'We'll have to walk the rest of the way, it's only about ten minutes down that path,' Smith says, pointing to a narrow path that runs along the cliff top then tails off into an unmade track that leads down to the beach.

Morgan instantly regrets his decision not to return to his room to collect a hat, when he opens the car door and steps out into the furnace of the summer heat. Carrying the two bottles in one hand, he follows Smith down the path, sweat dribbling down the nape of his neck and soaking into his cotton t-shirt.

The two men walk in silence, an anticipatory stillness lying heavily between them as they both think about what they are going to find at the end of the track. Without warning, the path abruptly ends and in front of them lies a shingle sand bank, peppered with the coastal plants that have adapted to survive in the harsh saline conditions. Just over the other side of the sandbank, close to a concrete path that runs along the Suffolk coast, a man is waiting for them.

'His poor kids found the body earlier, they were playing in the sand dunes, collecting shells and rocks,' Smith explains, looking at the man who is standing as far away from the body as possible. 'His name's Terry Faversham.'

'Jesus that's not good, they must be traumatised,' Morgan says as he strides across the beach to greet the man, his trainers sinking into the powdery sand with every step.

The man begins to walk towards them, not wanting to be on the beach any longer than necessary. 'Are you the detectives?'

'I'm Detective Inspector Morgan and this is PC Smith,' Morgan says as soon as he is within speaking distance. 'I'm sorry to hear what happened.'

'Thanks, it was a huge shock, especially for the kids.'

'I can imagine. Are you local?'

'No, we're staying at the caravan park near Sizewell.'

'Not what you want to find at any time, let alone when you're on holiday,' Smith says as he approaches. 'Can you show us where it is?'

'Sure, it's just behind that clump of grass over there.'

'Thanks, you can go if you want, we've got your phone number,' Morgan says, certain that Terry will want to return to his wife and children as quickly as possible.

Morgan and Smith wait until Terry has gone then make their way around the grassy outcrop that has been pointed out to them. They do not need to walk far to find the body, which is partially hidden by the tall grasses.

'What do you think?' Smith asks, crouching down to take a closer look.

'It's not him,' Morgan says with relief, looking at a figure who is walking towards them. 'Looks like the calvary has arrived.'

'Right, well, I'll take you back to the Hall then,' Smith says. 'Another unidentified body to deal with is not what I was expecting when I woke up this morning. We don't have one for ages, then we get several at once.'

'Like buses,' Morgan muses. The conversation reminds him that he should call Dr Bootle and find out if the post-mortems have been done yet.

'Yeah, bodies like buses. I'll have to remember that one,' chortles Smith, trying to make light of the situation. Any outsider overhearing the conversation would no doubt have been horrified by it, little understanding the need for the emergency services to cope with traumatic situations as best as they can.

By the time they reach the car, Morgan is glad to be out of the sun again. The two men drink their bottles of water whilst they wait for the air conditioning to stop churning out hot air, then Smith manoeuvres the car back out onto the road, makes a U-turn at the end of the track and heads in the direction of Bawdsey Hall.

~ Twelve ~

Dr Bootle is at his happiest when he is learning something new and today is certainly fulfilling that need. The pathologist stands back to look at the three cadavers lying on stainless steel tables in the centre of the postmortem room. Harry, who has already photographed and fingerprinted the deceased as well as taking samples from their hair and clothing, is busy preparing the autoclaved instruments that are needed for the examination.

The two men busy themselves as they wait for the arrival of forensic archaeologist Dr Clive Dunning, who is going to assist. In the viewing gallery that overlooks the postmortem suite, a group of university students from the faculties of forensics, archaeology and pathology, are eagerly awaiting the session to begin. They do not have long to wait as Dr Dunning finds his way into the mortuary suite only five minutes later than anticipated.

'Good morning,' Dr Bootle says cheerfully. 'I hope you managed to find our little hospital ok?'

'Yes thank you. It's nice to get the chance to see some of the beautiful Suffolk countryside again. It's been a while since I've been back here,' Clive Dunning replies.

'Ah a local, then I don't need to give you any background on the history of the area. I hope you don't mind but I've already sent some photographs of the uniforms to the British Museum who have confirmed that they are World War Two Home Guard uniforms.'

'Excellent, that saves me a job. I don't suppose you have any idea as to the identity of the three men?'

'Well, actually we do have some information. It just so happens there was a training course going on at Bawdsey Hall near where the bodies were found and the course task was to find out what happened to three Home Guards who disappeared in August 1940 after going out on patrol on the beach near Bawdsey. It seems the task has ended up being a little more realistic than intended.'

'Isn't that the place where a course trainer also recently disappeared?'

'Yes, quite a coincidence, isn't it,' Dr Bootle surmises. 'Shall we get on, there's a group of students in the viewing gallery who are eager to watch the proceedings.'

'Yes of course,' Clive Dunning replies curtly, whilst deftly concealing the irritation that he is already feeling at the pompous attitude of the pathologist.

Dr Bootle begins by visually examining each of the three bodies in turn, explaining aloud his every observation for the benefit of the students in the viewing gallery. Although the existence of an unusually large audience in the parochial postmortem suite has given Dr Bootle an unprecedented feeling of stage fright, as a pathologist who adores teaching students, their presence is still a welcome addition to the typically empty gallery.

The pathologist stands in front of the viewing gallery to address his awaiting audience. 'This is a most unusual postmortem and one you may never come across again. I'm sure you will find the experience to be very valuable. My colleague Dr Clive Dunning is here to answer any questions of an historical nature that you may have.' Dr Bootle turns to look at Clive Dunning as way of introduction to the students before turning his attention back to the wall of glass, behind which are some twenty young people eager to learn.

'To set some context to the importance of today's proceedings, it is very rare for cadavers from the Second World War to be discovered in the UK, they do occasionally crop up in Europe though when a search for a missing person or an accidental finding might happen across one. It is certainly a rarity to find such a case though on British soil and I have no doubt that the press will take a keen interest.'

With his opening comments made, Dr Bootle turns his attention to the three bodies and begins to examine each one in turn with Clive Dunning on hand to assist. The postmortems take less time than usual as although the bodies are in remarkable condition given their age, they are in an advanced state of decay and it is not possible to even remove the men's uniforms. Instead, x-rays are taken to examine the structure of the body beneath the fragile green material that still proudly exhibits the emblem of the British Home Guard.

Once the examination is complete, the students from the viewing gallery file into the mortuary suite and stand at a respectable distance so that they can observe the bodies more closely.

'Can anyone tell me how these three men died?' Dr Dunning asks the students, who immediately look at the bodies for clues.

'I can,' a small voice from the back of the room pipes up.

'Can you indeed Poppy, do tell us then,' Dr Bootle responds, not expecting to hear the correct answer from his quietest student.

'I noticed when Dr Dunning was examining the third body that there is a hole in the side of his head,' Poppy replies shyly.

'Excellent, well noticed,' Clive Dunning replies, moving across the room to stand next to the third body. 'If I turn the head slightly, can you all see the entrance hole made by a bullet?'

The students murmur amongst themselves as they jostle for a position that will allow them to see. 'What about the bullet, is it still in there?' One of the students asks, clearly captivated by the whole thing.

'If you move to the other side of the skull, you can see there is also an exit wound,' Clive Dunning responds. 'Now can anyone tell me how we can find out the type of gun used?'

Poppy raises her hand, 'we can find out from the bullet?'

'Yes that would help. We can also tell a lot by the size of the entry and exit holes as well as the trajectory the bullet has taken and the extent of damage it has made. I don't know the answer to this one at the moment, I'll need to do some more research on the tissue damage. I also want to see if we can find the bullet that killed this man,' Clive Dunning explains to the students, who have now moved to the other side of the cadaver so that they can see the exit hole.

'I'll ask the SOCO team to take another look in the pillbox and see if there are any bullets or casings in there. Perhaps one of your team would like to assist, the pillbox is rather buried in sand and may need excavating?' Dr Bootle suggests, stepping closer to the body so that he too can observe where the bullet entered and left the body.

'Sounds a great idea, I would be delighted to help,' Clive Dunning says, glad that the trip out to the Suffolk coast has been fruitful for more than one reason. Fostering relationships with external partners is all part of the job, however tedious he might find it.

'Perhaps one of my students could also tag along, how about yourself Poppy?'

'Yes please,' Poppy says, her eyes shining at the thought of getting some real work experience.

'Well, that's settled then,' Dr Bootle says officiously. 'Now can we assume that all three men died in the same way?'

'Yes they did and in my opinion, they have all been executed,' Clive Dunning says, taking off his gloves and throwing them into the hazardous waste bin.

'Well, that is interesting. I will give Detective Inspector Morgan the good news that he now has a triple murder to investigate alongside the missing person case,' Dr Bootle concludes as he also removes his gloves before he leaves the postmortem room in search of a strong coffee to accompany his lunch, which is already sitting on his desk.

The coolness inside the Hall is an almost welcome respite from the intense heat outside, though Morgan knows full well that he will soon be complaining about the damp chill, which will leave him longing to be outside in the sunshine again. He finds the others where he left them - still pouring over the documents that were compiled by Bobby Chalnor, what now seems to have been a very long time ago.

'Ah Detective, I'm glad to see you're back. Jane has arranged for some lunch but we wanted to wait for your return.'

'That's very kind of you Mrs Fields, though I'm not sure I feel like eating at the moment,' Morgan replies, the image of the dead man with flies buzzing around him still fresh in his mind.

'Well perhaps you will join us in a little while. We'll go on ahead and give you a moment. Is there anything I can help with?' Camilla asks, ushering Fallow and Foster out of the room.

'Thank you but no and before you ask, there's nothing to report on Mr Chalnor either.'

'That may be a good thing, judging by the expression on your face. I can tell you've had a difficult morning,' Camilla soothes before stepping out of the conference room and marching down the corridor towards the dining room.

Morgan sits down at the table that is now unoccupied. He pulls towards him the documents that his colleagues have just been looking at, wishing that he could work out what it is that is puzzling him. The events of the past couple of days all seem to be too coincidental and as Camilla said, it rather feels as if they have been set up. The question is of course who has set up this escapade and why.

~ Thirteen ~

It is only a simple meal of sandwiches, fruit and sea-salted crisps but it gives Morgan the boost that he has needed ever since he left behind the body on the beach that was not Bobby Chalnor. The coffee too, of course also helps and by the time Morgan has sat for a while on the veranda, gazing out across the river as he drinks a large Americano, he is feeling decidedly better than he felt earlier.

The detective takes the opportunity to phone his wife Celia, who listens supportively as best she can despite their puppy vying for her attention by leaping up and down, trying to catch hold of the phone. Although the idea of the dog was to keep Celia company whilst her husband was working, it has in fact ended up being more Morgan's dog. The sound of Bailey barking in the background gives Morgan a slight pang for home but it is a feeling that is quickly replaced by the certainty that as always, his job must come first.

'I thought I might find you out here,' Camilla says as she steps out into the midday sun. 'It is a little cool inside the building.'

'...and then you get too hot when you've been outside for more than ten minutes,' Morgan continues.

Camilla smiles then pulls out one of the rattan chairs to sit down, placing her leather handbag close to her court shoes. Morgan cannot help but wonder if Camilla ever wears more casual attire, he is certainly unable to imagine it.

'The others are looking over the display in the dining room, it's quite a fascinating insight into the history of the area and of course this building. Did you know that King Edward once visited the Hall whilst he was trying to decide whether or not to abdicate and marry Mrs Simpson. It caused quite a stir, I can tell you. They were in Felixstowe for a time as well.'

'I didn't know that, it seems there's always something new to learn,' Morgan says, taking another sip of the rich coffee. 'Can I get you a drink?'

'Thank you but I'm fine,' Camilla responds, gazing wistfully out across the River Deben towards Felixstowe Ferry. 'I wonder....'

'Sorry, what did you say?' Morgan asks, his attention re-focusing on Camilla who has stopped talking and is staring at the sailboats that are bobbing about gently on the tidal river.

'Oh, it doesn't matter, I'm just thinking aloud,' Camilla says before standing up again. 'Shall we go and join the others? I think Jane has now reappeared.'

'Yes of course. I wonder where Jane keeps disappearing to?'

'So do I, perhaps another mystery for you to solve?' Camilla teases.

Morgan smiles, knowing full well that the elderly councillor is of course taunting him. It is however something that he would genuinely like to know the answer to.

Fallow and Foster are at opposite ends of the long room, peering closely at each of the exhibits in turn as if hoping that they will somehow reveal something monumental to them. Morgan makes his way across the room to stand next to Fallow, who is looking at a map of the Bawdsey area in 1940. The map shows the placements of the barricades on the beach, along with the line of pillboxes that were constructed at regular intervals along the beach.

'It's fascinating isn't it. You can almost imagine what it might have been like to be here at that time,' Fallow says, squinting as he tries to decipher the writing at the bottom of the map.

Morgan cannot imagine how utterly terrifying it must have been, especially for the Home Guards who had been tasked with patrolling the beaches day and night, despite the area being littered with landmines and being very vulnerable to invasion. The detective takes a step to one side to look at the photograph on the wall to the right of the map, which shows the beach with its fortifications in place. Underneath the photo, the text states;

It was a well-kept secret that Bawdsey Hall was home to some of the clandestine experiments conducted during the early part of the Second World War. These deadly experiments involved the use of flames and how these might be used on the sea to defend the coastline from German invasion.

'That's interesting, wasn't there a rumour about there being a failed German invasion somewhere around here?' Morgan asks no one in particular. Fallow, who is standing nearby, hears Morgan's comment and sidles closer towards the detective.

'Yes, it is, apparently the sea was set on fire and bodies were found on the beach at Shingle Street. Can I take a look at that photo?' Fallow asks.

'Sure, it makes it a lot easier being able to visualise what the area looked like during the war.'

'Hmmm, yes, I guess so,' Fallow says, peering at the photo. 'Did you see the photo with the Canadian airman? He was seconded to the RAF during the war. I wonder if he's our mysterious diary writer Oswald Turner.'

'That's a good point. Are there any names on the photo?'

'I'm afraid not, it's a group photo taken on Martlesham airfield. I do think though the man in the centre though looks quite similar to Mr Chalnor.'

'Well, that's not very likely is it, I don't think Bobby Chalnor is quite that old,' Morgan says, rolling his eyes.

Fallow does not respond, he has learnt by now when not to bother trying to defend himself to Morgan. 'We haven't finished interviewing all the staff yet,' Fallow reminds Morgan.

'Why don't you and Foster go and chat to whoever is next on the list then, if you're so keen. I really can't see how it's going to find Bobby Chalnor.'

'It might help to find out more about the bodies found in the pillbox though,' Fallow says quietly as he pads across the deep-pile carpet to the other end of the room, where Foster is still perusing the wall display.

'Find out anything interesting?' Foster asks as Fallow stands next to him.

'Not really,' Fallow replies, feeling rather despondent after the uncomfortable encounter with his senior team member. 'Morgan's asked us to carry on interviewing the witnesses.'

'Sounds a better plan, I can't see what we'll find looking at a bunch of old photos,' Foster grumbles, clearly bored of looking at the historical documents.

'You'd be surprised what you might learn from history Detective Constable Foster,' Camilla says a little sternly, as she crosses the room to join the two men.

Foster smiles tight-lipped but does not respond, clearly not agreeing with his older peer. 'We're now off to carry on interviewing the staff.'

'Ok, good, well I'll finish off looking at the photos then make a start on that diary,' Camilla says, staring at a photograph behind Foster's head. The picture shows a group of Home Guards who were stationed at the Hall at the start of the war and there is something about the photo that has caught Camilla's attention.

Next on the list of witnesses to interview is the kitchen hand. Foster and Fallow find Maisie in the pantry, sorting through tins and packets of food.

'Hallo,' Maisie says cheerfully, holding a tin of baked beans in one hand.

'Sorry to disturb you but we're doing the task that was set by Mr Chalnor for the course. We're hoping it might give us some idea of what's happened to him. I think we're supposed to question you about it?' Fallow explains.

'Oh, do you think it will help to find him?'

'Honestly, I don't know but right now it's the only thing left we can do, there's already a lot of people out there looking for him. It might help of we can work out why he's disappeared and finding out more about him and his work could help with that,' Foster justifies from his position standing in the narrow corridor that connects the kitchen and the pantry that at one time would have been outside of the main building.

'That's true, I didn't think of it like that,' Maisie says, putting the tin that she's holding down onto one of the painted shelves. 'Shall we go into the kitchen, there's a bit more room in there?'

Fallow and Foster shuffle backwards against the wall to allow Maisie to exit from the pantry then they follow her into the kitchen, where a delicious scent of something slow cooking in the Aga reaches their senses before they have set foot in the room.

'What's for dinner then?' Foster asks cheekily.

'Spring chicken casserole. Reece kindly dispatched one of our chickens this morning,' Maisie says, watching the expression on the two men's faces change to one of abject horror. The young woman chuckles, having correctly deduced that the detectives are not very well acquainted with rural life.

'We've got a list of questions that we're supposed ask you,' Foster says, trying to put the thought of the recently deceased chicken out of his mind.

'And I have a piece of paper that tells me what I need to say to answer them,' Maisie responds, rummaging through a pile of cookery books to find the print-out that Bobby Chalnor gave her. 'So, I'm to tell you that I'm the kitchen maid and my name is Sarah. I'm only sixteen and have worked at the Hall for two years.'

Foster pulls out his notebook and jots down a few details. 'What did your job involve?'

'I cooked, cleaned, looked after the chickens, much the same as I do now. I did however have a pot boy to wash up in those days, I wish I still had one,' Maisie laughs.

'Don't you have a dishwasher?' Fallow asks sincerely.

'Err yes, shall we carry on with the questions,' Maisie says, sitting down on a nearby stool.

'Ok, so what's next,' Foster says, running a finger down the sheet of questions until he reaches the ones for 'Sarah Pearson'. 'Do you live here at the Hall?'

'Yes I do.'

'Who else is staying at the Hall?' Foster asks rolling his eyes, surely they could ask some more interesting questions than these?

'I've got a list written down, see here,' Maisie replies, showing the two detectives her answer sheet, which is similar to the one given to the gardener Reece Browne.

Esme Smart – Administrator
Mrs Maggie Adams - Cook
Molly Jasper – Maid
Sarah Pearson – Kitchen Maid
Oswald Turner – Instructor
Eleanor Fulcher – Trainee Radio Operator
Fanny Minter – Trainee Radio Operator

'It's a shorter list than the one Reece had,' Foster deduces as he reads through the list.

'That list was for the people who were working here and stationed here, this one's for the people who were actually staying at the Hall,' Maisie explains. 'Some of them would've been living in nearby Alderton, which was evacuated of its residents at the start of the war.'

'There's Oswald Turner's name again,' Fallow says, pointing at one of the names on the piece of paper. 'He's the one who wrote the diary.'

'What diary?' Maisie asks, picking up a potato from the pile of vegetables on the worktop and starting to peel it.

'Morgan found a book trapped inside the interconnecting doors between our two rooms,' Fallow explains.

'Oh! I wonder how that got there?' Maisie says, putting the potato down.

'Where is it now Fallow?' asks Foster.

'I think it's in Morgan's room, why?' Fallow replies.

'Just wondered, that's all. We should get back to looking at these questions,' Foster instructs, pulling the document towards him. 'So, the next question is asking where you were on the night of 25th August 1940.'

Maisie checks her answer sheet, then replies, 'I was on duty that night, that's the answer I'm supposed to give you. Do you know, this sounds really familiar, I'm sure my grandma said that she was working here that summer, though she's not on that list.'

'What did she do at the Hall?' asks Foster.

'She was a maid but also helped out in the kitchen as well. Her name was Sally Price.'

'Right well let's add her to the list then,' Fallow says, handing his pen to Maisie so that she can amend her answer sheet. 'Are there any more questions we're supposed to ask the kitchen hand?'

'No but the instructions say that we can ask our own questions,' Foster replies, reading through the sheet again. 'What happened on the night of 25th August 1940?'

'Well, I know the answer to that one without looking at the answer sheet, it was the night there was supposed to have been that German invasion. I remember my grandma telling me about it. She said that it was a stormy night, there was thick cloud cover making it feel really humid and sticky and when it got dark it was the blackest night she'd ever seen.'

'It was also the night the three Home Guards disappeared,' Fallow says slowly.

'That's right, it's all coming back to me now, my grandma told me that they patrolled up and down the beach just in case the Jerries decided to invade but one night they went out and never came back. Everyone thought they'd gone AWOL, it happens you know, especially in wars. They get scared you see and I can't blame them really.'

'Did she say anything else about that night? Foster asks, seemingly becoming more interested in the story.

'She said that she couldn't sleep because it was so hot and sticky, even with the window open. When she did eventually get to sleep something woke her up. She couldn't see anything out of her bedroom window so she went back to bed again but was too frightened to go back to sleep. I think she thought the Germans had invaded the beach, so she laid there all night, waiting for them to turn up at the Hall.'

'Did they?' Foster asks, tilting his head to one side as he ponders on the information they have just heard.

'Well now, that's the question isn't it. Something happened that night, those three boys went missing from Bawdsey and then there was that rumour of the German invasion. Funny things happened though in those days and it's hard to say what the truth of it was.'

'The myth said there were bodies found on the beach, did your grandma see anything?' Fallow asks.

'No she didn't but they were all kept inside the Hall and questioned about the missing Guards. Have you talked to the gardener yet?' Maisie asks, picking up another potato to peel.

'Yes we have, he wasn't much help really, just told us what was on the answer sheet,' Foster replies.

'No, I mean the old guy, Cedric. He was here in the war, he wasn't fit enough to fight so he helped out here doing the gardening.'

'Not yet, though it sounds like we should do,' Fallow says. 'Right, we'd better leave you to get on with the dinner. If you think of anything else though, please let me know.'

'I sure will. I hope you get to find Mr Chalnor soon, he seemed a real nice man even if I did find his accent a bit difficult to understand,' Maisie says, as the two detectives move towards the door.

Fallow stands in the doorway and looks at Maisie, who has now started peeling carrots. He did not notice Bobby Chalnor having a strong accent when he spoke to him the evening before he disappeared. Perhaps the course trainer was trying to hide his accent from the attendees and if that was the case then they need to find out why.

~ Fourteen ~

The sun is as relentless as it was the last time Morgan had found himself standing on the beach at Shingle Street, staring at a half-buried pillbox. This time though he is accompanied by Dr Dunning along with Len Bootle's student Poppy, who has an expression on her face that reveals her excitement at the opportunity to do some actual field work.

Morgan presses his back into the cold cliff face, a welcome respite from the searing heat that has been beating down on him for the past half-an-hour. He almost wishes he was back at Bawdsey Hall, helping Camilla look through the rest of the photographs in the dining room.

The entire area is still cordoned off, not only due to the discovery of the bodies but also due to the precarious state of the cliff that runs from Sizewell to Bawdsey. The current absence of tourists and fossil hunters has left the place with an almost eerie silence that is only broken by the rhythmic swishing of the waves crashing onto the nearby shoreline and the occasional comment from the three people who are standing in the place where the bodies of three Home Guards were recently discovered.

'Poppy, please could you grab the camera and take some photos of the area. Try to avoid the detective if you can, I'm sure he'd prefer not to be in them,' Clive says jovially as he kneels down next to the only window of the pillbox that is visible in the mound of sand and debris that covers most of the decaying concrete structure. The experienced archaeologist is relishing the challenge of something new, something out of the ordinary. Not that his job is mundane of course but just occasionally something unusual turns up that reminds him why he does this job.

'Poppy, do you know why there are different layers in the cliff face that look like stripes?' Clive asks, eager to teach at every opportunity.

'Are they layers from different time periods?'

'Thats right, they're mostly glacial deposits but could also be chalk or sandstone. Can you see there's water dripping down the cliff?'

'Yes, is there a river nearby?' Poppy asks, shielding her eyes so that she can see the cliff face more clearly.

'It's rainwater from the storm. The land has soaked it up and stored it but there's only so much it can absorb. Unfortunately it can make the cliff unstable.'

'I thought that landslides are caused by coastal erosion?'

'They usually are, especially around here. The North Sea is pretty fierce and the cliffs are quite soft so they erode easily. Further up the coast whole villages have been lost to the sea and even now several feet of land are being lost each year.'

'Can't they stop it?'

'They won't do anything here as there aren't any expensive houses to protect,' Clive bitterly explains. 'Sometimes nature is just left to take its course, a bit like getting older and needing to stay out of the sun.'

Clive Dunning looks in Morgans direction, who has of course heard every word of the conversation. Morgan rolls his eyes theatrically, knowing full well that the archaeologist is only joking. He is however grateful to be out of the sun for a while, even if being in such close proximity to a cliff that has recently collapsed is more than a little disconcerting.

'Anything of interest yet?' Morgan shouts across the sand dune, conversationally rather than out of any need for the question to be answered.

'Not yet, I'm going to have to go inside the pillbox,' Clive grimaces. Since the three bodies were removed from the pillbox, there have been further landslips from the cliff above, undoing some of the excavations made by the SOCO team and leaving the structure in an even more precarious position than it was already. Now the only entrance is through the narrow window, which looks entirely uninviting.

'Can you fit through that tiny hole?' Morgan shouts across the quiet space, eliciting a mock stern glare from the archaeologist.

'Do you want me to go in there?' Poppy asks earnestly, crouching down to look inside the pillbox.

Clive Dunning looks at the narrow opening and for a moment is almost tempted to take the student up on her offer but he knows that if something catastrophic did happen he would never forgive himself and nor would the University, which does not have insurance for students to accompany archaeologists out in the field on police business.

'Thanks but I'll manage. Perhaps you could get me a torch though, there's one in my rucksack,' Clive says, pointing to the filthy bag close to Morgan's feet.

'Sure,' Poppy replies, her voice revealing her disappointment as she locates the requested object and passes it to the archaeologist.

Clive Dunning uses a trowel to sweep out some of the loose sand that has found its' way into the pillbox, driven into the narrow space by the force of the wind hurtling across the North Sea. When a big enough gap has been dug out, he switches on the torch then lowers himself down flat onto the sand so that he can wriggle into the dark chasm beyond. The archaeologists heart pounds as he enters the enclosed space and he fights to control his panic, pushing aside all thoughts of what could happen to the fragile structure that he is now inside. In less than half a minute, Clive Dunning has left the warmth of the sunshine behind and is now deep inside the cold, damp pillbox.

Morgan is standing underneath the cliff, trying not to feel concerned that the archaeologist is working alone in a place that was once a coffin to three soldiers who were not expecting to die that night. A drop of water plips onto the detective face, interrupting his thoughts. The droplet is quickly followed by a shower of red grain that whooshes down the cliff directly onto him. Automatically Morgan moves, even someone unused to the countryside, would recognise the signs that something concerning is happening. He runs across the sand dune towards Poppy, who is still diligently taking photos of the pillbox and the surrounding area.

'Hey, did you see that?'

'What is it?' Poppy asks, putting down the camera.

'Some debris just came down the cliff face. I swear I heard someone on the path above me as well.'

'The path's closed though, isn't it?'

'Yes it is. I'm worried there might be another cliff collapse, I think you should step back a bit, I'm going to check on Clive. Here's my phone just in case anything should happen.'

As Morgan strides across the grassy knoll to the pillbox, a shadow moving on the cliff top above momentarily catches his attention then it is gone again, as if it were never there. When he is only a few feet away from the pillbox, Morgan shouts out to get the archaeologists attention. 'Hey Clive, I think you should get out of there.'

Immediately Clive's face appears at the pillbox window. 'What's up?'

'I've just seen some debris coming down the cliff from the path above, I think you should get out of there, it might not be safe.'

'Sure thing, sounds sensible,' Clive says, wincing with concern. 'I'll just grab the torch and trowel then I'll be right out.'

Morgan takes a few steps back from the concrete structure so that he is a safer distance from the cliff, which is showering tiny grains onto the beach below. The detective's shoes sink into the soft sand now saturated with salt water from the waves that are beginning to creep further up the shore. It is then that the unthinkable happens and Morgan can do nothing but watch as a large chunk of the cliff face breaks away and collapses downwards, burying the pillbox.

~ Fifteen ~

By the time the dust settles, Morgan has already brushed off the worst of the debris from his orange-stained clothes. His first thought is to check on Poppy, who is standing several feet away from him and has managed to miss the cliff fall entirely. Then he remembers about Clive Dunning.

'Poppy, can you see Clive?' Morgan tries to shout to the student, though only managing little more than a whisper as he is still struggling to breathe from inhaling the cloud of sandstone that enveloped him when the cliff collapsed.

'No,' Poppy says quietly. She sits down on the shingle and stares at the pile of rubble that now covers the pill-box.

'Do you still have my phone?' Morgan asks, checking that he is unhurt as he gingerly stands up from the stoney ground that he has fallen onto.

'Yes,' Poppy says, her voice barely audible.

'Ok, I need you to listen Poppy and do exactly what I tell you, can you do that?' Morgan says, staring at the youngster, willing her to shake herself out of her shocked stupor.

Poppy nods, still staring at the spot at the bottom of the cliff where the pillbox was only moments ago.

'Ok, I need you to dial 999 and ask for the police, ambulance and coastguard. Can you do that?'

'I think so,' a quiet voice says, almost drowned out by the roar of the waves that have grown exponentially since they first arrived on the beach. The tide has turned and is coming in fast.

Morgan pauses for a moment to check that Poppy has registered his words and is putting them into action, then with a brief glance at the cliff above, he runs over to where the landslip is and begins digging with his hands. Maybe they will get lucky and Clive Dunning has enough oxygen in there to keep him alive until help arrives but he cannot take that chance.

Not for the first time that week, Morgan chastises himself for putting off taking up running again. After moving several large boulders and chunks of fallen sandstone, the detective is too exhausted to continue. Poppy, having now recovered from the shock a little, finds a bottle of water in Clive's rucksack and hands it to Morgan. He looks at the plastic object then looks back at the place where the archaeologist is buried before putting it back down again. There is someone else here who has a far greater need for water then he has. Morgan just hopes he gets the chance to give it to him.

With the sun beginning to set in the West, the worst of the days heat begins to subside. The cooler air makes the task of shifting rubble a little easier for Morgan, who has recovered from his earlier exertion and is now feverishly digging again. Even though his muscles burn, protesting at the unexpected exercise, Morgan wills himself to continue excavating, spurred on by the fear that in a few hours it will become dark and with the incoming tide, the need to get Clive Dunning out of the pillbox is becoming increasingly more urgent. Morgan tries not to think about what it must be like in there, entombed alive with no way of knowing if you will ever get out. It then occurs to Morgan that perhaps he should try shouting the archaeologists name, in case he can hear him through the thick pile of concrete, sand and rubble.

'Clive, can you hear me?' Morgan shouts, crouching down and putting an ear to the rockfall.

Poppy, seemingly fully recovered from the shock of the rock fall, gingerly picks her way through the debris to kneel down next to Morgan, where she too begins calling out for the trapped archaeologist.

'Can you hear something?' Poppy asks, putting her ear to the ground.

'I'm not sure, try shouting again.'

Poppy calls out again. 'There, did you hear that?'

'Yes I did, come on, let's keep digging.'

Encouraged by the thought that Clive Dunning could still be alive, the pair move the rubble as quickly as they can, whilst keeping a careful watch out for any further landslips.

'I definitely heard something,' Morgan declares, using the bottom of his t-shirt to wipe away the perspiration from his forehead.

'Well, that's good news,' a voice says from someone who is clambering over a sand dune. 'We'll take over now.'

Morgan stands up, his legs gelatinous after crouching for so long. 'We've heard a few noises, they seem to be coming from over there,' Morgan says, pointing to the area where the window of the pillbox was once visible.

'Go and take a break, get some water. There's some in my bag,' says the Fire Officer who is striding purposefully across the sand towards the exhausted pair.

Morgan places a hand on Poppy's shoulder and gently steers her towards the group of people who have now gathered behind them. 'The experts have arrived, we need to leave them to get on with it,' Morgan gently explains.

Poppy hesitantly smiles as she looks back again at the landslip, then turns around and makes her way over the grassy knoll to the sea beyond. The student takes off her sandy trainers and holding them in one hand, walks through the cool water, the fresh tidal waves washing over her tired feet.

'Poppy,' Morgan calls, running after her. 'Do you want me to take you home?'

'Not yet, I want to be here when they get Dr Dunning out. I want to see that he's ok.'

Morgan nods his head, not wanting to say what they are both thinking – if they get him out alive.

The sun has almost set, leaving the rescue team with the decision to either halt the search for the night or find some emergency lighting, which could be challenging given their remote location. They decide to press on until the last of the light has dwindled, concentrating on the area where the noises seem to be getting louder and with one final push they drive through the crushed rock and sandstone. A hole appears and the void underneath it is quickly filled by a smile that can only belong to Clive Dunning.

Poppy and Morgan, who are sitting on the beach, no longer able to bear to watch the search, hear a cry from one of the Fire Officers. The pair look at each other, wondering if they dare to raise their hopes. Then another shout is heard and this time they are certain – Clive Dunning has been found.

'Hey, you two, you might want to come and take a look,' one of the Coastguards says, walking across the sand to find Morgan and Poppy.

'Is he ok?' Poppy asks nervously.

'Pretty good considering, they've still got to dig him out but you can speak to him.'

Poppy looks uncertain as to whether or not she wants to go over to the pillbox, the memory of the afternoon still fresh in her mind.

'It will help Clive,' Morgan says gently, 'Knowing that we're still here, it will give him hope.'

Poppy nods, understanding that the archaeologist's needs are more pertinent at this point in time than her own. 'Has he had some water?'

'Yes, we squeezed a bottle in through the hole. You've both done a great job you know, helping us to locate him.'

Poppy tentatively smiles then steels herself against the task ahead by fixing a smile firmly on her face. Then she strides across the grassy mound to the group of strangers who are still working to free the archaeologist.

Morgan follows closely behind Poppy, anxious as to what he might find. He is pleasantly surprised however to see the archaeologists usual cheerful grin peering through the dark chasm.

'How are you?' Morgan asks as he carefully kneels down, trying to avoid sending any more loose shingle back down into the hole again.

'I'm ok, not too bad considering. I think my wrist is broken though, so I won't be doing any excavations for a while.'

'Perhaps you could help Dr Bootle out with his students, I'm sure he'd relish the opportunity to learn more about your field.'

Clive Dunning chuckles at the thought of having to spend time in close proximity to Len Bootle, who is renowned for his difficult persona. Not many people could stomach working closely with the pathologist, except of course Harry, who seems to be immune to his blunt ways.

'I'm glad you're still here Morgan, there's something I need to tell you, something that I found.'

'Oh, what's that?'

The conversation is abruptly interrupted by the rescue team, who have finished their short break and are keen to get the archaeologist out before the light completely fades. Morgan steps back to allow them to work, curious as to the meaning of Clive Dunnings words. Perhaps he has found the missing bullets or their casings? Or is there something else, buried deep beneath the sand, overshadowed by the cliffs that tower over the beach at Shingle Street. Something that should not be there.

~ Sixteen ~

Morgan drops Poppy off at her parent's home in Deben Quay then drives onwards in the car that he borrowed from Jane Stokes, to his own house. He feels a pressing need to see his wife and dog even if it is just for a short time. He will not be able to speak to Clive Dunning again until he has been freed from the pillbox and taken to Hemley Hospital, where he is certain that Len Bootle will take the opportunity to fuss around the well-respected archaeologist.

The detective pulls up in front of his house and switches off the engine, allowing the quietness to envelope him, soothing him after the drama of the afternoon. It is only then that he remembers that Fallow, Camilla and Foster are still at Bawdsey Hall and most probably wondering where he is. Morgan pulls out his mobile phone to find that the battery is almost dead. Quickly he messages Fallow to let him know that he will be back later and will explain it all to him then. With the message sent, Morgan takes off his seatbelt, opens the car door, locking it behind him and walks towards his front door, leaving all that has happened behind for a short while.

The occupants of Bawdsey Hall remain blissfully un-aware of the drama that has been unfolding further up the coast until Morgan returns, still covered in dirt.

'Oh my, whatever's happened?' Camilla asks, walking across the hallway to greet Morgan, who has just come in through the front door, leaving a trail of dust behind him.

'It's a long story and I really need to go and take a shower first.'

'Of course, I'll ask Maisie to prepare some food for you whilst you get cleaned up.'

'Thank you and perhaps also a cold beer if there is one.'

Camilla nods then immediately steps into the dining room to make the arrangements - it is clear that the detective is not in the right frame of mind to talk at the moment.

'Did I hear Morgan?' Fallow asks, having heard voices in the hallway. He stands up from the comfy armchair he has been sitting in, next to the window in the adjoining snug.

'Yes, he's gone to have a shower. It appears that something very serious has happened. I'm going to ask Maisie to find some food for him, perhaps you could get the detective a beer? I'm sure you know better than I do what he likes to drink,' Camilla says, heading towards the door that leads into the kitchen.

Camilla finds Maisie still washing up from dinner, which prompts her to recall that during the war there were staff who would wash up the pots and dinner plates.

It seems ironic in this modern day that staff are still needed to do menial tasks despite the available technology that has the capability to do it for them.

'Maisie my dear, Detective Inspector Morgan has just come back and is in need of something to eat. Do you have anything that you could rustle up?'

'Yes of course, there's some leftover casserole in the fridge, I'll warm it up for him now.'

Camilla thanks Maisie then returns to the dining room where Fallow has located several bottles of cold beer. Whilst she waits for Morgan to return, Camilla peruses the wall display again to see if there is something that she might have previously missed amongst the photographs. It then occurs to her that there is a small library in the sitting room at the back of the Hall, which is rarely used by guests who have little time for reading when attending the intensive training courses. She makes her way back into the hallway, which is dark in comparison to the room she has just left, then pads across the soft carpet to the sitting room.

Camilla opens the door to find Jane Stokes sitting in one of the comfy armchairs, reading a newspaper. 'Oh hello, I wondered where you'd got to,' Camilla exclaims.

'Do you need me for something? I was just taking the opportunity to catch up on the local news.'

'Anything of interest in there?'

'There's an article about Bobby's disappearance. It's so odd, him leaving like that. I do hope nothing's happened to him.'

'Have you known Mr Chalnor long?'

'He's only been working here for a few weeks.'

'I see, well hopefully we'll get some news soon. I must say it's very unsettling not knowing what's happened to him.'

'Yes it is,' Jane agrees, placing the copy of '*The Suffolk Times*' down on the small table next to her chair. 'I wish I could understand why he left.'

'How much do you know about Mr Chalnor? Presumably he does not make a habit of just disappearing?' Camilla asks, sitting down in the chair opposite Jane.

'I don't think so, not as far as I know anyway. I don't know much about him, he was hired by the Halls owner.'

'Ah the mysterious owner who never comes here.'

'Some people buy properties for investment,' Jane explains.

'I would have thought that the fact that one of their employees has disappeared would have enticed some communication from them though?'

'They don't know that Bobby's missing,' Jane admits, looking at Camilla to see her reaction.

'Oh, why not?'

'I didn't tell them, I didn't want Bobby to get into trouble.'

Camilla nods her head thoughtfully, 'so you think that he'll return then?'

'I don't know,' Jane says quickly. 'Please excuse me I think I'll get an early night.'

'Of course. Before you go, I wonder if you could point me in the right direction of any historical books about the Hall. I'm particularly keen on anything from the Second World War.'

'Yes of course, they're over there,' Jane says pointing at a low bookcase in the corner of the room. 'I really must go and lie down, I have an awful headache.'

'Probably all the stress, I hope you feel better soon,' Camilla says, striding across the room to look at the books. She pulls out a few of the books that look like they could be of interest, then takes them back to the dining room, where Morgan has just returned.

'Do you feel any better?' Camilla asks, pulling out a chair at the table where Morgan is now sitting, waiting for his re-heated casserole to arrive.

'Yes, thank you, it's been quite a day,' Morgan mutters as he picks up a bottle of beer and drinks deeply from it.

'Would you like to talk about it?' Camilla asks with her usual sense of diplomacy.

Morgan takes another swig from the bottle of beer then places it down on the table. 'I had a phone call from Dr Dunning, the forensic archaeologist who's been helping Dr Bootle with the postmortems of the three Home Guards. Dr Dunning and one of Dr Bootle's students were on their way to the pillbox where the bodies were found and asked if I could go as well, in case anything was discovered.'

Camilla nods thoughtfully, 'please do continue.'

'There was a landslip from the cliff above the pillbox, poor Clive was inside it when it happened,' Morgan says, shuddering at the recollection.

'Bloody hell,' Foster exclaims as he walks into the room, catching the end of the conversation. He sits down at the table, Fallow following suite. 'Is he ok?'

'It was a close call, Poppy and I heard him call out so we knew the area he was in for the rescue team to search. They'd just located him before it got dark.'

'How is he? Did you get to speak to him?' Camilla asks, her forehead wrinkling with concern.

'For a few moments, he said there was something he needed to tell me, something he found in the pillbox.'

'I wonder what he meant by that?' Fallow asks, filling a glass with water from a jug in the middle of the table.

'I don't know, I'll have to wait until he's fit enough to talk to me,' Morgan explains.

'Well I expect that won't happen this evening so I suggest that you relax a little and perhaps we could take a look at that diary later?' Camilla says, also filling a glass with water.

'That sounds a good plan,' Morgan replies, putting the empty beer bottle down on the table.

Maisie arrives with a plate of food for Morgan, then swiftly leaves again. The room lulls into a comfortable silence, each of them deep in thought, mulling over the news of what occurred earlier that day. Eventually Morgan breaks to silence by pushing back his chair and padding across to the door to the veranda. He pauses for a moment, looking back at the trio who are still sitting at the table. He smiles thinly at them, then heads out onto the patio where it is still warm despite the late hour.

Morgan sits down on one of the wicker chairs, strategically placed for an optimal view of the river and contemplates if the vista has altered much since the Second World War. He imagines that it has changed little, except for the bright lights of Felixstowe that have no doubt increased in the last eighty years. The view of the stars twinkling in the dark sky above the Hall however are unlikely to have altered and Morgan leans back into the chair to gaze at them for a while.

Feeling more relaxed than earlier, Morgan takes a few deep breaths then pushes himself up from the chair. He takes one last wistful look at the river, taking in the sound of ropes clanging against the masts of the sailing boats moored in the deepest part of the river, the soothing rhythm of the North Sea waves crashing onto the shingle shore on the other side of the building and the quietness that seems to have descended as if the storm has now passed and all that will come now is closure of what has already occurred and acceptance of what will soon be forthcoming.

Morgan reluctantly leaves the peaceful ambience of the garden and steps back into the bright dining room. Camilla is still seated at the table, engrossed in reading the diary that Morgan found hidden between the two inter-connecting doors. Fallow and Foster have disappeared, presumably tired and of need of an early night, leaving Morgan and Camilla to talk freely.

'Have you found anything interesting?' Morgan asks as he rejoins the table.

'I certainly have, Oswald was quite a character and certainly had a likening for the ladies,' Camilla tuts disapprovingly.

'Oh, well I guess they were exceptional times.'

'I guess so,' Camilla says, sounding unconvinced. 'Listen to this, I'll read some of it to you.'

May 10th, 1940
I've just met the most beautiful, vivacious woman on this earth. I am totally in love, even though we've just met and she doesn't even know my name. I'm sure though that I will win her affections. The problem is what do I do about S?

'See, he's a rogue, wanting another woman when he's already seeing someone.'

'It does look that way,' Morgan reluctantly admits. 'What else does it say?'

May 17th, 1940
How quickly things change, I never expected my
life to get this complicated. At least I have N here
with me though, the only person I can trust, the
only one who understands what's going on.

'Sounds rather intriguing, perhaps he's got caught up
with something clandestine?' Morgan suggests, trying to
peer over Camilla's shoulder so that he can read the diary
more quickly.

'It would appear so. There were all sorts going on in
those strange times, covert operations, spying for the enemy, it must have been difficult to work out which side
anyone was on and who to trust in it all.'

'I imagine it was, it's a wonder people coped with it all
so well. I can't imagine that sort of bravery happening today.'

Camilla rolls her eyes, 'trust you to say that, there are
plenty of heroes in today's society, the problem is that
journalists like to report on the miserable things that sell
papers.'

'I guess that's true and of course you would know all
about the press in your line of work,'

'Shall we read a bit more?' Camilla says, deftly avoid-
ing answering the retort.

May 19th, 1940
It's happened, I was dreading it, didn't know what
to expect but in the end it wasn't as bad as I
thought it would be. I took one of the cycles that
are kept near the kitchen and rode all the way to
the meeting place without being seen, a miracle
in itself and a sign that I'm doing the right thing.
Well that's what N said when I got back. I'm glad
it's over, until the next time anyway.

'It definitely sounds as if our Oswald was doing something he shouldn't have been doing,' Camilla says, putting the diary down. 'I wonder if we can find out more about what who was in the Hall at that time and what they were doing?'

'I completely forgot that Fallow and Foster have been interviewing the staff,' Morgan exclaims, slapping himself on his forehead. 'I'm such an idiot at times.'

'You're too harsh on yourself, you've had other things to occupy your mind like poor Dr Dunning.'

'Have Fallow and Foster gone to bed?'

'Yes I'm afraid so and so has Jane who has a headache. Perhaps we should as well, you've had quite a time of it and I can't stay up late these days,' Camilla says smoothly, picking up the diary and the other books that she found in the sitting room earlier.

'You're right, I'm too tired to think clearly,' Morgan admits as they leave the dining room. He follows Camilla up the stairs and stops outside her bedroom. 'Well, I hope you sleep well, we can carry on with it in the morning.'

'Thank you, you too and yes we will continue tomorrow. Goodnight Detective,' Camilla says before closing the bedroom door.

Morgan stares at the closed door for a moment, wishing that he had asked for the diary so that he could continue reading it. He pauses with his hand raised near the door, ready to knock but then thinks better of it - he is exhausted and really needs to get a good night's sleep. The diary can wait until morning. Morgan strides across the landing and unlocks his bedroom door then he takes off his shoes and climbs into bed, instantly falling asleep, with the sound of the sea soothing away the events of the day.

~ Seventeen ~

Morgan wakes up to find that it is overcast and dull, a stark contrast to the brilliant sunshine they have become accustomed to. With the sun veiled by a thick layer of cloud, the detective has failed to awaken at his usual hour, which automatically puts him in a bad mood. If there is one thing that Morgan cannot stand it is being late.

As soon as has fully awoken, Morgan's thoughts immediately turn to Clive Dunning and the events of the previous day. He reaches across to the bedside table to grab hold of his phone then opens up WhatsApp to check if there are any new messages. A brief text was received at 3am by Dr Len Bootle, informing that Dr Dunning has been admitted to Deben Ward and is keen to speak to the detective as soon as possible.

Morgan pulls on a pair of beige chinos, realising too late that he should have collected some more clothes when he stopped off home yesterday. Hopefully he will not be here much longer though Morgan muses as he searches through the pile of used t-shirts to find one that is not too dirty.

With some acceptable clothing located, Morgan pads across the deep-pile carpet, down the ornate staircase and through the hallway. He peers into the dining room, which is empty as the few other occupants of the Hall are either still in their rooms or perhaps have found something else to amuse themselves with whilst they wait for the others to awaken. Even Jane Stokes is not at her usual place in the small office next to the front door and nor is there any sign of Camilla Fields, which is surprising given her eagerness to solve the mystery they have become entangled in. The thought of Bobby Chalnor and the three Home Guards brings Morgan's attention back to the task at hand. The car that he borrowed from Jane yesterday to go to Shingle Street is still in the driveway. Morgan fishes the keys out from his trouser pocket that he forgot to return yesterday evening then sets off towards Hemley Hospital.

The traffic is surprisingly light which Morgan guesses is because most of Deben Quay's residents are either on holiday or making the most of the school holidays to get into work early and avoid the usual commuter traffic. The car swiftly weaves through the one-way streets, cutting through the Hartsmere estate to reach the car park of the town's only hospital. As always, the sight of the hospital brings back memories that Morgan would rather forget from the last time he was here, when he visited two young girls from the nearby estate who had become embroiled in the convoluted lives of the gangs who were fighting for control over the area. Since the riot, the estate has largely fallen into a quiet lull, with the majority of the gang members either in prison or being moved onto other areas. The more cynical observer might of course deduce that the problem had not been solved but simply moved away from the quaint, riverside town. It is a sentiment that Morgan himself echoes but would not dare to voice, especially within earshot of Chief Superintendent Bennett whose instructions on the dispersal of the gang members had of course been followed to the letter.

The thought of Bennett reminds Morgan of the reason why he and Fallow had been made to attend the course at Bawdsey Hall. It is a well-known secret at the station that Morgan has taken a dislike to the young officer since his arrival and it seems that this fact has reached the ears of Fallow's uncle, Chief Superintendent Bennett. To say that Bennett was not amused to hear that his nephew was being so openly disliked is a vast understatement and subsequently both detectives were swiftly booked onto the first team-building course that had availability, despite the elevated cost of it being in such a luxurious location. Seemingly for Chief Superintendent Bennett, protecting Fallow's reputation was worth the cost to the small training budget.

Of course, Morgan knows that he has been too harsh on the rookie detective but he cannot help being irked by the quiet youngster - the fact that Fallow has such open patronage from his uncle does not help matters. Morgan does however fully recognise that he should learn to leave his personal feelings about work colleagues outside of the station walls, especially if he wants to keep the job that he has worked so hard to get.

It takes little time to locate an empty space in the car park closest to the morgue, which sees few visitors and is often less busy than the rest of the site. Morgan finds a ticket machine that is not broken and places the ticket inside the windscreen where it can be clearly seen by the warden, who is at the far end of the car park doing his morning rounds.

As Morgan strides across the car park towards the main entrance to the hospital, it begins to drizzle, the weather suiting his sombre mood. He steps through the automatic doors to find the emergency room unusually quiet, especially given the difficulties that residents are having in obtaining GP appointments, which has led to them seeking other means of obtaining medical attention.

'Excuse me, I'm looking for Deben Ward?' Morgan says to the man sitting behind the reception desk, sorting through a pile of documents.

'Just down the corridor mate.'

Morgan tries not to roll his eyes, when did staff at the hospital start behaving so unprofessionally. He makes his way towards the long corridor that connects the emergency department with the wards beyond. The ward where Clive Dunning has been admitted is at the far end of the corridor, in a much quieter part of the hospital and with the added advantage of having a view over the sparse courtyard where a few Sparrows and Robins can usually be seen milling about on the bird table.

The forensic archaeologist is looking surprisingly well considering the day before he had been buried alive by a landslip. He is lying in a bed at the far end of the room, next to a metal-framed window that is partially open, allowing droplets of rain to blow in with the periodic gust of wind.

'How are you?' Morgan asks as he approaches the bed. He pulls up a chair and sits down next to the archaeologist, who immediately struggles to sit more upright amongst the plethora of soft pillows that seem to be drowning him.

'Nice to see you, Morgan. I really can't thank you enough for yesterday and Poppy of course.'

'That's quite alright, you'd have done the same. How are you doing?'

'I'm a bit sore, my wrist is broken so I won't be working for a while.'

'That's bad luck though also very lucky that you were inside the pillbox when it happened, the concrete roof must have saved you from the worst of the fall.'

'Yes it did. That's what I wanted to talk to you about,' Clive says, pulling himself even more upright so that he can sip some water from a glass on the nearby table.

'When you were in the pillbox, you said there was something you wanted to tell me. Did you find any bullets or casings?'

'Three of them, not far from where the bodies were found. I don't know how SOCO missed them.'

'Bennett won't be happy about that, he's been arguing for us to keep using the local forensics team when it would be more cost effective to use the central one. This will go against them for sure.'

'I'm sorry about that, it's not good to have all these service cuts. Anyway, that's not what I wanted to tell you. I saw something else in the pillbox, something that was definitely not there the last time SOCO were there - there's no way they could've missed it.'

Morgan leans forward, eager to hear the archaeologist's words. 'What did you find?'

'Another body. I think we might have found your missing course trainer.'

'Bobby Chalnor?'

'I think so, I caught a glimpse of him before the landslip.'

Morgan leans back in the chair, his right foot pumping up and down on the floor. 'It can't be, it doesn't make sense?'

'I told you it was interesting, didn't I,' Clive Dunning says, his eyes shining with enjoyment at seeing the detective's reaction.

'I wonder where he's been all this time? Did he die in the pillbox do you think?'

'I doubt it, there was no blood and a wound like that would leave a lot of evidence.'

'What kind of wound?'

'He was shot in the back of the head, poor man. Looks like he was executed.'

'Just like those three lads from the war,' Morgan murmurs softly. He stands up and moves across to the window to gaze at the rain, which is now pelting down with some force, flooding across the worn, grey patio slabs that circumvent the small courtyard.

'Exactly like the three soldiers,' Clive Dunning says solemnly. 'There's got to be some connection.'

Morgan turns around to look at the archaeologist, 'yes there must be, I always thought there was but now I'm sure of it.'

~ Eighteen ~

Jane Stokes is sitting at the desk in her compact office at Bawdsey Hall pretending to work as she stares at the computer screen. The sound of car tyres crunching over the gravel driveway, stirs her from her thoughts. Shutting down her computer, Jane pushes back her chair then steps over the trailing power cables to stand next to the window overlooking the grand driveway that sweeps across the front of the building. Pulling down one slat of the venetian blind, Jane sees that her car has returned and with it the somewhat scruffy-looking detective. She lets go of the slat again, allowing it to ping against the one below before settling back into its' original place again, then she strides across the utilitarian carpet to greet Morgan.

'You went out early?' Jane says, holding open the enormous oak door to allow the detective to pass through.

'I needed to see Dr Dunning, he's still in hospital. I hope you don't mind, I borrowed your car again.'

'How is he?' Jane asks, following Morgan into the dining room, where she deftly pours out two mugs of coffee from the machine and hands one to the detective.

'Not too bad considering. He had something to tell me though and I think I should tell everyone together. Do you know where Mrs Fields, Fallow and Foster are?'

'They're in the conference room, still looking over the task that Mr Chalnor set. I'll go and call them in,' Jane says smoothly, placing her coffee down on the nearest table.

'No, don't worry, we can go in there,' Morgan replies stiffly before marching out of the room before his host can respond.

'Good morning detective,' Camilla says brightly as Morgan walks into the room. 'How are things, any news on that poor archaeologist?'

'That's why I'm here, I have some news for you all,' Morgan replies gravely. He walks to the front of the room to stand in front of the whiteboard as if waiting to give a presentation.

'What's happened Morgan?' Foster asks, having now finished his conversation with Fallow.

'I just need to wait for Ms Stokes to join us,' Morgan says, just as Jane enters the room and sits down at the top table, gracefully crossing her legs.

'What's wrong? Has something else happened?' Camilla asks, placing her pen down on the table so that she can give Morgan her full attention.

'So, as you know Dr Dunning examined the pillbox yesterday to see if he could find any evidence relating to the three Home Guards that might have been missed by SOCO,' Morgan begins to explain.

'And then there was a cliff fall,' Fallow continues, wanting to be helpful as always.

Morgan smiles thinly at the rookie detective then turns his attention back to the others who are all waiting to hear what it is that he has to say. 'When he was trapped in the pillbox, Dr Dunning told me that he had found something.'

'Found something? What did he find?' Camilla asks, her eyes narrowing as she tries to guess.

'Unfortunately he was unable to say any more than that yesterday so I've had to wait until this morning when he was well enough for me to visit him.' Morgan pauses, looking at each person in turn to ensure they are listening.

'What did he tell you detective?' Jane enquires.

'Just before the landslip, Clive found another body in the pillbox.'

'Another one? Do you mean another soldier from the war?' Camilla exclaims, leaning in closer towards Morgan.

'No, this one is more recent,' Morgan says slowly, unsure of quite how to break the news to them all.

'Not our Mr Chalnor by any chance?' Camilla asks, almost shrieking at the thought that the missing course trainer may have been found.

A gasp is heard from the left side of the room, Morgan turns to look where the sound has come from and sees Jane Stokes pale face staring at him.

'I'm sorry to say that it does look as if we've found Mr Chalnor,' Morgan says still looking at Jane, who looks as if she might feint.

'Well, I never expected you to say that,' Camilla responds, breaking the silence that has descended.

'Neither did I,' Foster says softly, also looking at Jane Stokes who is now sitting down on a chair and seemingly staring at the blank wall behind Morgan.

'How come he wasn't discovered the other day, when the others were found?' Foster asks the question that is one everyone's mind.

'Because he wasn't there then,' Camilla says quietly, looking at Morgan. 'Am I right Detective Inspector Morgan?'

'Yes, you're right. We will need to wait for the body to be removed and for a PM to be carried out to be certain but going from the description, it's likely to be Mr Chalnor.'

'It can't be,' sobs Jane, looking utterly bereft and confused by the news.

'I'm sorry my dear, it must be such a shock for you,' Camilla soothes, moving over to the distraught woman and placing a hand on her shoulder.

'We weren't just work colleagues,' Jane says just loud enough for Camilla to hear.

'What was that my dear? What did you just say?' Camilla asks firmly, looking at Jane, hoping that she might explain further.

'We weren't just work colleagues. Bobby was my cousin, well half cousin.'

'I see. Is that why he came all the way here to work? He's not from England of course, even though he did try to hide his accent,' Camilla says as she pulls up a chair to sit next to Jane.

'Yes, we found each other through a family history website. We had the same grandfather.'

'And would that same grandfather be a certain Canadian airman who was seconded to Bawdsey Hall during the Second World War?' Camilla responds confidently.

Jane Stokes nods, tears cascading down her cheeks.

'Detective Constable Foster, please could you go and fetch a tot of whisky from the dining room. I think Jane could do with one,' Camilla instructs.

'Yes of course,' Foster responds quietly.

'Where has Mr Chalnor been all this time?' Fallow asks, looking at Morgan for a response.

'We don't know yet, that's one of the things we need to find out,' Morgan replies, sitting down on the nearest chair.

'There seems to be a lot of things that need to be explained,' Camilla says evenly, patting Jane's shoulder. 'Ah, here's the detective with your drink.'

'Dr Dunning thinks there must be some connection between Bobby's death and the three Home Guards,' Morgan suggests, looking at each person in the room in turn.

'Yes I agree. The questions is, what do we do next?' Camilla responds. She sits back down in the chair that she has occupied since early morning to read through the documents compiled by Bobby Chalnor.

'I don't know,' Morgan admits.

'I do. We need to solve the mystery of the Bawdsey Boys then we need to find out what the hell that's got to do with Bobby Chalnor,' Morgan spits.

'Yes, we do detective and we need to do it quickly, before anyone else gets hurt,' Camilla responds, looking at Foster as if there is something she knows but is keeping to herself.

'I think I'll go and lie down for a while,' Jane says softly to no one in particular. The administrator keeps her head bowed down as she passes by the three detectives who have fallen silent from their excited chatter.

'Why don't we carry on going through that diary?' Fallow suggests, looking at Morgan.

'Good idea, can I leave it with you?'

Fallow nods, then picks up the diary that is lying next to the pile of documents the trio were working through before Morgan returned to the Hall with the news that they had all been dreading to hear.

'Inspector, shall we go through the photographs in the dining room again and have another look at the library? I'm sure there must be things that we've missed, especially now we know a little more than we did a few days ago.'

'Sounds a good plan Mrs Fields. Foster, why don't you carry on interviewing the staff then go back to the ones you've already spoken to and find out where they were the night Bobby Chalnor disappeared. Someone must know something, people don't just vanish without a trace and they certainly don't just turn up dead several days later without anyone knowing where they've been all this time.'

'I'll get onto it straight away. Where's the list? I think we covered most of the staff from Mr Chalnor's task.'

'It's here,' Camilla says, pushing a piece of paper towards the detective. 'Would you like one of us to accompany you?'

'Nah that's ok, I'm from London, I reckon I can manage a few country bumpkins,' Foster chuckles as he disappears through the doorway then continues down the corridor of the old servant's quarters towards the back door.

'Where would you like to start?' Morgan asks Camilla as he waits for her to stand up.

The councillor winces as she rises from the chair, her aging knees complaining at the movement. 'I think the dining room, it will be the faster of the two tasks.'

Morgan follows Camilla into the dining room again, which is dark considering the time of day. He strides across the deep-pile carpet to gaze out of the French doors. Above the Hall, ominous clouds are beginning to gather, threatening to unleash yet another torrent of rain over the already saturated ground.

'I hope that the forensics team manage to get Bobby out from the pillbox soon, if we get more rain then there could be another cliff fall.'

'So do I, it would be terrible to lose him again, especially so soon after he's been found.'

Morgan turns to look at Camilla, uncertain if her comment was a serious one or contained a hit of sarcasm. 'I'll find out how forensics are getting on soon, for all our peace of minds. Would you like to start at this end of the room and I'll start at the other? We could meet somewhere in the middle.'

Camilla smiles, then pads across the room to the end of the display that mostly focuses on the Hall during the Second World War when it was acquisitioned by the War Office. Before then, the Hall had been occupied by the Cobbold family and there are photos of the family throughout the building's history, starting with a stern looking Victorian family, followed by the glamour of the 1920's cocktail parties and the innocent gaiety of the pre-war 1930's occupants who did not yet know of the hell that was about to be unleashed upon them.

Camilla pulls her reading glasses out from her handbag then places them on her slender nose so that she can peer at the small text of the labels underneath each photograph. The councillor peers at each item in turn, squinting to read the labels whilst grumbling to herself about the small font size. The display soon transforms from pictures of the Hall as a home, to the building being occupied by a seemingly never-ending plethora of soldiers, airman and high-ranking individuals whose occupations were mainly classified. The whole area was heavily infiltrated by the US Airforce during the later part of the war, but in the early part, the Hall had been predominantly occupied by the local farmers who comprised the Home Guard and the women who were trained to be radio operators. A photograph that Camilla had not spotted before catches her attention, or rather the label beneath it;

Billy Foster, Frederick Longcroft, Harry Norman.

'Morgan, come and look at this,' Camilla says, peering over the top rim of her glasses to get a better look. 'Doesn't this chap look like our DC Foster?'

'Let me take a look,' Morgan says, striding across the room to look at the photo. He squints to read the small text, then stands back to look at the photo from a distance. 'You're right, it does look like Max, this must be his grandfather.'

'Perhaps you could ask him about it when he returns,' Camilla concludes before moving onto the next set of photos. 'Ah there's one of our mystery Canadian airman.'

Morgan follows Camilla's gaze to see that there is indeed a photo of the airman, standing with a group of pilots at RAF Martlesham. 'I wonder what he was doing here?'

'Perhaps we might find something in the library to help answer that,' Camilla surmises.

'And the internet as well, there's all sorts of information on there,' Morgan replies, still staring at the photograph.

'Look at the dates on the photos, Inspector. They were all here at the Hall in the summer of 1940.'

'Interesting, especially given what we've already read in the Canadians diary, about there being something fishy going on.'

'Who else was here at that time I wonder?'

'Well if the task that Mr Chalnor set is based on the real mystery then the list that Foster has got might very well tell us.'

'Of course, now we know that all of this is connected I think we must assume that the task Mr Chalnor set us is a genuine one that he wanted to solve.'

'And who better than a group of detectives.'

'Indeed, the question though is why?'

'Presumably he wanted to find out something about his grandfather, the Canadian airman. I wonder what happened to him after 1940, perhaps Jane knows?'

'Good point, I'll ask her as soon as she is feeling up to talking again. I must say she seemed very shocked at the discovery of Mr Chalnor's body, almost as if she was not expecting him to turn up dead.'

'I thought so as well. I don't know why but I somehow feel as if we've all been set up.'

'I know what you mean Inspector, it's as if someone wants to find out something and is using us to do just that.'

'And someone else does not want us to find out,' Morgan concluded.

~ Nineteen ~

There are two members of staff listed on the task sheet set by Bobby Chalnor that have not yet been interviewed. DC Max Foster stares at the list for a moment, trying to decide which one of them he should visit first. With the decision made, he sets out across the well-kept grounds once more, striding across the grass that is still damp with morning dew.

The overhanging branches from a lilac tree drip their wet fronds onto the detective shoulders as he squeezes past them. It is a wonder that the path is so overgrown considering the gardener lives on site, grumbles Foster to himself as the droplets of dew drip down onto his t-shirt. Even Foster must admit though that the morning wetness has brought a welcome break from the tense humidity that has yet again befallen the peninsula, leaving the occupants with little doubt that another storm is brewing far out across the North Sea.

The thought of the sea reminds Foster of the time he visited the area when he was just a young lad. It had been a rare treat for an inner-city boy whose mother could barely pay the bills let alone afford a holiday. Somehow though she had managed to scrape together enough pennies to pay for the train fare to Woodbridge, then a taxi to the caravan site at Hollesley Bay, not far from the prison, which in those days was a borstal for Suffolk's wayward youth. Foster did not of course question at the time the reason why his mother had chosen this exact location for their only holiday, it was only later, when she was almost dead from lung cancer, that she revealed her father had been lived in the area and had been stationed at Bawdsey during the war. After his mother's death, Foster had discovered a box in the small loft space containing a letter from his grandfather to his baby daughter, dated the day that he disappeared.

The childhood remembrance fades as Foster reaches the end of the concrete path, which leads to a small barn that has been converted into a museum. A sign on the door to the museum states that it is open to the public during the summer months and for other special occasions, which can be pre-booked. To the left of the door, a blue plaque on the wall states that the museum is dedicated to all of those who passed through Bawdsey Hall during the Second World War in recognition of their bravery and their service.

Foster pushes open the door, which he is surprised to find unlocked and steps straight inside the main room of the museum. Oversized boards that have been pinned onto the walls, exhibit similar information to the display in the Hall's dining room but with greater detail about the role of the estate during the latter part of the Second World War when it was used for the development of radar systems. An entire wall is dedicated to the history of radar development, accompanied by a multitude of photographs of the enormous masts that were erected close to the beach and whose role was to monitor aircraft movement so that warnings of possible enemy attack could be given.

Foster scans through the information on display then makes his way through to the small room at the back of the building that is used as an office. According to the list compiled by Bobby Chalnor, he should find Fanny Minter in the museum, who trained as a radio operator at the Hall. As if somehow knowing that there is a detective standing in the museum waiting for her, the outer door to the converted barn opens to reveal a short, stout woman, with varifocals perched on the end of her nose.

'Hallo can I help you? The museum isn't open today I'm afraid.'

'Hi, I'm staying at the Hall, for the training course.'

'The course has been cancelled, hasn't it? I heard about poor Bobby. I'm Kerrie Mason by the way.'

'DC Foster. Yes it's been cancelled but we think the task set by Mr Chalnor might be connected to what's happened to him. It says on my instruction sheet that I'm supposed to interview Fanny Minter?' Foster explains, showing the woman the piece of paper that details the list of witnesses.

'I see, well I'm not sure how it could have any connection to what's happened to Bobby but of course I'm happy to help.'

'What information were you supposed to tell us about Fanny Minter?' Foster asks, sitting down on one of the wooden chairs next to a Typex machine that was used to send encrypted messages during the war.

'Ok, let me think, I'll see if I can remember. I threw the paper away when I heard about Bobby going missing, I wasn't expecting anyone to ask me about Fanny.'

'Thanks, anything you can recall would be helpful.'

'So, let me think. Ah yes, I remember, Fanny was being trained at the Hall during 1940, she was going to be a radio operator. They trained quite a few women here around that time.'

'Do you know the names of any of the other women who were here in the spring and summer of 1940?'

Kerrie screws up her face, trying to recall what it was she was supposed to have learnt for the course task. 'I can't, sorry. I can tell you though that Fanny stayed on here after the training was completed and helped with the radar development research. It was vitally important work you know.'

'Yes, I gathered that from all the stuff in here and at the Hall.'

'The Hall's very proud of its' history and the role it played in the war.'

'What else went on here during the war?'

'Well there was a lot of secret stuff of course, which Fanny probably wouldn't have known about.'

'Is there anyone who would have known about it?'

'Ah well, people gossip of course so others might have known though I doubt they would've openly admitted it. There were spies as well, it was difficult to know who to trust, some of them were double agents, feeding false information back to the Germans and Russians.'

'Why did they do that?'

'It was called black propaganda. Let's say the Germans heard about some new test the British were doing such as using flames to set fire to the sea, what do you think their reaction would be to it?'

'It would put them off invading?'

'That's right. So, some of the information getting back to the enemy was released to them on purpose.'

'But not all of it was fake?'

'No and that made it very difficult to know who to trust. Imagine not knowing if someone you were working with might have been a spy.'

'And if they were, not knowing which side they were on,' Foster says, nodding his head. 'Who was training Fanny to use the radio equipment?'

'Ah that would have been Captain Oswald Turner, a dashing Canadian. He was seconded to the RAF to help with training though it's suspected he was also involved in some of the hush hush stuff as well. Apparently, he was very popular with the ladies,' Kerrie chuckles, abruptly halting when she sees the stern look on Foster's face.

'Was it unusual having a Canadian stationed here?'

'It was unusual during the early part of the war, of course later on the entire region was overrun with Americans.'

Foster stands up to look at some of the photos on the display board. 'There's a photo here of Oswald Turner in June 1940 but none of him after that date?'

'Perhaps something happened to him or maybe he was posted elsewhere?' Kerrie replies, standing next to Foster so that she can also look at the photo. 'I can have a look through the old paperwork and see if I can find out if you like?'

'Please, I'd like to know.'

Kerrie looks at Foster, alerted by the subtle change of tone in his voice that makes her wonder if perhaps there was more to his question than he was letting on. 'Sure, I'll let you know if I find anything else out about him.'

'Thanks, I think I'll head back to the Hall now. Next on my list is Esme Smart.'

'That will be Jane Stokes. Esme Smart was one of the WAAF who worked here in the office during the war, typing up letters etc.'

Foster opens the door to find that the clouds overhead have darkened. 'Thanks again, I look forward to hearing more about Oswald, if you find anything out of course.'

The detective allows the door to slam shut behind him then makes his way back up the path again towards the Hall. In the distance there is a feint rumble of thunder, spurring Foster on to quicken his step before the storm arrives. The incoming storm prompts him to wonder if

Bobby Chalnor's body has been removed from the pillbox yet before the storm makes conditions on the beach even more perilous than they already are.

The imminent arrival of the incoming storm has not gone unnoticed by the team who are frantically working to release Bobby Chalnor from the pillbox, where he is entombed by sand along with the recent rock fall from the cliff that towers above the place where they are now standing.

Morgan is, as always, overseeing the procedures, having left Camilla to peruse through the books in the library alone. The detective watches from the shingle bank that has built up following last night's high tide. It has always fascinated him how the coastal landscape can shift and change so quickly and with such apparent ease. Of course these changes are not always benign Morgan reminds himself, staring up at the cliff top where a large section has given way. This part of the coast has always been susceptible to coastal erosion but it has certainly not been helped by the effects of climate change, which has led to much more severe storms and unprecedented deluges of rainfall along with the steadily rising sea levels.

The sun is hidden behind a blanket of dark clouds that threaten to unleash its full force at any moment. Typical, grumbles Morgan quietly to himself as he recalls his wet weather clothing is at home. He really should be used to the unchangeable nature of the British weather by now. Fleetingly Morgan wonders what the weather is like in Italy, then immediately regrets the thought, given it should have been himself and Celia sitting at the poolside sipping cocktails and Cook standing here in the bracing North wind watching a body being removed from a World War Two pillbox that has just been dug out by a very hot and weary forensics team.

'Detective,' shouts one of the team who is striding across the shingle bank towards Morgan, one arm held up in the air that appears to be waving.

'Yes, what is it?' Morgan shouts back, trying to be heard over the wind that has begun to increase in strength.

'We've released the body and are ready to take it to Hemley Hospital. Do you want to come and take a look and ID it?'

Morgan grimaces then walks over the dune towards the body bag that has been left slightly unzipped. Taking a deep breath, he bends down to take a look inside. A quick glance at the deceased is all Morgan needs to identify the man as being the missing course instructor.

'Any idea yet how he died?' Morgan asks, recalling Clive Dunnings words but still needing confirmation from someone who has not recently been entombed in a pillbox with a dead body and could still be in shock.

'Oh yes that's very obvious, if I turn his head sightly you can see for yourself,' one of the forensics team says, standing beside Morgan. The woman, covered in white overalls that dwarf her slight figure, gently cups Bobby

Chalnor's head in her small hand then twists it a little to reveal a neat hole at the back of his head.

'Is it self-inflicted?'

'Possible but from the angle of the trajectory of the bullet, it's unlikely. There's something else that I can tell you about Mr Chalnor's death,' the woman says, gently replacing the head again and zipping up the bag. She stands up, flexing her back to ease her aching joints.

'Oh, what's that?'

'The gun used was from the Second World War.'

'Are you sure?'

'And it wasn't a professional hit, they left the bullet behind.'

Morgan stares at the woman for a moment, trying to comprehend how it is that he came to Bawdsey for a team-building course and now he is being told that the course trainer has probably been murdered using a gun from the same era of the task that they were due to solve.

~ Twenty ~

When Morgan returns, he finds Camilla Fields in the library, reading through a collection of newspaper clippings from '*The Suffolk Times*'.

'How did it go Detective?' The councillor asks, looking up from the newspaper clipping that she has been reading.

'As well as can be expected, though also not what I was expecting.'

'What on earth do you mean by that?'

'Sorry, I didn't mean to sound so cryptic. Mr Chalnor's body has been recovered, it's definitely him, I checked.'

Well, that's good, I guess. At least Jane can have some closure now. So, what else happened, it's obvious that something did?'

'It appears that Mr Chalnor was shot dead by a Second World War gun.'

'Oh my goodness, I see what you mean, that is rather unexpected.'

'Yes it is, though I don't know why I'm surprised really given everything else that's gone on here over the last few days.'

'It makes it all seem rather more serious though now, doesn't it?' Camilla says in a manner that assumes her question, which is more of a statement, will simply be agreed with.

Morgan nods, 'I should go and talk to Ms Stokes.'

'Let me go, I don't wish to be rude but I think I might make a better job of it.'

Morgan smiles, 'you could be right.'

Camilla places the newspaper clippings onto a small table next to the fireside chair that she has been sitting in all afternoon. 'Anyway, I could do with a break. You could always carry on looking through these?' Camilla suggests, pointing at the pile of papers.

'Ok, I'll just grab a coffee first.'

'And perhaps get something to eat as well seeing as you missed lunch again. Maisie might still have some pastries from this morning if you ask her nicely.'

Morgan smiles tight-lipped, he is of course used to the light-hearted banter of the station but is starting to wonder if perhaps Mrs Fields has a point and he is not coming across to others as being as friendly as he thought.

The sound of singing directs Morgan to the kitchen, where Maisie is washing up the dishes from lunch whilst keeping a close watch on a chicken that is roasting in the enormous oven.

'Hallo Detective, I thought I might see you in here, you must be hungry.'

'I am, do you have anything I could eat?'

'Of course, I saved you a plate of Danish pastries and there's some sandwiches over there. A pot of coffee is brewing in the dining room.'

'You're an angel, Bawdsey Hall is lucky to have you.'

'I feel as if I belong here, my family having served here and all that.'

'I can't imagine feeling like I belong in my family home.'

'Where's that?'

'It was a farm, not too far from here actually, near Felixstowe.'

'Was it sold off? A lot of them are you know, there's not much money in farming anymore.'

'Something like that,' Morgan mutters quietly. 'Well, thanks for the food, I'd better get on, Mrs Fields asked me to look at some papers.'

'You'd better get on with it then,' Maisie chuckles, clearly knowing how persuasive Camilla Fields can be in getting her own way.

Morgan carries the plate through to the dining room, where he collects a mug of coffee, then takes them through to the library. With the small table now occupied by the plate and coffee mug, Morgan removes the historical documents to another larger table.

The newspaper clippings begin from just before the start of the Second World War and give an insight into the Hall and the family that occupied it before it was requisitioned by the War Office. Morgan picks up a ham sandwich to nibble as he flicks through the clippings until he reaches the ones from 1940. He pulls out the relevant articles then picks up each one in turn from the pile, skimming through the text before placing it back down again. In the middle of the heap there is one article that immediately catches his eye. Morgan puts down the remainder of the sandwich so he can pick up the article then he walks across the room to the small window where the light is better, though only just, as the ominous dark clouds are still lingering above the hamlet.

The fragile newspaper clipping has yellowed with age but Morgan can still read the print clearly.

The Suffolk Times

August 1940

Disaster At Shingle Street

An Aldeburgh resident has reported that whilst attending a dance at Jubilee Hall on Saturday evening, a siren sounded. All of the soldiers who were at the dance were instructed to attend an emergency further south along the coast. Later that evening there were reports of an orange glow being seen on the sea at Shingle Street, which was believed to be flames. Some local residents inland also reported that they were awoken in the early hours of that same night by trucks full of soldiers racing though the country lanes. One resident who did not wish to be named, believed that the trucks contained injured soldiers who were being transported from the coast to specialist burns hospitals outside of the County. Residents reported to The Suffolk Times that there had been a German invasion at Shingle Street, which was targeted due to its close proximity to the strategic points of Bawdsey and Felixstowe. The War Office have not yet confirmed or denied the rumour.

Very interesting, mutters Morgan to himself as he flicks through subsequent newspaper clippings to see if there are any further reports on the incident. There are no more from that time period but there are a few more recent ones from when secret documents were released by the Government following an embargo. The more recent articles reveal that the now released documents confirmed Shingle Street residents were evacuated in 1940 but there was no mention of a failed German invasion or any plausible explanation as to what really happened that night.

'Ah I see you've reached the more interesting articles,' Camilla exclaims on her return from visiting Jane Stokes.

'How was Jane?'

'As well as can be expected, hopefully she'll join us later for dinner. What do you think then?'

'Of the newspaper reports? Well clearly something happened that night but whether it was a failed German invasion or something else happened, I don't know. What do you think?'

'I think that whatever happened, the Government wanted to cover it up.'

'Why would they do that?'

'If it had been a German invasion then they wouldn't have wanted the public to know about it. At that time, the British public were already terrified and telling them that they were in even more danger than they thought, would not have helped morale.'

'What if it was something else that happened? What is it that they would've wanted to cover up?'

'Well, I would've thought that a friendly fire incident or something of that sort would be something the Government would not want to be made public. I found some more information in a history book about Shingle Street. The author believes the German invasion is a myth and that there was in fact another disaster that night. There was a report of a group of barges being accidently attacked by the British. They were incorrectly identified as German and when the boats were attacked, they panicked and ran into a minefield. There were a lot of casualties with burn injuries. It's also possible that the whole myth was created as black propaganda. There were experiments going on here during the war, testing flame warfare on the sea and so forth. Perhaps the British Government wanted the Germans to think we had succeeded. The use of fire in naval warfare is one that would strike abject terror into even the bravest of seamen.'

Morgan tilts his head to one side, mulling over what he has just learnt. 'So, either of those theories could account for the fire seen out at sea and the reports of injured soldiers. Where do our three Home Guards fit into it all?'

'Ah well that's a question I'm not able to answer, for now in any case.'

'And let's not also forget Oswald Turner, could he also be connected?'

'I think it's likely, especially given that his diary suggests he was up to something clandestine.'

'Was there any mention of Oswald Turner in the newspaper reports?'

'Well, it just so happens....' Camilla starts, then stops again when she hears a noise behind her. 'Ah Fallow, how's the reading going? Anything interesting in the diary?'

'Yes there is, take a look at this,' Fallow says, walking across the room and placing the book onto the table. He opens the book at one of the pages he has marked with a yellow sticky note.

Morgan cannot help but wonder why Fallow would have something like sticky notes with him but decides not to ask. Instead, he peers over Fallow's shoulder and tries to decipher the scribbly writing that the detective is pointing out.

> 1 August, 1940
> Things are starting to get hot here and I don't mean the weather. I'm still doing what N asks, how could I resist such a beautiful woman, she is everything that I've ever wanted. Lord knows what will happen when it's time to go home.

'Look at this one,' Fallow says, taking hold of the diary and flicking through the pages to reach the next yellow sticky note.

20 August, 1940
A note was pushed under my door last night in my room
at the Hall. Someone's worked out what I've been doing
and wants to meet me on Saturday night. Whoever it is
thinks I'm a traitor and maybe they're right but I'm doing
it for the right reasons. Whatever happens I have to
protect N.

'Well, I see what you mean about it being interesting. I wonder what he's referring to?' Camilla ponders, standing back a little from the table and removing her reading glasses.

'Whatever he was up to, someone wasn't happy about it,' Fallow says, stating the obvious.

Morgan ignores the comment and manages to stop himself from rolling his eyes. 'Do you think there could've been more than one person who wanted to meet with Oswald?'

'Yes, I thought that as well. Perhaps 'they' are the three Home Guards that you found,' Camilla concludes, turning to look at Morgan.

Camilla takes out a small notebook from her handbag then places her glasses back onto the end of her nose. 'Let me see, yes here it is, I've written down that there was an article in '*The Suffolk Times*' that mentioned three Home Guards disappearing on the night of 25 August 1940 and that it was thought they'd gone AWOL. What else does Oswald's diary tell us?'

'That was the last entry,' Fallow admits.

'I thought as much. I also found a newspaper article that might tell us what happened to Oswald. I copied down the information into my notebook.'

'That's very helpful Mrs Fields,' Morgan says, unsurprised by the elderly woman's resourcefulness. It occurs to him that the purpose of the training course had been to get them all to work together as a team and here they are, doing just that.

'What did the article say?' Fallow asks, becoming impatient as Camilla searches through the notebook.

'Ah here it is,' Camilla replies, flicking to the last note in the book. 'It says that a man was killed by a landmine on the beach at Shingle Street on the night of 25 August 1940. Well that is very interesting, there seems to have been a lot going on that night.'

'There certainly does, doesn't there and let's not forget the alleged failed German invasion as well,' Morgan recalls, trying to read through Camilla's notes before she closes up the book again.

'Where's Foster?' Fallow asks, suddenly realising that it has been some time since they last saw him.

'Good point, I haven't seen him since he went out this morning to carry on interviewing the staff.'

'And so I did, well the lady in the museum anyway. Jane Stokes is next on my list but I wasn't sure she would be up to it at the moment,' Foster explains, appearing at the doorway.

'Where have you been then all this time?' Morgan demands, disappointed by the lackadaisical attitude of the detective.

'Walking along the beach, nowhere in particular,' Foster murmurs. 'Have I missed anything?'

Morgan glares at Foster then sighs theatrically, not wishing to repeat all that has happened that day to someone who is clearly not taking the situation very seriously.

'Come with me detective, I'll fill you in on the day's events,' Camilla purrs, taking hold of Foster's elbow and steering him towards the dining room. 'Shall we go and find some tea?'

Morgan watches as the pair head towards the dining room and then no doubt on to the veranda to watch the sun sink lower below the trees that line the outer perimeter of the estate. Not for the first time, Morgan wonders why it is that the councillor decided to book onto a team building course. It does not seem to him that she is in need of any training on how to work well as part of a team, she seems to do that very well already.

~ Twenty One ~

The heat of the day has barely receded by the time the three detectives and one local councillor sit down for dinner in the relative coolness of the dining room. As there are so few guests left at the Hall, there is only a set meal available but still they all eagerly await the food to arrive, whatever it may be.

'I think there's another storm coming,' Fallow says nervously.

'I should think so, I just hope the Hall doesn't flood given that there's also a high tide tonight. Did you know that the area flooded very badly in 1953, a lot of people died that night in the freezing water, not a pleasant thought,' Camilla declares as she pours water from a jug into a glass for each of them.

'It's not just the sea that we have to be worried about, the river floods as well and when that happens, the Hall often gets cut off. That's why there's always a good supply of food and bottled water in the pantry,' Jane Stokes explains as she approaches the table.

'How are you, Jane?' Camilla asks with genuine concern.

'Not too bad thank you. I thought I'd join you all for dinner though I don't think I can eat very much.'

'I'm not surprised Jane, it must have been such a shock to you, especially when you and Mr Chalnor had only just started to get to know each other. Was it you who brought Bobby to work at the Hall?'

'I thought it would be good to get to know him and he was keen to find out more about our grandfather.'

'Oswald Turner was married to Bobby's grandmother, is that right?' Camilla asks.

Jane nods,' yes they were already married when he volunteered to fight.'

'But they have different surnames?' Morgan points out.

'Oswald's wife changed back to her maiden name after she found out what her husband got up to when he was stationed over here.'

'Who was your grandmother?' Morgan asks.

'My grandmother was someone who worked here, Oswald Turner treated her appallingly.'

'I'm sorry to hear that, though they were difficult times and people did behave in ways they would not have normally done,' Camilla says diplomatically.

'I suppose so and to be fair I don't think he knew that my grandma was expecting a baby.'

'What was your grandmothers name?' Fallow asks, searching through his notes for the list of names he had written down detailing the occupants of the Hall in 1940.

'Molly Jaspar,' Jane replies.

'So not the mysterious 'N' then,' Morgan muses.

'Who's that?' Foster asks.

'Someone who was mentioned in Oswald Turners' diary,' Morgan explains. 'It also looks like he was found out, whatever it was that he was doing that he shouldn't have been doing.'

'How do you know that?' Foster asks, taking a sip of water.

'From his diary, it's very interesting,' Camilla says smoothly. 'I'm looking forward to reading through the rest of it. Fallow, do you have the diary?'

'Yes, I'm going to carry on reading it this evening.'

'Do we know who else was at the Hall in 1940?' Camilla asks.

'Only from the list that Bobby Chalnor made for the task, which we're now assuming to be based on real people,' Morgan replies.

'Don't forget the photos as well,' Fallow says, pointing towards the display on the longest wall of the dining room. 'We could cross check them against the list, see if we can figure out if the names on Mr Chalnor's list were real people?'

'They are,' Jane interjects. 'It was me who set the test. Bobby went along with it as he also wanted to find out more about our grandfather.'

'What was it that you wanted to find out?' Camilla asks, placing her now empty glass down onto the table. 'Ah, here's the starter.'

Maisie approaches the table carrying a large tray, which is filled with four bowls of spring vegetable soup. 'Hello Jane, I didn't realise you were here as well, I'll go and get you some soup.'

'Thank you, most kind,' Jane murmurs, her attention seemingly captivated by the wall display showing the history of the Hall, as if seeing it for the first time. She walks over to the cluster of photographs nearest to the table where they are seated then stoops down to get a closer look at one of the photos. 'There's Oswald, handsome chap.'

Camilla immediately joins the administrator. 'Yes, he was, I'm sure he had a lot of female attention, especially with so many young men off fighting elsewhere.'

Jane diverts her attention from the photo to smile at Camilla then looks beyond her towards the table that is laden with food. 'Shall we eat before it gets cold?'

'Good idea,' Camilla soothes, rubbing Janes shoulder sympathetically. The poor woman has been through quite an ordeal over the last few days.

The conversation drifts onto less fractious topics and the group quickly forget about the stresses of the last few days, for a short while at least. The air is still thick with humidity though, lessening their appetites for consuming anything too heavy. The main course of roast chicken is consumed with gusto but the deserts are left uneaten, the sweetness of the cheesecake apparently unpalatable in the sticky atmosphere of the awaiting storm.

'Shall we move onto the veranda, we should have a good view from there of the approaching storm,' Camilla suggests, picking up the cup of black coffee that Maisie has just brought out for her.

'Good idea,' Morgan replies, looking sideways at Fallow, who looks tense at the suggestion of another storm.

Morgan moves onto the veranda, pulling out one chair for Camilla and another for Jane before settling into his own at the far end of the table where he has a good view across both the River Deben and the North Sea. In the distance, dark clouds rumble over the French coast, prompting Morgan to consider the time when soldiers were sat in this very place, wondering what was happening to their friends who were fighting on the other side of the grey water.

'I wonder what it was like,' Camilla murmurs reflectively, gazing out across the sea, her thoughts also focused on the past. 'It must have been terrifying.'

'They certainly were very brave men,' Foster says, drinking deeply from the cold pint of Suffolk ale that Maisie has brought outside for him.

'And women as well,' Camilla tuts, glaring at the detective.

'Ah yes of course, though they weren't in the firing line were they,' Foster retorts.

'What makes you think that?' Camilla says tersely, still staring at Foster who seemingly has not noticed the elderly woman's dark eyes boring into him.

'Well, they weren't the ones who were over there, getting killed. They were all back here in blighty, in their safe little jobs,' Foster states, his attention still focused on the calm river in front of him.

'Well, you're wrong about that assumption, very wrong indeed,' Camilla spits, pushing back her chair. 'I will bid you all good night. Fallow, please let me know if anything else of interest comes up in Oswald's diary.'

Fallow nods his head then looks sideways at Morgan. The rest of the group have fallen silent, seemingly a little taken aback by Camilla's unexpected outburst.

Morgan knows that as the most senior officer, it is his duty to smooth over the fraction within the group. Instead, he decides to ignore the situation, 'I hope you sleep well Mrs Fields, I mean with the storm and all that.'

Camilla stares at Morgan for a moment as if she is about to speak but then decides better of it and instead tuts loudly before moving back into the dining room and disappearing out of sight.

'Blimey, what rattled her cage,' Foster says, rolling his eyes.

'Well clearly something you said did,' Morgan snaps, tiring of Foster's attitude. It is now becoming apparent why the detective was booked onto the team-building course.

'There were women who had dangerous jobs during the war,' Fallow interjects, his need to correct the factual inaccuracy more pressing than his desire to avoid confrontation.

'Yeah right,' Foster snorts, draining the remainder of his pint.

'Some of the spies were female, they were called SOE's - Special Operation Executives. Some even went to France undercover,' Fallow explains before exhaling loudly, also seemingly tiring of Fosters attitude.

Foster glares at Fallow, his dark eyes glinting in annoyance at being corrected. 'Haven't you got a diary to read?'

'Yes, you're right, I should get back to work,' Fallow says stiffly, pushing back his chair and walking off without saying goodnight.

Morgan stands up and goes back inside the building where he pours himself a glass of Merlot from one of the opened bottles behind the bar. With a large glass filled, he heads back outside to sit on the veranda to watch for the impending storm.

Far out to sea, lightning arcs between the voluminous clouds, followed by a deep rumble of thunder. The storm is fast approaching and will be overhead in the next couple of hours if the wind continues to blow it across the sea towards them and does not instead turn up the English Channel.

'I'd better go and find Reece, make sure he's prepared in case there's a flood. It's bad timing having a storm at high tide,' Jane says quietly, having managed to hold herself back from reacting to the previous conversation. Fallow is not the only member of the group who prefers to avoid conflict but the administrator has heard more than enough narrow mindedness from the London detective this evening. To avoid putting her job in jeopardy by reacting in the way she dearly wishes she could, Jane instead makes her excuses to leave then steps onto the neatly cut lawn and disappears into the darkness.

~ Twenty Two ~

Dr Len Bootle would not usually have arranged to carry out a postmortem at this late hour and only agreed on this occasion as Clive Dunning has been tied up with classes for most of the day. Only the most pressing emergency of national importance could have taken Dr Dunning away from lecturing his first-year students on human evolution, a course that he designed and has proudly delivered for the past seven years. There had of course been no question of the archaeologist not assisting with the PM, having discovered the body himself just before a cliff fall had entombed him in the pillbox alongside the cadaver.

Another reason for delaying the examination until the evening was Clive Dunning's hope that one or two of his students might have the opportunity to also attend the postmortem with it being scheduled after class. Alas though, Dr Bootle has stayed resolute on his decision that there should be as few attendees as possible given that it is likely the PM report will form part of a murder investigation. The pathologist did however agree to the session being recorded, not only for future educational purposes once the evidence is deemed to be no longer sensitive but also as a safeguard against any maligned accusations that might occur. Unfortunately in this age of online living, professionals need to take precautions against the faceless social media trolls whose only aim is to discredit them.

'Ready?' Dr Bootle asks the university-based archaeologist.

Clive Dunning is standing next to the cadaver, peering at it with great interest. 'Yes of course, please go ahead.'

Dr Bootle nods to indicate that he has heard then begins the examination without any preamble, knowing that his colleague has sufficient experience to not need it. The pathologist automatically goes into the zone of deep concentration that he usually finds himself in when he is at work. This time though he is not accompanied by Harry who he works with like a well-oiled engine and he has to pull himself out of his hyperfocus intermittently to give instructions to Dr Dunning on any actions that are required in his temporary role as pathology assistant.

Clive Dunning watches as the pathologist swiftly and expertly manoeuvres around the cadaver, his head titled slightly to one side as he concentrates on his colleague's actions.

Len Bootle seems to have momentarily forgotten that he is not alone as is muttering to himself. 'Well there's still some rigor mortis so our Mr Chalnor has not been dead for as long as I would've expected given the length of time he has been missing.'

'Do you think he died where I found him in the pillbox?' Dunning asks, more out of the desire to make conversation than to affirm what he already knows.

Dr Bootle looks up in surprise at hearing another voice in the room. He quickly regains his composure then clears his throat. 'I don't think that's very likely, you would've seen more blood in the sand. Presumably SOCO didn't find much in their samples?'

'I can check, if its ok to use your laptop?'

Dr Bootle nods thoughtfully then bites his lip as he realises that he has yet again forgotten to put a password on the device despite receiving a reminder from the IT team that morning.

Clive Dunning switches on the laptop, opens up a web browser and logs onto his email account. He scrolls through the unopened messages to see if there is one from the forensics team and soon spies a new email that was sent to him after he had already left the university to travel to Hemley Hospital. The archaeologist double clicks on the mail icon to open the email, reads through the text then closes up the laptop again.

'You're right, forensics didn't find a lot of blood in the samples from the pillbox, so Mr Chalnor must have died elsewhere.'

'Killed elsewhere you mean. I don't think there's much chance he managed to commit suicide given the angle of the bullet trajectory.'

'Well that's what I thought but I like to keep an open mind until after the PM,' Dunning bristles, instantly realising why Harry was so grateful to be given the evening off. He takes in a deep breath to quell his irritancy a little.

'I wonder if it's the same gun that was used to kill the three Home Guards,' Bootle mutters to himself, barely loud enough for anyone else to hear.

Dunning is uncertain if he is meant to respond or not, given the pathologist was not directly speaking to him. His earlier enthusiasm at being given the opportunity to assist on such an interesting case is rapidly beginning to wane. 'Surely it's unlikely to be the same weapon given the extensive time between the two events? That would be a very strange coincidence indeed.'

'Well not really, it's possible that whoever killed the three Home Guards kept the gun as a memento and then it was used for this more recent murder,' the pathologist explains.

'Sounds a bit creepy to me.'

'Perhaps if you feel that way then this is not the right line of work for you,' Bootle retorts, clearly also not enjoying the temporary partnership.

Clive Dunning holds back the words he wishes he could utter and instead silently vows never to volunteer to assist Len Bootle again. Even the arrogance of his third-year students cannot match up to the level that is currently exuding from the pompous pathologist.

'Right, well let's get back to the reason why we're here, shall we?' Dr Bootle prickles before turning his back on the archaeologist. He returns to his previous position next to the cadaver's head then begins to talk out aloud for the purpose of the recording more than for Clive Dunnings benefit.

'There is a close contact gunshot wound on the side of Mr Chalnor's head that could not possibly have been made by him and therefore it is my conclusion that this man has been murdered.'

The remainder of the evening passes with little being said between the two alpha males who are clearly not suited to working with each other. It is almost 9pm by the time Len Bootle pulls off his gloves and casually throws them into the hazardous waste bin next to the door.

'Well, thank you for your assistance this evening, I'll write up the report and send you a copy of it. Now I really must get home before the storm reaches us, a flood warning's been issued and the road leading to my house often floods.'

Clive Dunning smiles tight-lipped then pulls off his gloves and heads straight for the exit. It will be a long drive home and he does not want to spend any more time than has to making polite conversation with a man that he can only describe as 'odious'.

Morgan's evening is faring a little better than earlier, as he sits on the veranda sipping the fruity red wine that he helped himself to after the spat between Foster and Fallow. The quietness is welcoming after the events of the day and Morgan savours the opportunity of being left alone after the exiting of both detectives following their heated disagreement as well as by Jane Stokes who decided to make a detour enroute to see Reece Browne, so that she can check if Maisie has left sufficient supplies in the kitchen for a few days in case the Hall is cut off by the storm.

Whilst Morgan is contemplating what he should do next, his phone bleeps, notifying him that he has received a new message. He reaches for the phone that is lying on the table next to his glass of wine and opens up the messaging app to find an unread text from Tom Cook.

Tom

How's it going?

Just waiting for another storm to arrive, seems to be some concern that the roads around here might flood. Luckily Bobby Chalnor has already been moved to the mortuary. Len's doing the PM this evening, I'll let you know when there's any news

Ok cool the rest of the team will come and help as soon as they can, there's been an incident on the Hartsmere estate so they need to deal with that first

I'll be fine, stop worrying and remember you're on holiday!

Now that Bobby Chalnor's case has changed from missing person to one of suspected murder, it has been officially been assigned to the Serious Crime team. The thought of working with his team again lifts Morgan spirits, along with the knowledge that this is at least a situation he has been trained to do and one that means he is no longer frustratingly consigned to the background, waiting for another team to do the work.

Morgan looks out across the calm river, trying to imagine what it might look like in a few hours when the storm hits the Suffolk coast. Despite the difficult circumstances and the anticipated rough night ahead, the detective is feeling more relaxed than he has done for a long time. He mulls over everything that has happened then decides that first thing tomorrow, he will interview the staff. They need to find out where Bobby Chalnor went to after he disappeared as well as who could have a possible motive to kill him. The case of the murder of the three Home Guards will now have to wait.

'Ah Morgan, I thought I might find you out here,' Foster says, lighting up a cigarette as soon as he steps onto the veranda.

Morgan glares at the London-based detective, one thing he really cannot stand is someone smoking near him. 'Actually I'm just going to have a walk before the storm reaches us.'

'Good idea, I'll come with you.'

Morgan rolls his eyes. The last thing he wants is for Foster to come with him. He trips down the shallow stone steps and onto the shingle bank that leads steeply down to the rocky outcrop where he found Bobby Chalnor's shoes the morning after he arrived at the Hall - a day that now seems so long ago.

The two detectives stand close to the water's edge, near the outcrop of rocks, observing the array of small boats moored in the river. Eventually Morgan interrupts the quiet ambience, 'I still don't understand why Bobby Chalnor's shoes were left here?'

'Perhaps they were a red herring, left there to make us think that Mr Chalnor had gone into the water?'

'Perhaps,' says Morgan quietly, unconvinced by the explanation.

'I wonder where he's been all this time?'

'We need to interview the staff tomorrow, once this blasted storm has gone. I do think they're overreacting a little, surely a flood can't be that bad?'

'Yeah, I totally agree. Maybe they just want us to wait a bit longer before talking to them all about Bobby. Maybe they want to buy some time to get their stories straight,' Foster deduces.

'You could be right. Perhaps we should go for a walk now in the direction of the gardener's cottage and back around the estate, see if any of the staff are about?' Morgan suggests. Without waiting for a response from Foster, Morgan retraces his steps up the beach again and back onto the now familiar path that will lead them through the estate grounds to the gardener's cottage.

~ Twenty Three ~

Despite the lateness of the hour, rivulets of sweat are dripping down Morgan's back by the time he has fought his way through the overgrown shrubbery to reach Reece Browne's cottage. Behind him, Foster is grumbling quietly, also seemingly not enjoying the evening stroll.

'Is it much further?' Foster groans, echoing Morgan's own discomfort at being outside in the tense humidity.

'Not too much further now,' Morgan pants, wishing yet again that he had not put off taking up running as his lack of fitness is becoming more and more evident with every step.

The path takes them towards the edge of the estate then suddenly curves eastwards. As the two detectives reach the sharp bend, the estate worker cottage's loom into view, though still partially shielded by the shadows cast from the gigantic Poplar trees at the far end of the grounds. The left-hand cottage is encased in darkness, seemingly unoccupied. Morgan raps loudly on the door then listens as the echo bounces through the cramped space.

'Where the hell is he?' Foster grumbles, fumbling in his pocket for a packet of cigarettes and a lighter.

'I wouldn't smoke here, not with all these trees,' Morgan warns sternly. It is blatantly obvious that Foster is a city-dweller and one who has little understanding of the tinder-dry summers in rural Suffolk.

Foster reluctantly pushes the packet back into his jeans, then hearing an unfamiliar noise, turns to look at Morgan. 'What was that?'

'I didn't hear anything,' Morgan replies quietly, feeling a little uneasy at the quietness coupled with the tense atmosphere of the awaiting storm that is moving ever closer to them. Even though Morgan considers himself a country lad at heart, he still finds the stillness of the sparsely populated countryside a little unnerving, especially in the dark when they know there is someone here on the estate who is responsible for the death of Bobby Chalnor.

'There's no one here,' Foster reluctantly admits, his head titled to one side as he listens intently for any further noises. 'I'm sure I saw a light on though a moment ago.'

'Could it have been the reflection of the moon on the window?' Morgan responds, looking at the gap in the thick cloud cover that is momentarily allowing the light of the full moon to shine onto the path below their feet.

Suddenly there is a noise behind them, Morgan swings around, wishing that he'd had the sense to bring something with them that could be used as a weapon, especially given there is a murderer on the loose. Foster also hears the noise and jumps back into the enormous Wisteria that is growing around the gardener's cottage door.

A window opens in the adjoining cottage and the outline of a stout figure can be seen in the light of the moon. 'Who's that?' A voice says from within the dark building.

'It's Detective Inspector Morgan and Detective Constable Foster.'

'Hang on, let me come to the door,' a thin voice begrudgingly says.

A few minutes pass then the door to the cottage opens. A yellow beam from a ceiling light revealing the buildings' occupant to be Cedric Browne. 'What do you want?'

'We're looking for your grandson,' Morgan replies.

'Well, don't look like he's here does it,' Cedric Browne spits, starting to close the door again.

'Do you know where we might find him?' Foster asks.

The old man stares at Foster as he chews on his bottom lip. 'I expect he's putting sandbags out, there's a storm coming in case you haven't noticed.'

'Ok thanks,' replies Morgan, realising that little more will be gleaned from the elderly man. 'Sorry to have disturbed your evening.'

Cedric Browne grunts an unintelligible response then begins to close the door. Suddenly the movement of the door stops and is slightly pulled back open again. The elderly man stares out of the opening at Foster, who is now quite visible in the moonlight. 'Here, do I know you lad?'

'I don't think so,' Foster says slowly. 'Perhaps you saw me the other day when I was talking to your grandson?'

'Nah it's not that. You look familiar, that's all.'

'Maybe I look like someone you used to know,' Foster says smoothly, trying to placate the old man who has no doubt confused him with someone else.

'Hmmm well it will come to me, it always does,' Cedric mumbles before shutting the door.

'Well, he wasn't exactly friendly,' Foster says, pulling a face.

'And not very helpful either,' Morgan agrees. 'Shall we carry on looking for Reece and Jane?'

The rain begins pelting down just as Morgan finishes speaking. He looks up at the menacing sky, 'great, that's all we need.'

'We'd better get back to the Hall, if this storm's as bad as everyone thinks then we want to be inside when it hits.'

'You're right, I guess. Hopefully Jane has returned by now as well and Reece has found cover, wherever he is.'

Morgan takes the lead back down the path again. Even though the darkness has receded a little with the emergence of the moon from behind the thick clouds, it is still difficult to see the path ahead and Morgan trips more than once on roots and low branches that overhang their route.

'Watch your step, god knows what I just tripped over but I nearly broke my bloody neck,' Morgan snaps, pushing an overhanging branch out of his way. 'That gardener obviously isn't doing his job properly.'

'To be fair it's a big estate to look after and he's doing it all on his own. Years ago, there would have been lots of staff here,' Foster says, uncharacteristically diplomatically.

Morgan grunts and says no more on the subject but lets out a sigh when he reaches the end of the path, relieved when his shoes make contact once again with the gravel driveway. By the time both men reach the centre of the driveway, the moon is once again hidden by a blanket of cloud and the two detectives have to make their way back to the Hall using the light from the hallway as a guide. They have barely had time to step inside the front door when a loud rumble of thunder crashes overhead followed seconds later by a sheet of white lightning that illuminates the nearby river with its small boats rhythmically bobbing up and down on the incoming tide.

'Good timing,' Morgan says as he peers out of the hall window at the rain that is lashing down.

'So that's what all the fuss is about,' Foster mutters, as he stands next to Morgan and stares through the window at the river beyond. Even in the short time since the storm has moved inland, the river level has begun to rise as the strong winds push the vast depth of water up the small channel that is already swollen by the sheer quantity of rain that has fallen recently.

'I can't see anything,' Morgan says, squinting as he tries to see into the darkness.

'Wait for some more lightning, then you'll see.'

Morgan waits for a few minutes for another flash of lightning to light up the dark sky and when it does, he sees that the river is now almost halfway up the riverbank.

'It's pretty high already and it's not even high tide yet,' Foster says sounding a little more concerned than he was earlier as he continues to look out into the darkness.

Morgan shivers, being cut off from flooding on the main road is one thing, but being cut off in a building that is surrounded by water on two sides is quite a different matter altogether.

'Let's go and find the others,' Morgan says, hoping that they are all in the Hall, safe from the torrential downpour that is deluging the already saturated ground outside.

Morgan does not have to wait long to find Camilla Fields, who is already making her way down the sweeping oak staircase, having heard the sound of the two detective's voices from her small bedroom close to the top of the stairs.

'Did you find Jane?' Camilla asks, holding onto the banister as she carefully makes her way down each step.

'No, nor the gardener,' Morgan replies, watching the elderly woman to ensure she does not slip. He cannot help but wonder how old she is and when she will decide to retire from public duty.

'Ah, I see,' Camilla replies.

Morgan stares at Mrs Fields and waits for her to continue speaking but instead she smiles knowingly and says no more on the subject.

'The river's already rising,' Foster informs the elderly councillor with a hint of concern in his voice.

'I thought it might. I don't think the Hall has ever badly flooded, perhaps its luck will continue,' Camilla soothes.

'Have you seen DC Fallow?' Morgan asks, suddenly remembering about his team member.

'Not since he retired to his room to read the rest of Oswald's diary,' Camilla replies.

'I'll go and check on him,' Foster says, running up the staircase before anyone can respond.

'Shall we go and find some coffee?' Morgan asks Mrs Fields, pointing towards the dining room where there is a coffee machine.

'Good idea,' Camilla says, moving towards the room.

From somewhere upstairs they can hear Foster knocking on a door, then the next moment, the Hall is plunged into darkness.

'Oh, not again,' Camilla says crossly.

'I'm afraid we might have had another power cut,' Morgan says, stating the obvious.

The sound of footsteps in the dark hallway silences the conversation.

'It's just me,' Foster declares, feeling his way into the room then walking over to the French doors that lead out onto the veranda where there is at least some light from the moon.

'Is DC Foster ok?' Camilla asks, joining the detective by the window.

'He's asleep, I didn't want to disturb him. Anyway, the lights went out so I thought I'd come back here,' Foster explains. 'Is there any whisky behind the bar Morgan?'

'There is, I saw some earlier,' Morgan replies, feeling his way towards the bar. He pulls out his keyring from his trouser pocket, which has a small penlight attached, then uses the thin beam from the torch to locate three glasses and a bottle of whisky. Holding the narrow cylindrical torch in his teeth, Morgan takes the objects over to the table nearest to the veranda.

'Shouldn't we be higher up, in case it floods?' Foster asks, sounding troubled.

'I'm more worried about where Jane has got to,' Morgan says quietly.

'I wouldn't worry about Jane, she will no doubt be with Reece,' Camilla purrs before taking a sip of the fiery liquid that Morgan has now poured out into the three glasses.

'There wasn't anyone at the gardener's cottage,' Foster says, seemingly immune to Camillas inferences.

'How do you know that?' Camilla asks.

'Well, the lights were all off and no one answered when we knocked on the door,' Foster responds.

'Indeed, though that doesn't mean the building was unoccupied,' Camilla says, winking at the detective.

'Seriously Foster, surely you don't need us to spell it out for you,' Morgan chuckles, also taking a sip from his glass.

Foster does not reply but instead gulps down some of the molten brown liquid, wincing as it hits his stomach.

'Well now, I think we should all go to bed, I'm sure the Hall won't flood too badly and in any case, we will be safer upstairs,' Camilla decides, placing her empty glass down onto the table just as another deep rumble of thunder rolls overhead. 'Now which one of you gentlemen will accompany me to my room, I would hate to slip in the darkness.'

'We both will, you're right, there's nothing else we can do but wait for the dawn and hope that the sandbags Reece put out earlier will hold,' Morgan agrees, shining his penlight towards the hallway so that they can find their way back to the staircase.

Morgan keeps the beam of the small torch a little way ahead of him so that Camilla and Foster can safely make their way upstairs. They reach Mrs Fields room first and Morgan shines the light into the room so that the elderly councillor can locate the lantern that she kept from the previous power cut.

'Good night gentleman,' Camilla says before closing the door.

'Well, this is my room,' Foster states, turning the handle of the door and shuffling into the dark space.

'Try and get some sleep, I'm sure Mrs Fields is right and we'll all be safe up here,' Morgan soothes, seeing the concern on the detectives face even in the dim light.

'Good night Morgan,' Foster says quietly before he too closes his bedroom door.

Morgan stands on the other side of the door for a moment in the corridor that is shrouded in darkness, then he strides across the landing to his room. There is something in the tone of Fosters voice that is niggling at him. It was not what he said but the way that he said it. It almost sounded like he was saying goodbye.

~ Twenty Four ~

The storm hits the Suffolk coast in the early hours of the morning, just as the tide is at its highest. Just as Jane Stokes predicted. Unseeingly in the dark, the tide pushes the slow-moving river water upstream, where it rises and swells, overflowing into the smaller inland streams and tributaries. It does not take long for the water to find its way onto the main road that leads to Bawdsey Hall, cutting it off from the outside world until the tempestuous waters decide that they will once again subside. For now at least, the small hamlet of Bawdsey has become an island, trapping inside it all those who have chosen to stay within the estate's boundaries.

Morgan first becomes aware of the flood when he looks out of his bedroom window to gaze across the river that has now increased enormously in both girth and height. If he had also opened the small side window and craned his head around to the right, the detective would have also been able to see the moonlight reflecting on the dark water that now covers the main road. This is not what Morgan chooses to do though, instead he continues to stare out across the River Deben towards Felixstowe, at the point where the tidal water merges with the

North Sea. The water has made its way up over the giant boulders that serve to protect the lower parts of the town from the relentless onslaught of the sea. Morgan's gaze follows the trail of water uphill, where it gradually comes to a standstill just before the towns' golf club. On the left, the sun is rising, the first rays of dawn sparkling on the sinister mass of water that was not there the previous night.

A gentle knock on the door stirs Morgan from his quiet purveyance of the temporarily changed vista. He draws back into the room again, automatically reaching for the light switch, which emits a dull click. It is then that Morgan remembers about the power outage. The knock comes again, a little more insistent this time.

'Detective? Are you awake?'

Morgan smiles, immediately recognising the polite voice coming from the other side of the door. 'Yes Mrs Fields, I'm awake.'

The door is locked and the key stiff to turn. By the time Morgan has opened the door, DC Foster is also waiting impatiently in the dark corridor.

'Morgan, I'm a bit worried about Fallow, I didn't hear anything in the room next to me during the night and I've just knocked again and there's still no answer.'

'That is worrying,' Camilla asserts, looking back down the landing towards the room where Fallow has been staying.

'Ok let's take a look,' Morgan says confidently, striding across the carpet to the far end of the corridor. He knocks loudly then tries the handle – the door is locked. 'Has anyone seen Jane Stokes this morning?'

'No, I haven't. I would've thought she'd had the sense to stay where she was last night, especially given what's happened,' Camilla replies.

'What do you mean?' Morgan asks, his forehead creasing in puzzlement.

'The flood. She was right, you know. I went outside a little earlier, the road to the Hall is completely impassable,' Camilla explains.

'I didn't see that, I was just looking out of my window,' Morgan muses.

'Well perhaps you weren't looking in the right place,' Foster says facetiously. 'It seems to have become a habit.'

Morgan smiles tight-lipped, knowing that the detective is right but not wanting to admit it. 'Well let's go and see if the office door is unlocked, there must be spare keys in there for all of the rooms.'

'Perhaps Max would like to go to the gardener's cottage and see if he can locate the whereabouts of Jane and Reece?' Camilla suggests.

'Sure thing, I could do with a walk anyway. I'll take a look at the road as well, see if the flood has caused much damage,' Foster replies as he walks towards the staircase that sweeps downwards into the hallway below.

'Ok, let's go and see if we can find a key for this door,' Morgan says, following closely behind Foster who is already moving down the stairs.

Foster reaches the end of the hallway first, opens the front door then strides across the sodden driveway in the direction of the two cottages that are nestled within the grounds.

Morgan waits for Camilla Fields to catch up to him, then tries the handle of the office door, which to his relief, is unlocked. He pushes it open and automatically flicks on the light switch before remembering yet again that the power is off.

'If my memory is correct, there's a key cupboard next to the notice board,' Camilla instructs as she follows Morgan into the centre of the room. Camilla walks over to the window at the front of the building and draws back the heavy curtains to allow daylight to flood into the room.

'You're right, it's here,' Morgan says, moving behind the desk to stand in front of the noticeboard. 'Not exactly very secure is it.'

'Luckily for us, no. Perhaps a lesson on security is needed once all of this is over.'

Morgan starts to speak but then stops. At this precise moment he cannot imagine this situation will ever end, they seem to be lurching from one disaster to another and he is starting to dread what might come next. What he really needs now is support but his team cannot reach him through the flood water.

'Look, there it is, that's the one,' Camilla says, pointing to one of the keys hanging on a neatly labelled hook. Above each key is a small light that would once have been used by the family who lived here to summon a servant to cater for their needs.

Morgan grabs hold of the correct key then strides back out into the hallway. Without waiting for the elderly woman to follow, he trips up the stairs two at a time, eager to find out what has happened to Fallow.

The key turns easily in the lock. Morgan presses down on the handle and pushes the door inwards to find the room encased in darkness with the heavy curtains still drawn.

Camilla, who has now caught up, immediately opens the curtains to reveal what they have already guessed; Fallow is not there.

'The beds still made so he hasn't been here all night,' Morgan groans.

'There's something else missing,' Camilla says, slowly looking around the room.

Morgan grunts, too focused on his absent colleague to care what else might have disappeared. He walks over to the window to take a look outside. The room overlooks the gardens at the back of the building. In the distance, Morgan can just about make out the gardener's cottage behind a dense thicket of trees that are swaying in the strong breeze coming over the sand dunes from the North Sea.

'The book's gone,' Camilla tries again to catch Morgans attention.

'What book?' Morgan snaps, still looking out of the window. He watches as Foster walks up the narrow path towards the cottages until it curves out of sight and is hidden by a thick blanket of shrubs.

'The diary. Oswald Turners diary has gone.'

The words have their desired effect. Morgan immediately withdraws from the window and purveys the room, his eyes resting on the bed that has not been slept in and the empty side table next to it. Camilla is right. Fallow had the diary with him last night and now both of them are missing.

The door to the cottage opens after the second knock, revealing a sightly dishevelled gardener behind it.

'Yeah, what's up?' Reece says sleepily, leaning a toned arm on the doorframe.

'I just wanted to check up on you and Ms Stokes, make sure you're all ok. Is Jane here?' Foster asks, peering over the gardener's shoulder to see inside the dark cottage.

Reece glares at the police officer and immediately pulls the door almost shut, leaving only a small gap that is filled by his stout frame. 'No, she's not, why would she be here?'

'Mrs Fields seems to think that Jane might be here, we haven't seen her since yesterday.'

'Well she isn't here so if you don't mind, I've got lots of work to do with sorting out the mess from the flood and all that.'

'Sorry to have disturbed you, Sir,' Foster responds flippantly. 'If you do happen to see either Jane or DC Fallow, who also seems to have gone astray, please do come and let us know up at the Hall.'

Foster does not wait for a reply but instead turns around to walk back up the path again. As he moves past the cottages, the corner of the net curtain in the kitchen of Cedric Browne's cottage lifts up a little before swiftly dropping back down again.

Foster stares at the cottage for a moment as if deciding whether to knock on the door or not, then he continues walking up the path, past the overhanging trees that are dripping with moisture from the previous night's rainfall.

The detective has almost made it out of the small copse and back onto the neatly mown lawn that frames the ornate veranda of the dining room, when he spots Morgan walking at pace towards him.

'Has something happened?' Foster asks

'Fallows definitely missing, Mrs Fields and I checked his room.'

'That's really strange, I wonder where he's gone?'

'Or just importantly, why he's gone,' Morgan concludes. He turns around to walk back to the Hall again. As he reaches the end of the copse, Morgan stumbles over something that feels like a tree root. The detective stops, curious to discover what it is that he has tripped over. He pulls back a large Conifer branch that is drooping elegantly over the path, its' distinctive earthy fragrance filling the morning air then peers into the shaded area beyond. Further back, shrouded by the shadows cast from the towering tree, a dark object beckons to Morgan and his unsatiated sense of curiosity to find out what it is that he has just stumbled over; something that he does not recall being there the last time that he walked up this path.

The estate is silent bar from the rhythmic sound of waves crashing onto the nearby shingle, occasionally interjected by the soft cawing of seagulls soaring over the murky water that has now dulled to a gentler pace. The rising sun casts a ray of light through the dense fronds of the conifer, creating an eerie green light that compliments the quiet atmosphere. The beam of light caresses the object on the ground underneath the tree, which Morgan is now staring at, frozen like a deer caught in the headlights of a passing car on the narrow road that leads to the Hall. The detective does not need to step any closer, he recognises the outline of the object all too well. It is not the first time that he has seen a dead body.

~ Twenty Five ~

The sound of someone running across the stony driveway immediately attracts the attention of Camilla, who is still searching through the room at the top of the stairs where DC Fallow has been staying.

'Has something happened detective?' Camilla asks, walking steadily down the stairs, taking care as she transcends each step.

'A body,' Morgan pants, looking up at Camilla. 'There's a body on the path, I found it when I went to locate Foster. Jesus, that must've been what I tripped over last night.'

'Yeah must have been. No point worrying about that now though,' Foster soothes his breath calming a little to a more normal pace after the short run back to the Hall.

'Who is it?' Camilla asks quietly, her face ashen.

'I don't know,' Morgan replies as he reaches into his trouser pocket and pulls out his mobile phone. He flicks through his contact folder to find the number for Chief Superintendent Bennett - this case is now far too out of hand for him to manage on his own. The detective places the phone to his ear as he walks down the hallway so that he is out of ear shot of the others. Morgan turns to look at Camilla and Foster, a stern grimace on his face.

'That doesn't look good,' Foster says grimly.

'No it doesn't,' Camilla replies.

Morgan ends the call, returns the phone to his trouser pocket then strides back up the hallway again towards Camilla and Foster.

'Let me guess, the emergency services are all busy dealing with the flood?' Camilla states.

'I'm afraid so and in any case, no one can get through with the road being flooded. We're just going to have to manage as best we can for now. We can use the outdoor larder to store the body in until it can be collected and taken to Hemley Hospital.'

Foster opens his mouth and is about to say something when he is interrupted by a loud knock on the front door.

'Hallo, is everyone ok?' PC Smith says with his usual joviality.

'We were until you just gave us a fright,' Camilla snaps.

'What are you doing here?' Morgan asks.

'Checking up on you lots, after the flood and all that. There's been quite a bit of damage and this area's cut off for now,' Smith explains.

'What I meant to say is, how the hell did you get here given the road outside the Hall is flooded?' Morgan demands.

'I used my canoe of course, always handy to have one in case of emergencies,' Smith replies smugly.

Morgan is stunned into silence, why did it not occur to him to use a boat to leave the Hall?

'Well, I'm very glad to see you however you got here,' Camilla soothes. 'DC Foster and DI Morgan have just found someone deceased in the garden and we seem to have misplaced both DC Fallow and Jane Stokes.'

'All in one night, gosh that's got to be some sort of record,' PC Smith exclaims, ignoring the hard stare from Morgan. 'It must have been a very distressing night. So, what's the plan?'

'Unfortunately no one can get out here until the water subsides, so it's just us I'm afraid.'

'Lucky that I'm here as well then. What do you want me to do first?' Smith asks, a beaming smile appearing on his face.

'I'll go to see about locating some food and try to find a way to boil enough water for coffee,' Camilla mutters as she walks off towards the kitchen, not wishing to hear any more about the dead person who is in the garden, not very far from them.

'Have either of you got a camera?' Morgan asks the two police officers.

'I've got one on my phone, will that do?' replies Foster, taking his phone out of his waterproof coat pocket.

'Have you got enough battery if we need it for any emergencies? We can't charge it up until the powers back on,' explains Morgan, staring at Fosters phone, which is considerably more modern than his.

'I've got a spare battery pack. I always keep one just in case,' Foster replies smugly.

'Ok, well, let's go and take photographs of the area and be careful not to tread on anything that could be evidence. PC Smith perhaps you could go and see if there are anything like food bags that we could use to collect any evidence? Oh and look for some gloves as well,' Morgan instructs, automatically taking charge.

'Will do. Whereabouts is the body?' Smith asks as he makes his way towards the kitchen, where Camilla is noisily searching through the cupboards for something they could eat.

'It's on the path just behind those big bushes, on the way to the gardener's cottage,' Morgan explains.

'Ok, well I'll see you there in a bit,' Smith replies before disappearing into the kitchen.

From the porch, Morgan can see the glint of water on the road beyond. It is a wonder that the flood did not spread up as far as the house, he muses as he trudges across the shingle driveway towards the path that leads to the estate workers cottages. At the far end of the driveway, pulled in away from the flooded road is a kayak.

'Maybe Deben Quay Police Force should invest in one of those,' Foster says, catching up with Morgan.

'Somehow I can't see it happening, not with all the budget cuts again.'

Foster nods thoughtfully then overtakes Morgan to lead the way through the bushes to the place where the body is hidden from view. Gently he pulls back the overhanging branches to reveal the motionless shape beyond.

'What are we going to do, we haven't got a body bag or anything?' Morgan says, mulling over the best way to approach the problem. Whatever he decides, he cannot leave a body out here uncovered like that, apart from anything, the local wildlife will be helping themselves to a midnight snack.

'I've got a bag,' Smith responds, striding up the path at pace towards the two detectives. 'I put a couple in my rucksack, in case I found anyone caught out by the flood.'

'That's very resourceful of you,' Morgan mutters.

'Ah well us countryside bobby's need to be, it's a whole different game out here you know,' Smith explains. 'We get a lot of emergencies just like this one and of course all sorts of different crimes that you don't get in the towns. The poor farmers around here have no end of break-ins.'

'Really, I'd have thought they'd be safe out here in the countryside?' Foster says, sounding surprised.

'I wish that were true, it would make my life a lot easier. Trudging around fields at night looking for illegal hare coursers and people nicking farm machinery to order is the bane of my life,' Smith says. 'Anyway, how shall we do this? Shall I hold back the branches and you get the body out?'

'Let's just check first that there's no potential evidence in the area. Foster, can you take some photos around the tree as well as underneath it please,' Morgan barks, trying not to roll his eyes at the local officer who clearly has little understanding of how to secure a crime scene.

Foster immediately springs into action, snapping photos of the path and the tree as well as anything on the ground that looks as if it could be potential evidence. Despite the heavy rain on the soft ground, the ground beneath the tree is still relatively dry, protected by the discarded fronds from the conifer that towers above them, which also means there is little opportunity to capture any footprints that may have been made by whoever placed the body there.

Morgan stands back to watch, automatically taking on the role of senior officer. Despite his seemingly calm exterior, he is anxious to hell that he might miss something important and wishes for the third time this morning that his team could be here with him. The thought reminds him again of the still absent Fallow and his eyes are drawn to the dark shape resting beneath the tree.

'All done boss,' Foster says, taking a stick of nicotine gum out of a packet in his shorts pocket and chewing on it loudly.

'Smith, can you hold back these branches, Foster and I will go in and retrieve the body. There's not enough room to manoeuvre it into the bag where it is so we'll have to bring it out here.'

Foster steps in line with Morgan then they solemnly walk towards the tree. Both detectives need to stoop down to pass under the branches that Smith are holding up as high as they will stretch. Morgan moves towards the gnarled trunk and squeezes himself between it and the upper part of the body. Foster automatically manoeuvres around the other side so that he is opposite Morgan.

'Ok when I say, take hold of the body under the arm and let's pull it backwards until we're out onto the lawn,' Morgan instructs.

For a moment the woodland is encased in a taut silence that is only broken by Fosters size 11 feet crunching over the bracken and leaf fall from the autumn. Once the detective is in place close to the cadaver's shoulder, he looks sideways at Morgan, who in turn returns his gaze. They do not need to speak, both men are wondering the same thing; Is the body DC Fallow or Jane Stokes?

'One, two three, heave,' Morgan instructs, reaching his right hand under one arm and pulling the body out of the darkness and into the bright sunlight. As soon as they are clear of the tree, the exhausted detectives collapse onto the lawn that is now dry, the previous night's rainfall having already evaporated in the warmth of the morning sun.

'Shall I do the honours?' Smith asks, approaching the innate shape whilst still clutching onto a body bag that he has retrieved from his rucksack.

Morgan nods, a feeling of dread washing over him at the thought that the body in front of him could be the young detective who he has not treated as well as he should. He vows to himself that if the body is not Fallow's, from now on he will be a much better colleague to the youngster than he has been up to now. After all, it's not the lad's fault that he's related to Bennett and in any case, the connection could be more of a hindrance than an advantage to the young detective's career.

'Ok here goes,' Smith says, turning over the body that is encased with a sodden black waterproof coat.

All three men stare at the face that is now uncovered. For a moment, none of them speak, lost in emotions that they do not want to reveal in front of the others.

Morgan takes a deep breath then lets it out again in a steady flow, 'it's not Fallow.'

~ Twenty Six ~

The gentle lapping of the flood water that is now subsiding from the road circumventing the Hall's estate,
suits the sombre mood that has befallen the group. They
are standing protectively over the body of Jane Stokes,
who is lying on the neatly manicured lawn that sits between the elegant red brick building, which has seen so
much death already and the woodland that stretches out
towards the boundary of the estate.

The silence is unnerving, as if they are all just waiting
for the next person to die, having reluctantly succumbed
to the inevitable path that they have found themselves
on. A path that is not of their choosing, yet neither can
they deviate from. Not yet.

It is Camilla who speaks first, 'well, I'm lost for words,
which is very unusual for me. I suppose we should move
Jane to a more appropriate place so that she's not left exposed on the lawn for anyone to see.'

Morgan nods, holding back the retort that immediately comes to mind - there is no one else left here to
see the body. They have all gone and this odd trio are
the only ones left. Apart from PC Smith who, as always,
seems to appear when he is least expected.

As if hearing Morgans thoughts, PC Smith appears from behind the dense conifer tree that towers over them, the tough branches rustling in the breeze. 'Sorry about that, got caught short.'

Camilla rolls her eyes, 'surely you could've waited until we got back to the Hall.'

'I'm afraid not, when I need to go, I need to go. I'm sure you understand these things,' Smith says.

'What do you mean by that? Oh I see, it's because I'm a woman of a certain age. We don't all have weak bladders,' Camilla says pointedly, pursing her thin lips.

'Shall we get the body into the bag,' Foster suggests, trying to divert the conversation into something more congenial and failing miserably in the process.

'The body,' snaps Camilla. 'Do you mean Jane? She was a person once you know, not just a body.'

Morgan winces at the elderly councillor's words. Police officers can come across as being insensitive sometimes but it is just their way of dealing with all the trauma they experience.

'Foster, perhaps you could take hold of Jane's shoulders and I'll take her feet. Smith, please open the bag up as wide as you can,' Morgan says, steering the conversation away from the unpleasantness that seems to have descended. Not long ago, they were all working as a team but the comradery has disappeared as quickly as Jane Stokes life. Morgan of course understands full well what is going on. It is not just the fact that another person they know has died or that Fallow is still missing, it is also because they know that someone here is a killer.

Morgan is sweating profusely by the time the body has been carefully manoeuvred into the black body bag that Smith so helpfully thought to bring with him. The detective now knows what the term 'dead weight' means. He could never have imagined how someone so petite as Jane Stokes could have weighed so much. The thought strikes him that whoever killed Jane and moved her into the bushes must be fairly agile.

Despite the heat of the sun that is now above them, Morgan shivers. For the first time in his life, he actually feels afraid, not just for his own safety but for those who are still alive. And of course for Fallow. He must find him, whatever it takes.

An unusual sense of longing comes over Morgan to see the detective's serious face, to talk to him about the case and to work with him on solving it. Perhaps the training course has had the desired effect on him after all.

'I'll go and boil some water and make a pot of coffee. It's fortunate that the hob is gas and not electric,' Camilla states before marching off across the lawn towards the dining room where the door to the veranda is open.

Morgan watches as the elderly woman walks surprisingly spritely towards the building. He knows her well enough by now to know that although she wishes to give the impression that she is hardened to the sight of a body, in reality it is distressing her deeply.

'Let's get Jane into the outdoor larder, it's cool in there,' Morgan instructs, picking up one end of the body bag.

Foster immediately picks up the other end, almost shoving Smith out of the way. Morgan watches intrigued, Foster clearly does not like the local bobby.

Ten minutes later all three men are in the dining room drinking coffee, though without the usual chatter that would normally fill the room.

'I wonder how she died?' Foster asks, taking a sip of the hot liquid.

'We will have to leave that one for the pathologist,' Camilla says sternly, placing her now empty cup onto the table. 'Inspector, when will Jane be taken to the hospital?'

'I don't know yet, I'll give Dr Bootle a ring in a bit. They can't do anything until the water's subsided.'

'That could take days,' Camilla grumbles. 'We need to leave here, I know I'm old but I want to live a bit longer.'

'I agree but first we need to find Fallow. He must be here somewhere and I'm determined to find him,' Morgan says.

'You're right, I'm being selfish. We must find Fallow,' Camilla agrees. 'I'd just feel so much safer if there were more people here, if the emergency services could get here.'

'We could all get in a boat and leave here?' Foster suggests.

'Yes we could but I'm not leaving Fallow here alone,' Morgan responds, slightly exasperated at having to repeat himself.

'Detective Inspector, you're in charge so what should we do first?' Camilla says, skilfully altering the dynamics of the group to manoeuvre Morgan back into being in charge.

'Smith, Foster and I will start searching the grounds then move onto the beach this afternoon when the tide has gone out.'

'What about me?' Camilla asks.

'I think you should stay here, just in case Fallow returns,' Morgan says tactfully, aware that the elderly woman is not physically capable of searching the grounds.

'Right, well I'll go to the library then and see if I can find any more documents that might at least solve the mystery we were set to do by Mr Chalnor. Let's all meet back here again at lunchtime,' Camilla instructs.

By late morning, Morgan and Foster are thirsty, hungry and tired but neither of them voice their discomfort, determined to find the still-missing Fallow.

'I keep hoping that perhaps he just went for a walk and got stuck somewhere or even took a boat over to Felixstowe,' says Morgan as he steps over a low outcrop of grass on the edge of the beach.

'I know what you mean, he's a nice lad, it would be a shame for anything to have happened to him.'

Morgan remains silent, not wishing to share his personal thoughts about Fallow. Regardless of how he has felt about the young detective, Fallow is a member of his team and they do not lose teammates.

The pair walk on in silence, both lost in thought, both wanting to conserve their energy for finding the missing detective. The diary has been forgotten for now, finding Fallow is far more important, however much they wish to see the mystery of the Bawdsey Boys solved.

'Well there's no sign of him down this part of the beach, shall we cut through here and head back across the estate? We can search the outbuildings then head back to the Hall?' Morgan suggests.

'Whatever you think boss,' Foster says cheekily, trying to ease the uncomfortable atmosphere a little.

Morgan ignores the tone of Foster's comment. It is not the right time to make jokes, not with everything that's happened. He lengthens his stride and pushes ahead of Foster, wanting to put a little distance between them. There is something about Foster that Morgan does not like though he cannot quite put into words what it is.

'There's a light on in the barn,' Foster says, surprised that anyone should be there. It is unlikely to be the engineering apprentice Britany as she left the estate before the storm and so did Kerrie Mason, the museum curator. The only people who stayed on the estate are Reece Browne and his grandfather.

'Let's go and take a look,' Morgan says officiously as he pushes open the enormous door.

At first glance, the barn appears to be empty. It is only when the two detectives' step around a vintage combine harvester that they see Reece Browne.

'What are you doing in here?' Morgan asks, his voice echoing through the voluminous barn.

'Oh my god you made me jump,' Reece yells, instantly dropping the spanner that he was holding.

'Sorry mate, we're looking for DC Fallow, have you seen him?' Foster asks, approaching the gardener.

'No I haven't,' Reece replies tersely.

Morgan has been so focused on finding Fallow, that he realises they have failed to tell Reece about Jane Stokes.

'There's another reason for our visit,' Morgan begins, clearing his throat a little. 'We found Jane Stokes earlier.'

'Oh right, that's good,' Reece replies, bending down to retrieve the spanner.

'No, it's not, she wasn't alive,' Foster explains.

A sharp intake of breath is heard then Reece's face appears from the shadows. He steps around the machinery to stand next to the two men. 'I don't understand,' Reece says, his bottom lip trembling.

'I'm sorry to say that we found Ms Stokes dead this morning,' Morgan states with more diplomacy than his counterpart.

Reece's jaw drops open, 'she can't be, I only saw her last night.'

'What time was that?' Morgan asks, pulling a notebook and a small pencil out from his back pocket.

'It was in the evening,' Reece admits.

'Was she with you when I came looking for her?' Foster demands, looking slightly irritated.

'Yes, she was. She went back to the Hall soon after you left though and I didn't see her again after that.'

'Did you hear anything, I mean anything unusual?' Morgan asks, looking at the gardener with heightened interest.

'Once I'm asleep, that's it, I'm dead to the world,' Reece replies, his face draining of colour as he realises the significance of his words.

Morgan grimaces, 'well that should at least help with establishing time of death.'

'How did she die?' Reece asks.

'We don't know yet, we've moved her to the pantry but we're under strict instructions not to touch her.'

'I guess that makes sense, they won't be able to collect her until the water goes down,' Reece murmurs. 'If you don't mind, I'd like to be alone now, it's all such a shock.'

Morgan smiles grimly at the gardener then turns around and leaves the barn, Foster following closely behind.

'So, the old dear was right then,' Foster chuckles as soon as they are outside.

'Right about what?' Morgan snaps, growing tired of Fosters glib attitude.

'About Ms Stokes and the gardener. It's like something that happened in the old days, you know, the lady of the manor having a fling with the hired hand.'

Morgan glares at Foster for a moment, trying to decide if he should pull him up for his attitude then decides that it is not his job to do so, after all Foster is not a work colleague.

'Come on, let's go back to the Hall and find Mrs Fields and PC Smith, we can go and look again for Fallow after we've had something to eat,' Foster says.

Morgan waits for Foster to walk up the path ahead of him and watches as the London detective strides off at pace towards the Hall. Yet again he is struck with the notion of disliking the man without knowing why. Morgan takes a deep breath then follows in Fosters footsteps, he too wants to go back to the Hall but not for the same reason as Foster – he wants to take another look at the photographs on the display in the dining room, there's something about them that is bothering him.

~ Twenty Seven ~

The two detectives find Camilla Fields just where they expected her to be – in the small library at the far end of the building.

'Any news?' Camilla asks, looking up from the book that she is reading.

Morgan moves across the room to stand next to elderly councillor who is sitting in front of the window - the only source of natural light in the room. 'Sort of, you were right about Jane and the gardener,' Morgan admits, pulling out a chair and sitting down, ignoring the fact that it is the only other unoccupied seat in the room.

Foster clearly recognises a snub when he sees one and busies himself at the other end of the room. He pulls a book off from a shelf and pretends to read it.

'Oh I see, how did he take the news of Jane's death?'

'Not very well, he must've been fond of her,' Morgan says quietly. 'It made me think about Oswald Turner. We know that he abandoned the kitchen maid for someone else but we never found out who it was?'

'Do you think it's important?' Camilla asks, placing the book she has been reading down on a small mahogany table.

'Yes, though I don't know why.'

Camilla nods thoughtfully, 'you should always trust your instincts. Whoever the woman was, she could've had something to do with whatever was going on with Oswald Turner and the people who were blackmailing him.'

'Do you think?'

'Yes I do and I always listen to my instincts. People will do anything for someone they love and he had clearly fallen in love with this person.'

'Or maybe he thought he was. I'm sure he thought he loved his wife who he left back in Canada,' Morgan responds before standing up to look out of the window overlooking the garden that wraps around two sides of the building. The view is the same one that can be seen from Fallows bedroom, which reminds Morgan that they still haven't found the young detective. Where was he?

'Shall we get something to eat?' Foster suggests.

Camilla smiles, 'yes, that's a good idea then we can resume our search for Fallow. Have you heard any news on when help might arrive Inspector?'

'Not yet, they're all still tied up with the flooding plus the roads haven't cleared so unless someone came by boat, they'd have a problem getting here.'

'That reminds me, what's happened to our local police officer?' Camilla asks, gingerly getting up from her chair.

'That's a good point, I'd forgotten about him,' Morgan confesses. 'Foster and I went North and PC Smith went South.'

'I hope something hasn't happened to him?' Camilla says, her voice wavering a little.

'Perhaps he's been called away to something more urgent,' Morgan soothes. 'We'll take a look and see if his kayak's still there after lunch.'

'I'm sure you're right detective. I'd just hate for someone else to go missing.'

'So would I Mrs Fields, so would I,' Foster says from somewhere at the back of the room, making Camilla and Morgan jump, who have momentarily forgotten that he is still there.

'Let's go and see what we can find to eat in the kitchen,' Morgan suggests, moving towards the door. The others trail quietly behind him as if reluctantly following a funeral procession towards the lynch gate of Bawdsey churchyard.

In the kitchen, Morgan and Foster find some bread, cheese and left-over ham then set-to making some sandwiches, leaving Camilla to boil a saucepan of water to make a pot of coffee.

With the food and drink assembled, the trio make their way into the dining room and sit down at their usual table next to the French doors that lead out onto the veranda.

There is little conversation whilst they eat, the events of the past few hours weighing heavily on their minds. Morgan is the first to finish the meal. He brushes the crumbs from his trousers then pushes back his chair and wanders over to look at the display of photographs on the wall.

'Is there something you're looking for detective?' Camilla asks as she slowly walks across the room to join the detective.

'There's a photo I wanted to see, something that I wanted to check on but I can't find it now,' Morgan explains, looking over the display again.

'Was it here?' Foster asks, pointing towards a blank part of the wall that is slightly discoloured as if there had once been something there that shielded the wall from being bleached by the sun.

'It could've been, I honestly can't remember now,' Morgan answers glumly, frustrated that his memory will not reveal to him what it is he wants to know.

'Any food left?' PC Smith asks jovially as he steps into the room.

'I'm afraid not but I can make some more sandwiches?' Camilla replies diplomatically.

'That would be great, thanks,' Smith responds.

'Where have you been?' Foster asks, direct as ever.

'Looking for your mate, where do you think I've been?' Smith snaps.

'You've been gone a while, that's all,' Foster replies meekly.

'Well, that side of the estate takes longer to get around,' Smith says defensively. 'Did you two find out anything useful?'

'Yes, actually we did,' responds Morgan tersely, growing tired of Smith's attitude and wishing yet again that he had his team around him instead.

'Good, well I'm pleased for you,' Smith responds, taking hold of the plate of food that Camilla is holding out for him.

'We should get back to searching for Fallow,' Morgan says tight-lipped.

Foster nods, then goes behind the bar to retrieve some bottles of water from the chiller cabinet that are now warm as the power is still off. 'I hope the electric comes back on soon,' he grumbles, wiping a bead of sweat from his forehead.

'Don't we all,' Camilla muses. 'Don't we all. Well, I shall return to the books and hopefully you will come back with some better news this time.'

'We all hope for better news Mrs Fields, it doesn't seem to be very forthcoming though does it,' Morgan sighs.

'Don't lose hope Inspector, Fallow may still be alive and we know that help will be with us soon,' Camilla says softly.

Morgan nods thoughtfully. 'Mrs Fields, I wonder if you'd mind looking in the library for records of who was at the Hall in 1940. We've got Mr Chalnor's list of course and know a bit from what the staff told us but we don't know for certain if it's right or if there was anyone else here.'

'Good idea, I'll get onto it right away,' Camilla says enthusiastically, pleased to have been tasked with something that will allow her to be useful. 'I'll go to the museum as well, there should be a key for it in the office.'

'Thanks Camilla, please be careful though,' Morgan warns.

'I will, don't you worry about me, I'm a tough old girl,' Camilla replies, smiling broadly.

Morgan walks over to the French doors that lead out onto the veranda. As he steps out onto the small patio area to wait for Foster to join him, he turns around to take one last look at PC Smith and Camilla Fields. Now every time he says goodbye to someone at the Hall, he wonders if he will ever see them again.

~ Twenty Eight ~

The sun is beating down relentlessly on the path that takes Camilla through the shady woodland, past the two estate-workers cottages, past the barn that is now a workshop and onwards to the small museum that has not yet opened for the summer season.

Camilla fumbles about in her pocket for the museum key and is relieved to find that it is still there even though of course it is unlikely to have gone anywhere since she placed it there only fifteen minutes earlier. Not for the first time that day, Camilla senses a change in the atmosphere at the Hall and it is making her feel very uneasy. Of course the enforced isolation from the flood is not helping her feel less tense but really it is the knowledge there are now so few of them left on the estate and one of them is a murderer.

The elderly councillor winds her way up the path then gingerly makes her way up the steps to the museum, her aging knees complaining at the movement. She places the key in the lock, her weak hands barely able to turn the lock that is stiff with age. Camilla smiles at that the thought that key is as old and decrepit as she is then she returns her focus to the task ahead.

The wily councillor knows what she is looking for - proof that two particular people were here at the Hall in the summer of 1940; proof that her instinct is right, as always. Camilla thinks back to the photograph that she took from the wall in the dining room earlier that morning; the photograph that is now inside the handbag she has just placed on the desk in the museum. A photograph of a group of people who were staying at the Hall in 1940 and amongst them, someone who was there for a very different reason to what was officially recorded.

Camilla takes a dark brown envelope out of her bag, carefully opens it and pulls out a fragile photograph. It is of a young girl, dressed in her finest clothes, ready for an evening at the theatre. The girl's face is familiar to Camilla, she has seen it all her life, not just when she has taken the photograph out from the shoe box in her bedroom to gaze at it but also every time she looks in the mirror and sees the same blue eyes staring back at her, the same determined chin, slightly raised in defiance. The girl, who later became a woman, had the same never-ending sense of loyalty to her country as Camilla, one that is so intense that it overcomes even the strongest of fears. The woman in the photo also had the same sparkle in her eyes, a steely look that reveals that whatever happens, she will always do her utmost to succeed.

Carefully she returns the photograph to the envelope and places it back in her handbag, alongside the one from the dining room. Camilla places the bag onto the floor than begins to search through a large register that contains the names of every person who was billeted to the Hall during the war. The book is heavy, not only from the number of people who have passed through this place but from the stories that they could have told, if only they had lived to tell them. So many young lives lost, reflects Camilla sadly as she sits down to read through each name in turn.

Time passes quickly and it is an hour later when Camilla finishes reading through the book. The name she was hoping to see is not there. This is not entirely unexpected but disappointing all the same. If only she had Oswald's diary, Camilla muses as she pushes back the chair to stand up again. Oswald knew the identity of the woman, he must have done, her initial is written in his diary. Perhaps that should be proof enough, along with the photo, that the woman was here but somehow Camilla feels it is not. She wants to find out more about the woman, what she was doing here in 1940 and then later in 1942 when she returned to Bawdsey Hall after having the baby. Most of all though, Camilla needs to find out how the woman died - how her mother died.

'Do you think we'll find him?' Foster asks, quickening his pace to catch up with Morgan than immediately regretting the additional exertion in the midday sun.

'No, I don't but what else can we do? We can't just sit in the Hall and wait for the next person to die.'

'You're right, I just keeping hoping we'll find the little fella alive and well. I like him, in an odd sort of way. It must be awkward sometimes, having someone who's different on your team,' Foster says.

'What do you mean?' Morgan asks, stopping to face the detective.

'Well, I mean with his autism, it must be difficult sometimes though I guess you're all used to it.'

Morgan stares at Foster for a moment, trying to understand what he has just said. Of course in hindsight it's obvious why Fallow isn't like the rest of the team, it just never occurred to Morgan to find out.

The moment passes and Morgan, who is still grappling with the fact that he has completely failed to recognise that a member of his team needed support not criticism for being different, steps up the pace. The ground is still level but it has become more onerous to contend with as the dense sand has morphed into thick layers of shingle that give way underfoot.

The two men continue to trudge over the pebbles until they reach the worn, wooden steps that lead upwards to the top of the cliff. Morgan looks up at the towering structure, grateful that its' shadow allows some respite from the fierce sun.

'Do you want to carry on along the beach and I'll go up there?' Morgan says to Foster, as he too shelters in the coolness of the shade.

'Do you think it's safe?' Foster asks, looking further down the beach to the place where the cliff has recently slipped.

'I can't worry about that now, I need to find Fallow.'

Foster nods, understanding the burning need to find one of your own. 'Sure thing, I understand. I'll carry on searching on the beach then I'll head back across the estate and check if Smith's kayak is still where he left it.'

'Strange how he just went off like that,' Morgan ponders as he puts his foot on the bottom step of the ladder.

'I reckon something urgent came up.'

Morgan is about to reply when his phone bleeps, notifying him that a new message has arrived. He opens the message, which is from DCI Tom Cook.

Tom

Morgan, I'm on my way back, just about to board the plane. I'll ring you when I land. What the hell has been happening?????

Morgan puts the phone back into his pocket, not wishing to respond yet. He knows it's a long shot but hopefully they will have found Fallow by the time Cook lands at Stansted Airport and then there will be one less problem for him to relay to his boss.

When he is half-way up the rickety steps, Morgan glances down to watch Foster diligently searching around the outcrops of tall grasses. He wonders if middle age is starting to mellow him a little as a feeling of something that can only be described as pride is niggling at him, at the sight of the officer doing what he is trained to do. Perhaps he has been too quick to judge Foster as well as poor Fallow. Perhaps Cook was right to send him on the team-building course even though of course it didn't happen. Morgan has learnt far more than he could have ever anticipated by being here on the Suffolk Coast - not just about other people but also about himself.

The detectives' thoughts stray to his wife, who as ever has come second to his demanding job. A pang of guilt niggles at Morgan - he has not been a good husband in the past and even now, he has failed miserably to let his wife know that he is safe. In fact, since Morgan has been at Bawdsey, wrapped up in the events that seem to be never-ending, he has seldom thought about Celia. What Morgan can't decide though, is if that is a reflection on his hyper-focusing on work, his abject failure to even be a half-decent husband, or if it is a sign of something that he does not want to admit – that his marriage is not working.

Morgan pushes the uncomfortable thought to one side and focuses on reaching the top step whilst praying that the rickety ladder remains intact. It is so fragile that it could even have been built in the Second World War, Morgan decides as he pulls himself up onto the top of the cliff. For a moment he stands on the edge of the cliff and breathes in the welcoming fresh air that is blow-ing across the sea. It has always amazed him that just across this stretch of grey water there are entirely different countries lying unseen. Morgan wonders who else has stood here in this exact spot, looking out across the water. Perhaps even the three Bawdsey Boys, the farmers who signed up to serve their country without hesitation and never returned home again.

The thought then occurs to Morgan - where did the locals live before they were evacuated at the start of 1940? There must be some houses in the area, even if they were never occupied again after the war and are now derelict. Apart from anything, the two cottages at the Hall could not have possibly housed all the staff needed to run such a large estate and then of course there would have been fishermen and people who worked on the surrounding farmland - people like the Bawdsey Boys.

Morgan stands at the edge of the cliff and peers down below to see if Foster is still near enough to shout to but the detective has already moved out-of-sight and out of earshot. He pulls his phone out of his pocket and sends a message to Foster, though knows that it may not be received anytime soon with such a poor mobile coverage in this area. The detective pushes the phone back into his pocket and takes a conservative swig of water from the bottle in his rucksack – just enough to slightly quench his thirst but leaving him some for contingency. With the sounds of the waves crashing onto the shingle beach behind him, Morgan sets off along the overgrown path that will take him deeper into the Suffolk countryside.

~ Twenty Nine ~

Morgan does not have far to walk before his hunch is proved right. Not far from the cliff top, is a row of terraced houses that were once occupied by the fishermen that made their living from the nearby North Sea. A dilapidated picket fence leads Morgan to the front door of the first building, which has been propped open by a small boulder.

The detective peers inside to see a jumble of broken floorboards and a rickety staircase that is too precarious to attempt to climb. Morgan retreats then hops over a small hedge into the front garden of the adjoining property. A quick look through the window into what was once the front living room, reveals the building to be in a similar state to its' neighbour.

A low fence separates the middle house from the last one in the row, which is in better condition due to being slightly less exposed to the force of the wind coming off the North Sea. Morgan tries to push open the front door but it will not budge. An overgrown path leads him to the rear of the house, where a dilapidated fence separates the garden from the neighbouring scrubland. The wooden gate easily gives way when Morgan gives it a firm shove and he steps over a large stinging nettle onto an old concrete path that leads straight to the back door.

Morgan pushes open the door, his training as a police officer automatically kicking in as he cautiously peers around the door until he is certain there is no movement within the building. He steps inside what was once a small kitchen, with a sink underneath the window and a wooden table in the centre of the room. Even from the back of the building, the sea can clearly be heard. For some, the sound elicits a sense of calm, for Morgan though, it evokes a deep feeling of loneliness. He has never really liked the isolation of the countryside, preferring instead to have close neighbours nearby. The poor condition of the building adds to the eeriness of the situation and Morgan is suddenly struck with a strong desire to leave as quickly as possible.

Taking small steps to test the condition of the floor with each movement, Morgan shuffles into the adjoining room – a living room with a staircase on one side. The front door, which is at the far end of the room, has been blocked by a large boulder that no doubt came from the nearby shore. On one side of the room is an overturned wooden chair, lying prone as if its' previous occupant left in a hurry. Even from this distance, Morgan can see that the staircase is in too poor condition to attempt to ascend. He turns around and moves towards the kitchen again then stops. Out of the corner of his eye, he catches sight of something out of place, something that is not in-keeping with a building that has been clearly abandoned for many years.

Carefully Morgan treads across the floor, which creaks disconcertingly at his every move. Almost hidden in the dark corner, the detective spies some dark blue material that looks as if it could be part of a sleeping bag. Morgan stares at the object for a moment, trying to decipher what it is. It is no good, he will need to get closer to it. He takes another step towards the wall that separates the house with its' neighbour and is almost close enough to see the material, when there is a loud cracking sound and Morgans foot disappears into the chasm below.

From somewhere in the distance, a voice is calling for Morgan to wake up but for some reason he cannot make out where the sound is coming from.

'Just lie still for a bit,' the muffled voice continues. 'You've had a bit of a bump to the head.'

'What's going on?' Morgan says, his voice sounding slurred as he struggles to waken himself up more.

'You've had a bit of an accident, just as well I was nearby,' the voice continues.

The voice is starting to sound familiar to Morgan though he cannot yet work out who it is and neither can he turn around as his leg seems to be stuck. 'I'm stuck,' Morgan declares, stating the obvious.

The voice laughs, 'yeah I know you are. I'm just going to try and find something to break up the floorboard and then I can get your leg out.'

For a few minutes, the voice is replaced by a heavy silence again that is only broken by the soothing sound of the waves rushing up onto the nearby shingle beach. The sound of the sea penetrates through Morgan's befuddled brain and he suddenly remembers that he is at Shingle Street. As his awareness increases, so does the realisation that his foot is injured and that is hurting like hell. Morgan tries to wiggle the appendage and immediately regrets the action as the broken floorboards bite harder into his calf muscle.

'Just keep still, I'll have you out in a minute.'

Morgan tries again to turn around to see whose voice it is that he now recognises. His efforts though are unnecessary as the person steps around him, kneels down in front of the fragmented floorboard and begins pulling out the broken shards. It is PC Smith.

Morgan lets out a deep breath, he has never felt so vulnerable in all his life and is immensely relieved to see a familiar face. 'Thank god you're here, I had visions of me wasting away.'

'Yeah, it's lucky I was in the area,' Smith says, pulling out the last of the smaller pieces of wood. 'Can you move your foot?'

Morgan wiggles the foot again and winces, 'I can move it so it's not broken but it hurts really badly.'

'I bet it does. What happened?'

'I was looking for Fallow and saw something that I wanted to take a closer look at then this happened,' Morgan groans, pointing to where the floorboard gave way under his weight.

'What was it that you saw?'

'It's over there, near the wall, some blue material.'

Smith crawls over to the wall to avoid putting too much weight on the brittle floorboards. 'There's nothing there mate, perhaps you imagined it. I reckon you should get that head wound looked at, it looks a bit nasty. You must have hit it on the floor when you went down.'

Morgan suddenly notices the dull throbbing coming from the back of his head. Even with his still-befuddled brain, the detective knows there is no way he could have hit his head when he fell through the floorboards. Then he remembers, just at that moment when the floor gave way, he had heard something. There was someone else in the room, someone else was breathing behind him.

'I think I can walk now, thanks for your help,' Morgan says, suddenly feeling very afraid. He reaches into his trouser pocket for his phone. The battery is dead.

'You've been lucky,' Smith says, looking at Morgans phone. 'You should always keep your phone charged up when you're out in the countryside, you never know what might happen.'

'I'll remember that, thanks.'

'Do you reckon if you lean on me that you can walk back to the Hall from here?'

'I'll be fine honestly. You never said what you're doing here?'

'Same as you, looking for Fallow,' Smith replies smoothly as he takes hold of Morgan's arm so that he can lean on him. 'Mind yourself getting out through the door, we don't want any more accidents, do we.'

Morgan does not respond, he is too busy concentrating on every step that he takes as he traverses the kitchen then out through the open back door. Smith walks behind him, keeping a careful watch over the injured detective as he makes his way across the long, coarse grass that surrounds the house.

'How long do you think it'll take to get back to the Hall?' Morgan asks, grimacing every time he puts the injured foot onto the ground.

'At this rate, probably about an hour. Have you got any water?'

'A little,' Morgan replies wishing that he'd had the sense to bring more with him.

'Lucky that I came prepared then,' Smith chuckles as he pulls an unopened bottle of water out of his rucksack. The police officer unscrews the cap with a dull click then drinks deeply from the bottle before passing it to Morgan who follows suit.

With Morgan's thirst satiated, the daunting prospect of the long and painful journey back to the Hall seems to lessen a little. He wishes though that he could shake off the feeling of unease that descended on him just before he entered the fisherman's cottage and is still with him. His concern for Fallow is also ever present, even with the distraction from the pain in his foot. There is another thought though that is now running through Morgans mind, making him doubt his earlier decision to split up from his walking companion; where is Foster?

By the time Smith and Morgan reach Bawdsey Hall they are both exhausted, thirsty and soaked through with perspiration. The sound of footsteps crunching up the driveway alerts the occupants of the Hall that someone is approaching. The two police officers reach the front door of the building, just as it is opened by Camilla.

'Thank goodness you're back, I was getting worried.'

'I had a bit of an accident,' Morgan explains sheepishly.

'I can see that, what's the damage?'

'It's just his foot,' Smith replies as he helps Morgan to hop up the steps. 'Oh and a bit of a bang to his head.'

'His head? That's not good,' Camilla scolds.

'He hit it when he went through the floor in one of the old fishing cottages at Shingle Street,' Smith explains.

Camilla looks sternly at Morgan, 'shall we go through to the sitting room, there are some comfy chairs in there?'

'Sounds a good plan,' Smith replies jovially. He helps Morgan down the hallway and into the small sitting room that none of them have used since staying at the Hall. One wall is dominated by a large fireplace and cast-iron grate, whilst the rest of the room is adorned with comfortable chairs, fit for a stately home.

'PC Smith, would you mind looking in the kitchen for some ice and also bring back a jug of water as well, I'm sure you could both do with a drink,' Camilla instructs as she directs Morgan to place his injured foot onto a low footstool.

'Will do, I won't be long,' Smith replies.

Camilla waits until the officer has moved down the hallway, then sits down next to Morgan, who has now cautiously taken off the trainer and sock on the injured foot.

'What happened?' Camilla asks quietly.

Morgan looks up at the wily councillor who always seems to know what others are thinking. 'I don't know. I was walking across the room to get a closer look at something then my foot went through the floor, that's the last thing I remember.'

'Hmmm very difficult to hit your head when your foot has gone through the floor,' Camilla concludes, looking at Morgan to observe his reaction. 'What was it that you wanted to take a closer look at?'

Morgan nestles into the chair and thinks back to the moment just before his foot went through the floor. 'There was something blue at the far end of the room, I wanted to take a closer look at it.'

'That's interesting,' Camilla says, tilting her head to one side as if ruminating on it a little further. 'What's the last thing you remember before you lost consciousness?'

'Breathing, I could hear someone breathing behind me,' Morgan says, looking evenly at Camilla.

'And what is the first thing you remember from when you woke up?'

'I heard someone shouting. There's something else as well...,' Morgan begins.

'Right, here we are, some water and some ice for that foot,' Smith says, striding back into the room.

Camilla looks at Morgan, 'we'll talk again later when you've rested.'

'Well, it looks like Mrs Fields has got everything under control here and the flood water is starting to subside nicely, so I'd better get back to my usual duties,' Smith says cheerfully before downing a glass of water.

'What about DC Fallow?' Camilla asks, surprised that the officer is even considering leaving.

'Oh yeah, I forgot about him. I'm sure he'll turn up soon, he probably went out walking and got caught out by the storm. My guess is he's hauled up somewhere and might even be on his way back.'

Morgan stares at Smith, taken aback by his blasé attitude. 'Thanks for helping me out today.'

'No problem, just make sure that next time you go on a long walk that you take a fully charged phone and at least two bottles of water with you,' Smith chides, placing the empty glass down onto a small table before making his way towards the hallway.

'Thank you officer, very helpful,' Camilla replies in a tone that could be interpreted in many ways.

Camilla waits until she hears the front door shut then turns to Morgan. 'Where's Foster?'

'I don't know, we parted company on the beach near Shingle Street.'

'Oh god, I hope we haven't lost another one.'

The sound of footsteps approaching the servant's entrance interrupts the conversation. Camilla traverses the room to look out of the window to see who it is. 'Ah here he is now.'

'Thank goodness for that, I was getting a bit worried.'

'So was I. I wonder if he has any news on our missing detective,' Camilla mutters to herself as she walks back towards Morgan. 'You didn't finish what you were saying to me earlier.'

'No, well the thing is, I didn't want to say anything in front of PC Smith. It does seem awfully convenient that he was there just at that moment when I had the accident.'

'Yes, it does and now of course we have the return of DC Foster, who is also not to be trusted me thinks.'

'What makes you say that?' Morgan asks, pulling himself more upright.

'I don't know, call it instinct. I'm certain that there's something he's hiding.'

~ Thirty ~

'Well that was some walk,' Foster says, his face a deep crimson. 'Where did you end up getting to? I thought I might see you when I walked back across the estate.'

'I had a slight accident in an old fisherman's cottage,' Morgan explains, grimacing as he moves his foot onto the floor to see if the pain has now lessened.

'What happened?' asks Foster, taking hold of the glass of water that Camilla has passed to him.

'I put my foot through the floor,' Morgan admits. 'Bit of a silly thing to do as I couldn't get it out again.'

'Well you seem to have managed?' Foster points out, sitting down heavily into one of the wingback chairs.

'PC Smith found me and got me out,' Morgan explains, putting his foot back onto the low stool to ease the discomfort a little.

'That was lucky though you could've just phoned me,' Foster says.

'I couldn't, my phone battery had died,' Morgan reluctantly admits.'

'Anyway you're back now, that's all that matters. Did you see any sign of poor Fallow?'

'I don't think so,' Morgan begins to say then remembers that perhaps he should not say what is on his mind given that he has no idea who it was that hit him on the head. 'Did you?'

'I'm afraid not. I can't imagine if he'd gone out for a walk that he could've gone much further than where I went, not with that storm coming in and him being so scared of them.'

'I'd almost forgotten about the storm. It makes it less likely that Fallow chose to go out for a walk given how much he detests storms,' Camilla says, trying to catch Morgan's eye.

'Have you heard anything about when back-up will arrive?' Foster asks, kicking off his dusty trainers.

'I guess it will be tomorrow. The flood waters are subsiding according to PC Smith. I wonder if the electricity is back on?'

Camilla walks over to the light switch and flicks the switch. For a moment nothing happens but then the light flickers back into life. 'Oh good, that is a relief.'

'Just in time, I need to go and charge up my phone,' Morgan says, standing up to make the painful journey up the stairs to find his charger.

'Where is it mate? I'll get it for you,' Foster offers.

Morgan tries not to show his annoyance at the familiarity being shown to a senior detective. 'Thanks, that's very helpful.'

'No problem, we've all got to watch out for each other,' Foster says, leaping up. He takes Morgans phone from him then picks up his discarded trainers and pulls them on before heading towards the stairs.

'He's very sprightly for someone whose been out for such a long walk in this heat,' Camilla says wistfully as she watches Foster move.

'Yes he is,' Morgan replies.

'Now, what is it that you've been trying to tell me,' Camilla says, sitting down next to Morgan.

'There was something in the old fisherman's cottage that caught my eye.'

'Yes, I remember, something blue, wasn't it?'

'It wasn't so much the colour, it was the material. It was the type of material used for sleeping bags.'

'Oh really, well that is very interesting,' Camilla says. 'Perhaps if you tell me how to get to this cottage I can go and take a look?'

'Well, that's the thing I've been trying to tell you. When I woke up, it had gone.'

Morgan sleeps away the rest of the afternoon, which is unsurprising given the combination of heat and the exertion from his latest escapade. When he finally awakens, his first thought is of Fallow and then of Cook's message that he still has not replied to.

With his phone now fully charged, Morgan unplugs it from the charger then opens up his messages. Morgan pulls himself more upright, momentarily forgetting about his injured foot until a jolt of pain quickly reminds him. Trying to ignore the searing pain, he concentrates instead on finding the message that Cook sent him earlier, which is now so long ago that he is bound to have already landed back in the UK. Morgan finds the message and presses reply;

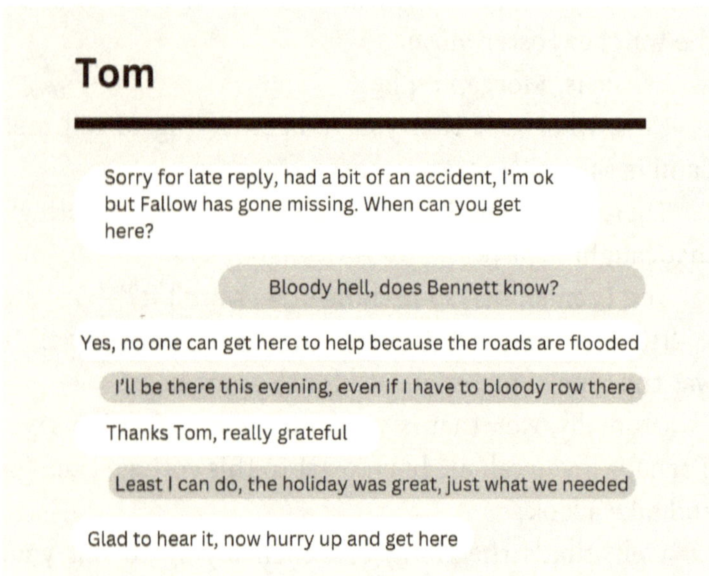

Morgan places the phone down on the bedside table, swings his legs over the edge of the bed then places his feet onto the floor, bracing himself for the inevitable sharp pain that immediately shoots through his foot. He sighs heavily, knowing that he has the choice of either staying where he is or to keep moving and put up with the throbbing pain that is a reminder of the day's events.

Steeling himself against what he knows will come, Morgan allows his weight to bear down on his foot then gingerly begins to shuffle across the carpet to the door.

When the detective opens the door that leads onto the landing, he is unsurprised by the quietness of the building but is taken aback to find that it is still daylight and that he has not slept for as long as he imagined. Morgan shuffles along the corridor until he reaches the top of the stairs where Fallow and Fosters rooms are. Tentatively he knocks on Fosters door, wondering if the detective is there.

When no answer is forthcoming, Morgan begins the painful journey down the stairs, hoping that he will find Camilla and Foster somewhere in the building. The silence of the Hall is unnerving Morgan a little, coupled by the very real fear that whilst he has been sleeping, Camilla and Foster may also have disappeared. His fears though are swiftly allayed when he hears the booming voice of Foster coming from the other end of the Hall where he is no doubt sipping a tot of whisky on the veranda.

Morgan makes his way through the empty dining room towards the direction of the voice.

'Ah Morgan, how's the foot?' Foster enthusiastically enquires.

'Painful,' Morgan replies, wincing as he pulls out a chair and sits down.

'Can I get you a drink? It might help to dull the pain a little.'

'Thanks, that's not a bad idea.'

Foster pushes back his chair and strides into the dining room. He stoops down behind the bar, moving out of sight. Just at that moment, Camilla walks assuredly across the pattered carpet carrying a wooden tray.

'I hope you slept well Inspector?'

'Thank you, yes. My foot's killing me though,' Morgan says before realising the inappropriateness of his words.

'Would a walking stick help? I'm sure I saw one on the coat stand in the hallway?'

'That would help enormously,' Morgan replies, taking a sip of the whisky that Foster has just placed onto the table in front of him.

Camilla purposefully strides off to locate a walking stick just as the dense clouds that have now blown over Bawdsey, unleash a torrent of rain.

'Typical,' Foster grumbles, heading back inside without waiting for Morgan.

Morgan pushes back his chair, trying to ignore the searing pain that jolts through him with every step. He steps back into the dining room again and sits down at the table where the group have sat for every meal they have eaten in the Hall since the disappearance of Bobby Chalnor.

'So much has happened since that first night when we all met,' Morgan says thoughtfully as he takes hold of one of the soggy ham sandwiches that Foster has now retrieved from the veranda.

'Yes it has, strange to think that this room is where it all started,' Foster considers as he stares at the display of photographs on the wall. He gets up from his chair and wanders over to look at them. 'This is where it all began, right here.'

'Well, I think technically it started when Jane Stokes booked us onto the training course and gave poor Bobby Chalnor the task of trying to find out what happened that night in 1940 when the Bawdsey Boys disappeared,' Camilla says as she enters the room holding a wooden walking stick.

'No, you're wrong, it started here,' Foster says, turning to look at Camilla and Morgan. 'I spoke to Bobby Chalnor that night. I told him why I was here.'

'What do you mean,' Morgan asks coldly. 'You're here for a training course, just like the rest of us.'

'That's not exactly true. I knew that Bobby was working here, I came across him on a military history website, one of those ones where you go to find out about your relatives who died in the war.'

A shiver runs down Morgan's spine as he wonders where the conversation will lead to next. 'So, you knew Mr Chalnor before you came here?'

'Not exactly. I knew *of* him. He was looking for information about his grandfather Oswald Turner. I knew who he was as soon as I saw that name,' Foster spits.

Morgan stares at the London detective, 'what do you mean?'

'It was him, the Canadian that my grandad was trying to stop passing on secrets to the enemy,' Foster explains as he walks towards the table where Morgan is sitting.

'You mean the person that your grandfather was blackmailing,' Camilla responds dryly.

'My grandad was one of those poor lads who signed up to patrol the beaches with no proper training. What they would have done if the Germans had actually invaded, I dread to think. They didn't know what they were doing, had no experience of war,' Foster explains.

'They knew what they were doing when they decided to blackmail Oswald Turner,' Morgan says quietly.

'They were trying to protect their country, our country. That bastard was passing secrets to the enemy,' Foster spits.

'What secrets?' Morgan asks.

'I don't know, all I know is that he was passing on information. Grandad wrote letters to his sweetheart - my grandma. She showed them to me, it says it all in there.. They all thought that the Bawdsey Boys had gone AWOL. There were so many rumours going about no one knew what to believe. Some of the locals thought that they'd run away, afraid of the Hun invading.

'Did your grandmother also show you the newspaper reports of a man dying on the beach the same night that the Home Guards disappeared?' Camilla asks, staring at Foster. 'And that the locals thought that the Bawdsey Boys had been involved with Oswald Turners death.'

'He died that same night?' Morgan asks, surprised that Camilla had not told him about this news before.

'Oswald was blown up by a mine on the beach, there is a copy of the report from '*The Suffolk Times*' in the sitting room,' Camilla explains.

'The Boys had been laying mines that day. So, you see, either way they got the blame and that sneaky Canadian got a hero's welcome,' Foster spits.

'I wonder what Oswald was doing on the beach that night,' Camilla murmurs.

'Exactly, if there was a German invasion then I bet he was involved in it. Maybe he signalled to the Germans, let them know where to come in on the beach,' Foster replies.

'Or maybe he was meeting the three men who were blackmailing him,' Camilla says quietly.

'Well this is all very interesting but I don't see what it's got to do with Mr Chalnor's death,' Morgan says, draining the rest of his drink.

'I told him, that first evening when we were waiting for dinner to arrive. He was looking at the photos on the wall, I told him my grandad's on there and so is that bastard Turner.'

'You told him what exactly,' Morgan says slowly, glaring at Foster.

'I told him why I was really here, that I was going to find out what happened to my grandad and clear his name. I knew my grandad would never have run away, apart from anything, those lads would never have left this place, it was their home and they would've done anything to protect it. I reckon Oswald killed them then got caught out by the newly laid mines on the beach,' Foster surmises.

'It is possible,' Camilla says thoughtfully.

'There's something that I'm a bit confused about,' Morgan says, looking up at the photos on the wall.

'Yeah, what's that?' Foster asks, turning to look at him.

'What made Mr Chalnor leave so suddenly?'

'That's what I'm saying, it's my fault. I told him I was going to find out the truth about what happened that night and whoever was responsible for my grandad's death was going to pay.'

'I see,' Camilla says slowly. 'I think that Detective Morgan and I need to have a private conversation.'

'Well then, what do you think about all of that? Could DC Foster be responsible for Mr Chalnor's disappearance?'

'It's possible that Bobby might have left if he felt threatened by Foster. It doesn't mean that Foster was responsible for his death though or for Jane Stokes either,' Morgan says evenly, trying to remain open-minded.

'But it could be him, he has the motive, wanting some sort of retribution for his grandfather's death?' Camilla says excitedly. 'It must have been a terrible stigma to live with, especially in those days. You know how people gossip, they would've all thought that Fosters grandfather was a deserter at the very least.'

'He was definitely a blackmailer and I have no doubt that Oswald Turner met up with them that night. It would explain why he was on the beach. Of course what we don't know is whether he killed the three lads to protect what he was doing or if someone else killed them and Oswald.'

'But Oswald died on the beach after stepping on a landmine?'

'Yes but we don't know that he was alone, someone could've forced him into the area with the mines. For all we know, the Bawdsey Boys could have killed Oswald then someone else killed them,' Morgan suggests, going through all the possible scenarios in his mind.

'Well either way, I'm not happy about DC Foster being freely able to wander about given we now know that he has a possible motive.'

'I agree. I think we should limit him to his bedroom for now, the door can be locked from the outside.'

'Agreed, let's go and tell him our decision,' Camilla states, stepping out of the conference room and back down the hallway to the dining room where they left Foster.

Morgan follows Camilla, taking care not to put too much weight on his injured foot. As much as he hates to lock up Foster, he cannot be certain that it was not him who hit him over the head in the old fisherman's cottage. He just hopes that they're right as if not, they will be taking out of action one of their allies.

'What's going on?' Foster asks as Camilla and Morgan arrive back in the dining room.

'Sorry Max but I'm going to have to ask you to stay in your bedroom for now,' Morgan reluctantly admits, still a little uncertain that he is making the right decision.

'Right, I see, well I guess I can understand it though I hope you'll apologise to me later when you find out I've not done anything wrong.'

'Apart from frightening poor Mr Chalnor,' Camilla interjects.

'Yeah, well maybe I was a bit hasty in thinking that anything I said made him leave. Anyway, it wasn't me who killed him,' Foster spits.

'C'mon, let's go upstairs. It'll only be for a few hours in any case as DCI Cook will be here this evening,' Morgan explains, taking hold of Fosters elbow and steering him towards the stairs.

'DCI Cook?' Camilla says, looking at Morgan. 'Is he one of your team?'

'My boss and a bloody good detective. He'll get this mess all cleared up, I'm certain of it.'

Camilla nods thoughtfully then follows the two detectives up the stairs. 'I think I'll go for a short nap.'

'Good idea,' Morgan replies as he waits for Foster to step inside his room then locks the door behind him. 'I'm going to sit on the veranda for a while, it looks as if it's stopped raining already. Enjoy your rest.'

'Thank you, Inspector, I shall.'

Morgan watches Camilla make her way towards her bedroom then disappear from view. As ever, he is unnerved by the silence and left wondering when Cook will arrive and who he will bring with him. Things are now becoming desperate, with both him and Foster out of action, there is no one left to search for Fallow.

As he delicately makes his way back down the oak staircase, Morgans thoughts automatically turn to the young detective, who has so often been on the receiving end of his insensitive sense of humour. Morgan knows that he should have behaved differently, looked out for Fallow instead of ridiculing him for being different. He just hopes that he gets the chance to tell him that and to prove that he has changed.

The rain has now stopped and Morgan makes his way back out onto the veranda, where he pulls out two chairs, one to sit on and the other to place his still painful foot on. He leans back into the chair, allowing his gaze to naturally fall upon the river and the boats that are bobbing up and down with the gentle ebb and flow of the tide. The river has now subsided back to its usual level, taking with it the water that was filling nearby Ferry Lane. The knowledge that they are no longer trapped in the hamlet comforts Morgan a little. He cannot relax completely though, Fallow is still out there somewhere and so is the person who killed Bobby Chalnor and Jane Stokes.

Detective Constable Max Foster sighs loudly as he looks at the rocks below his window that have been uncovered by the out-going tide. Whilst he understands why Morgan and Camilla have locked him in the bedroom, he cannot help but seethe over it. They have no right to keep him prisoner here, there is no evidence that he has done anything wrong.

The detective paces up and down the tiny room, looking at every inch of the wall, hoping that somehow it will yield some way for him to escape but there is nothing. The thought niggles at him though and he runs a hand over the wall, feeling the cold smoothness of the old plaster. Sometimes these old buildings had escape routes that were well hidden and difficult to find unless you knew where they were. Of course even if a miracle did occur and he found one, it may be blocked up or even collapsed.

Foster gives up and sits down heavily on the bed, which sags in the middle as the ancient springs give way to his weight with an audible creak. His eyes automatically focus on the wall opposite the bed and in particular, the built-in cupboard in the corner of the room. He walks across the room and opens the cupboard door, allowing it to rest against the wall. Placing a hand on the top wooden shelf, Foster feels about for anything that might be in there. His fingers touch something at the side of the cupboard. Foster stands up on tiptoe to see what it is then grabs hold of it. It is a piece of paper, a note with faded ink that is barely legible.

> We are in danger,
> someone knows what
> we're doing. Meet me
> tonight just before midnight
> in the usual place, take care
> you are not followed.

Foster turns the piece of paper over, hoping that there might be some clue as to who wrote it or who it was meant for but there is nothing. He stands on tiptoe again and sweeps his flat palm across the top shelf in case there is anything that he has missed. When he is certain that the shelf is empty, Foster moves down to the next shelf, which is also unfilled. The detective crouches down to look at the bottom of the cupboard. Lifting up the strip of old carpet that lines the cupboard, Foster peers into the dark void then thrusts a hand in to feel about and see if there might be anything in there. Only seconds pass before his fingers make contact with something towards the back of the cupboard, something that feels as if it is a push button. Foster stands up straight for a moment to stretch out his aching back, then kneels down on the floor next to the cupboard. He stretches out his fingers to locate the unfamiliar object again then presses down on the centre of it. At first nothing happens, then a feint whirring noise of a mechanism that has not been used for many years is heard and the back of the cupboard moves outwards.

The sound of the waves crashing onto the shingle beach hypnotises Morgan into a deep slumber. When he awakens, the sun is starting to set, streaks of gold and orange reflecting along the River Deben. Morgan shakes himself awake then checks the time on his wristwatch, the one that his wife gave him on their first wedding anniversary. It seems such a long time since he has seen Celia or their dog Bailey who has been such a blessing to them, especially for Celia, who has never really come to terms with the fact that they are unable to have children.

The soft cawing of seagulls swooping across the top of the dark, menacing rocks, stirs Morgan from his thoughts. His eyes drift to the shoreline and the satanic boulders closest to the house – the place where he found Bobby Chalnor's shoes. They never did work out why they were there or who put them there. Perhaps they will never know. Perhaps it does not even matter. Morgan watches as a seagull perches on the rock then takes flight again, soaring over the waves that pick up in height as they move further away from the coast.

In the distance, Morgan can see another outcrop of rocks, just below the window where Foster is staying. Morgan sighs loudly, as much as the detective has irritated him, he has helped a lot over the last few days and he really cannot imagine that Foster had anything to do with the deaths of Bobby Chalnor and Jane Stokes.

A thought begins to formulate in Morgans mind as to what the connection between Bobby Chalnor and Jane Stokes could be, there must be a reason why these two particular people have been killed. Morgan pulls himself more upright, his mind clearing a little more having shaken off the earlier sleepiness. Of course, the two people are connected, they share the same grandfather; the person who they know now was being blackmailed by Max Foster's grandfather. Two ideas begin to formulate at once, prompting Morgan to reach down for his phone to make notes. Morgan types;

"Who would want to kill Bobby and Jane?"

"Is there anyone else who could be in danger?"

Morgan leans back into his chair, his fingers drumming on the table as he considers the first question. What possible motive could there be for the deaths of these two people other than to hide a secret about Oswald Turner, a secret that someone does not want to be revealed. A secret that could have been revealed if the training course had gone ahead as planned.

The first thought that comes into Morgans mind is Foster, whose grandad blackmailed Oswald Turner as he believed that the Canadian airman was passing on secrets to the enemy. Could Foster be behind all of this? He has already admitted that he knew Bobby Chalnor was going to be working at Bawdsey Hall. Foster also admitted to frightening Bobby Chalnor that first evening, after he revealed his intention to find out what happened to his grandfather and to clear his name. At any cost.

Of course there were two other men who were blackmailing Oswald Turner during that summer in 1940, could they also have relatives that are here at the Hall? If so, who are they?

The detectives' thoughts turn to the task set by Bobby and Jane, who wanted to find out more about their grandfather. They still do not know for certain that Oswald Turner killed the three Bawdsey Boys or if Oswald Turners death was indeed an accident.

Morgan grimaces, feeling frustrated by the ever-increasing number of questions that he cannot answer. None of them though of course explains why Fallow has disappeared. Morgan feels certain that Fallow cannot have any connection to this mystery as his family originally came from Yorkshire. It is possible though that the young fella found out something that someone wanted to be kept a secret. Perhaps something in Oswald Turners diary, which is also missing.

Morgan looks down at the notes on his phone again, having come to no further conclusions about the first question. The second question is greatly troubling him. The last thing he wants is for someone else to die. He needs to focus though on the task ahead and not get side-tracked by his emotions, he must think logically, he is a detective after all.

The answer of course comes to Morgan the moment he stops thinking about it. If Bobby Chalnor and Jane Stokes were killed because of their connection to Oswald Turner, then anyone else who might have been connected to the Canadian airman will also be in danger. The question is of course, who?

~ Thirty Two ~

The sound of footsteps coming up the path stirs Morgan from his deliberations. He twists around to look behind him and immediately spots PC Smith striding up the path, a blue rucksack on his back.

'I thought you might all be a bit hungry, so brought some supplies.'

'That's very kind of you but haven't you got other stuff to be getting on with?' Morgan asks, wriggling more upright in his chair.

'Not really, I'm off duty now anyway.'

'How's the clean-up going after the flood?'

'All under control, the roads are now passable. Why, are you thinking about escaping?'

Morgan looks directly at PC Smith, trying to deduce if he is joking or not. The tone of Smiths voice makes Morgan think it is the latter so he decides to keep quiet about the expected arrival of DCI Tom Cook.

'What have you brought us?' Morgan asks, changing the subject.

'Just some local haddock and veg from my garden,' Smith responds proudly.

'I didn't take you for a gardener?' Morgan declares, unsure how his comment will be taken.

'Well, there's not much else to do around here, anyway I like it, it's relaxing,' Smith replies brightly, a large smile emerging on his face. 'Shall we go and see about cooking this lot then?'

'Sounds a good plan. Would you mind going upstairs for me to see if you can find Mrs Fields? My foot's still really painful.'

'Sure! What about Foster?'

'Ah, that's a long story,' Morgan grimaces, not wishing to explain any further.

'Right O, maybe a story for later then,' Smith replies, realising that it is a sensitive topic. 'Where's Mrs Fields room?'

'It's the third one from the top of the stairs.'

'Thanks, I won't be long.'

Morgan is left alone again to enjoy the peace and quiet of the river that is now almost back to its normal size again. Even though he knows that he is not alone, he feels it and cannot wait for Tom Cook to arrive; someone he knows he can trust. In all his life, Morgan has never felt quite as alone as he does now, nor so vulnerable he concludes, looking at his injured foot.

The sound of the dining room door opening heralds the return of PC Smith. Morgan cranes his neck around the chair to watch as the local police officer strides purposefully across the empty dining room. He can tell by the expression on Smiths face that something is wrong.

'She's not there,' Smith says, sounding concerned.

Morgan groans loudly, he really does not need to hear this news. 'Perhaps she's gone for a walk?'

'Maybe. I knocked on Foster's door as well when I was up there and there was no answer.'

'What! He has to be there.'

'Maybe he went out for a walk with Mrs Fields?'

'That's not possible, we locked him in you see,' Morgan admits, suddenly feeling awkward that perhaps he has overreacted by locking Foster in his room.

'What for? Oh I see, you think he murdered those two people,' Smith chuckles, pulling out a chair and sitting down. 'What gives you that idea?'

'Motive, other than that I can't say at the moment, you know how it is,' Morgan answers quickly.

'Well what do you want me to do, cook dinner or look for Mrs Fields?'

'Mrs Fields please but first could you check if Foster is in his room or not,' Morgan says, passing the key to Smith.

'Will do boss,' Smith responds, taking hold of the key.

Morgan takes a deep breath, his foot is beginning to ache again and he is finding it increasingly difficult to mask his intolerance at Smith's crass sense of humour. He listens for the sound of footsteps racing up the stairs followed by a key turning in a lock and a door opening. A moment later, the footsteps return down the stairs again, much faster this time.

'He's gone!' Smith says, panting from the exertion of running down the stairs.

'I guessed that, did he go out of the window?'

'Better than that, he found an old passageway through the back of a cupboard.'

Morgan starts to speak than stops, trying to digest the seemingly far-fetched news.

'I know what you're thinking mate but these old houses had all sorts of escape routes. My betting is that it comes out somewhere in the grounds, maybe even further along the beach.'

'Great, that's all we need and with Camilla going AWOL as well.'

'Stay here, I'll go and take a look, see if I can find them both.'

Morgan leans back into the chair again, more than a little frustrated that he too cannot be out searching. Then a thought occurs to him and he pulls out his phone to check through his notes. There is something that he can do, he can take a look in the library, the place where Camilla Fields has spent so much time, the place that may just be able to give him some answers.

The journey to the library exhausts Morgan to the extent that as soon as he reaches the room, he needs to rest again to ease the pain in his foot. He sits down in the wingback chair that Camilla favours and places his foot up on the small mahogany side table. On the table, there is a large book that Camilla has been reading. Morgan picks up the book and checks the title;

"Census of 1939".

'That's odd,' Morgan says quietly to himself, 'Why was Camilla looking at the Census?'

Morgan opens the book and begins to flick through the names of the residents of Bawdsey in 1939. There are several names that look familiar to him, relatives perhaps of the people he has met who are living in the area. Morgan scribbles down the names, then steels himself to get up again and take the piece of paper into the dining room.

It takes Morgan far longer than he envisaged to traverse the hallway again and make his way back into the dining room, where the display of photographs from the Second World War dominates the room. He stops at the first set of photographs he reaches, checking the names on the labels against those on his list, then he continues to walk along the room, checking all the names that he can find. There, in the centre of the display, is what he is hoping to find – photographs of all the residents of Bawdsey at the start of the war. Morgan checks through the names that he has taken from the 1939 Census, that confirms the three names of the Bawdsey Boys; William Foster, Frederick Longcroft and Harry Norman – the men who disappeared one August night in 1940, never to be seen again until their bodies were found in the old pillbox at Shingle Street only days ago.

Morgan is unsurprised to confirm what they already suspected, that the list of staff names given to them by Bobby Chalnor to investigate, were indeed real people. It now makes it clearer that the whole purpose of the training course task was to investigate what happened on that fateful night in late August 1940.

Morgan continues to look carefully at the photographs from 1940, noting Oswald Turner in several of them. In one photo, Oswald Turner is sitting on the steps at the front of the Hall with a group of staff. Morgan immediately recognises Maisie's grandmother and of course Cedric Browne, who must only have been about 16 at the time. The next photo is of a group of trainee radio operators. The photo is dated July 1940 but there are no names given for the group of smiling women who looked proud to be part of the war effort. Carefully Morgan lifts the photograph off the wall and hobbles across to the nearest table. He places the photograph face-down onto the table, then gently unhooks the thin cork back. In the centre of the document, in a light pencil scrawl, is written;

"*NF SIS*"

Morgan sits back into the chair, trying to work out what this could mean. Whilst still pondering on this new mystery, he hears the sound of the front door slamming shut. Without knowing why, Morgan rolls up the photograph and pushes it into his pocket. Seconds later, a shadow appears in the doorway.

'I'm back,' PC Smith says, stating the obvious.

'Did you find anyone?'

'No, the estate's really quiet, as if it's been deserted, it was almost creepy.'

'They must be here somewhere, we can't just lose so many people like that.'

'I agree. I'll just have a drink then I'll go and check the beach again.'

Morgan nods thoughtfully, 'did you check the gardener's cottages and the workshop?'

'Not yet, I'll head to the beach as far as Shingle Street then cut across the estate and back again.'

'That's the way I went yesterday. You never did say how you happened to be there at the fishermen's cottages?'

'I was checking the car park at Shingle Street to see if there had been any damage after the flood. When I was there, I remembered about the cottages and thought I'd check to see if DC Fallow could be there, same as you.'

Morgan tilts his head to one side as if he is pondering on saying something else but decides instead to check the time on his watch. Tom Cook should arrive soon.

Smith finds a bottle of lemonade behind the bar and pours some of the liquid out into two glasses before handing one to Morgan. The local police officer drains his glass in seconds and refills it before also emptying the glass a second time. 'Well, I'll be off again.'

'Take care, I don't want to lose another person,' Morgan says as he watches Smith leave. As soon as he is alone, Morgan returns his attention to the wall, where until a few moments ago there had been one more photograph on display; the photo that is now in the detective's trouser pocket. Next to the place where the photo was, there is another blank space that is paler than the surrounding wall, as if something had once been there, which had shielded the wall from being faded by the sun's rays. It is then that he remembers about the photograph that disappeared. It must have been something important, something perhaps to do with Oswald Turner?

Morgan hobbles towards the wall again, whilst pulling the photo out from his pocket. It was taken in the estate grounds, not far from the gardener's cottages. Morgan stares at the photo, looking at every detail of it. Then he sees it, something that he did not notice before; there is someone in the gardener's cottage, looking out of the window.

Morgan checks his watch again, hoping that time might have passed more quickly than it has, then he pulls out his phone from his pocket and messages Cook:

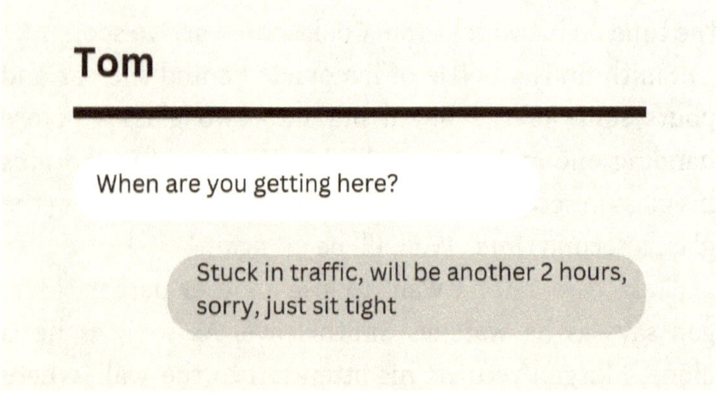

Morgan sighs, he cannot just sit here and wait another two hours for Cook to arrive. He needs to do something,

Fallow is still out there somewhere and so is Camilla. In any case, he does not feel safe being here alone in the Hall, especially with his injured foot making him vulnerable. He needs to go somewhere, but where?

With the photograph of the trainee radio operators still in his hand, Morgan makes his way to the hallway then out of the front door with the walking stick Camilla found for him clacking against the red floor tiles in the porch. Morgan stops to catch his breath as a wave of pain shoots through his foot. He leans against the red-brick archway and looks again at the photo. It is then that he realises, all that time ago when they started trying to solve the mystery of what happened that night in 1940, when they were given the task by Bobby Chalnor of interviewing the staff, there was one person they did not speak to, one person who was actually here at the Hall the night that Oswald Turner died and the three Bawdsey Boys vanished; Cedric Browne.

~ Thirty Three ~

The light is beginning to fade as Morgan slowly makes his way across the driveway and then onto the path that leads through the estate. The wind has picked up again and the leaves in the nearby trees whisper sinisterly as the detective travels along the narrow path, past the place where Jane Stokes was found. Morgan's thoughts automatically turn to the body that is still lying in cold storage at the Hall and he deliberates on when Harry, Dr Bootle's assistant will arrive to collect her.

The daylight has diminished even further by the time Morgan reaches the two cottages that sit side-by-side, unchanged since they were built at the turn of the century. The building on the left where Reece Browne resides, is encased in darkness. In the neighbouring cottage, where Reece's grandfather has lived since he was a sixteen-year-old lad who had desperately wanted to go to war but couldn't because of the limp he was left with after catching polio, there is a light coming through one of the downstair windows.

Morgan continues up the path, the wind swishing through the trees that are now behind him. The light from the cottage seems welcoming but still there is a tightness in Morgan's chest that was not there earlier. As he reaches the front door, his heart thumps faster and not for the first time, he wishes that his team were with him. He hopes that Fallow is still alive.

Although the electricity supply has been restored to the Hall, it seems that it has not yet been reconnected to the cottages. Morgan peers through the corner of the window and sees a hurricane lamp in the centre of the kitchen table. The lamp casts a yellow glow across the room, not quite covering the corner where the Aga is glowing a deep russet. Next to the Aga is a chair that even in the darkness of the shadows, Morgan can see is occupied.

Morgan pulls back from the window and takes a step to one side so that he is back on the path again. He knocks officiously on the door then waits for it to open, when it does, the face of Cedric Browne appears.

'Yeah, what do you want?'

'I thought I'd come and check up on you, with the flooding and all that,' Morgan states.

'Well, I'm fine,' Cedric snaps, beginning to close the door.

Morgan thrusts his uninjured foot into the gap before the door can close, 'I also wanted to talk to you about what happened in 1940.'

'What do you mean?' Cedric Browne sneers, looking at Morgans foot, which is preventing the door from being shut.

'What I mean is that I've spoken to everyone else on this estate about what happened here in 1940 except for you.'

'No you wouldn't, I wasn't part of that silly course. Waste of time if you ask me.'

'But you were here though, weren't you? In 1940 I mean.'

'So what,' Cedric spits, shuffling from one foot to the other to ease the pain in his leg a little.

'So it would really help me to learn more about what went on here during the war if I could come in for a chat.'

'I don't see how that will help you find your lost detective,' Cedric scoffs, looking at Morgan.

'Well I think it will, in fact, I think it will help a great deal.'

The door opens wider and Morgan stoops to pass under the low door frame. Once inside the cottage, which is a mirror image of the neighbouring one, he follows Cedric into the sitting room, where the elderly man lights another lamp.

'What do you want to know then?'

'What were you doing here during the war?'

'Well that's easy, I was the gardener, caretaker and handyman, bit like my grandson does now.'

'Did you have much to do with the people staying up at the Hall?'

'Not really, there was lots of hush hush stuff going on, I wasn't supposed to know about it.'

Morgan hobbles over to a chair and sits down without being invited. 'But you did know?'

''Course I did, I knew everything that went on here.'

Morgan reaches into his trouser pocket to extract the now crumpled photo. 'Do you know who these three women are?'

Cedric picks up his reading glasses from a small table next to the fireplace and puts them on, his forehead creasing as he tries to focus on the grainy image. 'Well that one there is Cynthia and the one on the right is Daisy.'

'What were they doing at the Hall?' Morgan asks, taking the photograph back from Cedric.

'They were being trained as radio operators.'

'What about this woman at the back of the photo?' Morgan says, passing the document back to Cedric and pointing to the unidentified woman.

Cedric wriggles his nose as he tries to see the figure more clearly. Suddenly the elderly man pales and reaches for a chair to sit down. 'Well I never, that's a face I haven't seen in a long time.'

Morgan leans in closer to look at the photo. 'Who is she?'

'Was, she didn't survive the war. Her name was Nell Fulcher.'

'I see, that explains the initials on the back of the photo,' Morgan says, turning the photograph over to show Cedric Browne. 'What does SIS stand for?'

'Special Intelligence Service,' Cedric reveals quietly.

'She was a spy?'

'Something like that,' Cedric replies. 'I wish there was a better photo of her, it's been such a long time and my memory isn't as good as it was.'

'Will this one do?' A voice says from the kitchen.

Morgan looks in the direction the voice is coming from then watches as a figure approaches. As the person moves into the light, Morgan sees that a black and white photo is being held out. The detective looks at the woman in the photograph, then upwards to the familiar face of the person who is holding it.

'Yes, thank you Camilla, that will do very nicely,' Morgan says evenly. 'Is that the photo you took from the dining room?'

'Yes it is, well done detective you worked it out. I wonder if you can work out the rest of our little mystery though,' Camilla challenges.

Morgan stares thoughtfully at Camilla, trying to decide how best to respond. 'Perhaps you'd like to enlighten us, you seem to know far more than I do.'

'What would you like to know?' Camilla asks.

'How about starting with that photo,' Morgan asks, pointing towards the document still in Camilla's outstretched hand.

'That's a photo of my mother, it was taken before I was born. It's so wonderful to finally find a picture of her, the only one I had was when she was a child.'

'Your mother?' Morgan repeats, not quite understanding what the elderly councillor has just told him.

'Nell Fulcher,' Camilla says proudly.

'Why are you here?' Morgan suddenly asks.

Camilla smiles, 'to find out more about my parents of course. The same reason why Bobby Chalnor and Jane Stokes were here.'

'But you're still alive and they're not,' Morgan says slowly.

A sudden movement to the side, draws Morgans attention away from Camilla. He takes a sideward glance and catches sight of the stubby end of a Colt revolver, pointing in his direction.

'I don't understand what's going on,' Morgan says quietly. He wishes he could check the time to see when Cook will arrive. He wishes he knew where PC Smith, Foster and Fallow are.

Camilla laughs, 'I know you don't and you thought you were clever, didn't you? But unfortunately, you're wrong, very wrong. You've been wrong all along.'

'Bloody police, think they know everything,' Cedric mutters.

'Why are you really here,' Morgan repeats, more softly this time.

'Ah you're beginning to understand. Of course, I didn't need to learn how to be a good team member, I already know all about loyalty and working together,' Camilla explains. 'My mother...'

'Your mother was the love of my life,' Cedric Browne suddenly says, beaming at Camilla.

Camilla smiles, 'yes, I know she was.'

'She was happy with me until that bloody Canadian turned up,' Cedric spits.

'Yes that was rather naughty of her but it had to be done unfortunately,' Camilla declares, inching closer towards Morgan.

'What do you mean by that lassie?' Cedric asks, his voice betraying his affection for the councillor.

'My mother wasn't interested in Oswald Turner, not in that way,' Camilla replies, taking another step closer to Morgan.

'Was it your mother who Oswald mentioned in his diary?' Morgan asks.

Camilla unhooks her bag from her shoulder then rummages around in it until she finds what she is searching for, 'do you mean this diary?' Camilla says, holding the book out towards Morgan.

'How did you get that? Fallow had it last,' Morgan spits, trying to hide the jolt of fear that has just shot through him.

'Ah yes, lovely man that DC Fallow. Don't worry, he's safe and well.'

From the corner of his eye, Morgan sees the hand that is holding the revolver creeping closer, before moving away from the shadows and out into the light coming from the lamp in the centre of the table.

'Yeah, don't worry he's not hurt or anything, just needed to take a little holiday along with that nosy policeman until we get all this mess cleared up,' Reece Browne says, moving into the centre of the room. 'The question is, what are we going to do about you, detective?'

~ Thirty Four ~

Morgan takes a deep breath then turns to look at Reece Browne who has now moved from the kitchen into the tiny sitting room, still holding the gun in his hand. 'Would someone please tell me what's going on here.'

Camilla laughs, 'ok detective it seems you are far more incompetent than I ever imagined, so I will kindly explain it all to you.'

'Can I please sit down first though, my foot is killing me,' Morgan says before moving backwards towards the nearest chair.

'Of course detective, we wouldn't want you to be in pain now, would we. So where shall I start?' Camilla says smoothly.

'What was the real reason for the training course?' Morgan asks, rubbing his foot, which is now throbbing.

'A few months ago, I came to Bawdsey Hall for a meeting with some parish councillors, the owners of the Hall had put in a planning application to build on part of the estate and we needed to assess the site,' Camilla begins to explain.

'And that was when you met Jane and Bobby?'

'I met Jane on that occasion, Bobby had not yet arrived but Jane was very keen to tell me all about their family connection and how they both intended on finding out what happened to their grandfather. They knew their grandfather had died on the beach at Shingle Street but suspected there was something more to it. They showed me the story in the local newspaper about the three Home Guards who went missing on the same night that Oswald Turner died on the beach.'

'What was Oswald Turner doing here at the Hall?' Morgan asks, settling back into the chair.

'Oswald was a radio operator trainer, or should I say, that's what people were told.'

'So he was a spy then and the Bawdsey Boys were blackmailing him to stop him passing secrets to the Germans?'

'That's right lad, he was a dirty spy and he needed to be stopped,' Cedric Browne spits, his eyes boring into Morgans. 'He was getting secrets from my Nellie, putting her in danger. Putting us all in danger.'

'Well, that's not quite right,' Camilla says slowly, moving towards Reece whose outstretched hand is still holding the gun.

'What are you talking about?' Cedric snaps, looking at Camilla.

A tense silence descends upon the cottage. Outside, Morgan can see that dusk has settled into night, leaving a thick blackness covering the estate that makes him feel even more isolated. Tension cuts through the room, leaving Morgan with the unenviable task of trying to diffuse the situation.

'When did you find out that Bobby and Jane were going to set the task to find out what happened to their grandfather?' Morgan asks Camilla, trying to steer the conversation away from Cedric Browne, who is still glaring at the councillor.

'Ah yes the task. Well Jane told me about her idea when I met her on the site visit, then she emailed me about the course and invited me to attend. I think perhaps she thought it would help to bring some business in, the Halls finances are in rather a precarious state. She told me everything, how they were going to get the course attendees to find out what happened to Oswald Turner and the Bawdsey Boys. She was certain the truth would come out.'

'And you decided that the course needed to be stopped but why?' Morgan asks.

'Well I should think that's obvious, I didn't want the secret coming out.'

'What secret is that then?' Morgan asks, half-wishing that he hadn't uttered the words but knowing that he has no choice but to ask.

'My mother had the most brilliant mind, so I'm told. I never met her of course. I was born in 1941 and then she went back to her work again. She was far too important for the Government to let go and in any case, she wanted to do her bit for the war.'

'What was your mother doing that was so important?'

'She was in the SIS, the Secret Intelligence Service, then after I was born, she became an SOE, a Special Operations Executive. She died in 1942 in France where she was a radio operator. They didn't last long in the field, the SS found her after she'd been in Paris for only a few weeks.'

'Was Oswald Turner in the SIS as well?' Morgan asks.

'My mother recruited Oswald to help her, he was passing secrets to the Germans as black propaganda, telling them about the experiments that were being done to set fire to the sea. He was in love with my mother and would have done anything for her. My mother had that effect on men it seems,' Camilla says, looking at Cedric Browne who is now sitting quietly in a chair next to the window.

'That man was a spy, Nell told me,' Cedric splutters. 'She was scared, she found out that she was expecting a baby and was scared of what would happen.'

'I imagine she was,' Camilla soothes. 'People say all sorts of things when they're frightened.'

'She told me that Oswald was blackmailing her, that she was terrified of him,' Cedric says, looking up at Camilla, his face pale in the lamp light.

'Oswald was the one who was being blackmailed, I found that out the first night we were all here. I overheard Foster telling Bobby Chalnor when we were all in the dining room,' Camilla says, looking back at Morgan.

'Who was it who killed the Bawdsey Boys?' Morgan asks, his nose wrinkling as he tries to take it all in.

'It was that filthy Canadian, that's who,' Cedric spits. 'He didn't want the truth to come out, that he was passing secrets to the Jerries'.

'That's right, ain't it grandad, it was all his fault those poor lads died,' says Reece.

'Ok, so now we know who killed the three lads and but what happened to Oswald Turner? Was his death an accident or not?' Morgan asks.

'I followed him that night,' Cedric says slowly, his eyes glazing over in remembrance. 'I saw him meet up with the three lads, saw what he did to them. Poor buggers had no chance.'

'What happened after Oswald killed them?' Morgan asks.

'I followed him back along the beach, saw Oswald walking in the area where the lads had been laying mines earlier that day. I knew what he'd done, dammed spy telling secrets to the Jerries then he goes and kills those poor boys who were just trying to protect their country. He got what was coming to him.'

'What happened Mr Browne?' Morgan calmly asks.

'I watched him set off an explosion at the bottom of the cliff, the rock fall covered the pillbox where he left those poor lads. It was completely buried, as if it had never been there. I saw him standing back, looking smug at his handiwork. He always was full of himself, it never occurred to him that someone might see what he did. He wasn't so cocky when he saw me standing there with my rifle.'

'So you took his gun then forced him onto the part of the beach where the mines had been laid so it would look like an accident,' Morgan concludes, beginning to piece together what happened.

Cedric nods his head.

'And the rumour about the German invasion, what was that all about?'

'It was my mother's idea, she couldn't risk her secret work being revealed,' Camilla explains.

'So she created the rumour as a cover, in case anyone heard the explosion that Oswald made when he covered up the pillbox. And of course if the bodies of the three Home Guards had been found, it would have been assumed that it was the Germans who had killed them,' Morgan says slowly. 'So Cedric killed Oswald to protect Nell, who he believed was in trouble.'

'Yes, I'm sorry to say that my mother was lying to you Cedric, she wasn't in love with you and she wasn't in any danger from Oswald. She would've done anything to protect the work she was doing.'

'How do you know all of this?' Morgan asks.

'Oswald wasn't the only one to keep a diary, my mother did as well. My grandmother, who brought me up, gave it to me before she died.'

Morgan nods thoughtfully, 'ok so I can understand why Cedric and Reece wouldn't want this secret to be found out but what I don't understand is why Camilla wanted to stop the truth from being discovered?' Morgan says, turning to look in turn at Camilla Fields, Reece

Browne and his grandfather. Now they are all next to each other, an idea has begun to formulate in Morgan's mind. The answer to his question is right in front of him.

'Well, this is all very interesting but Detective Inspector Morgan seems to be missing something very important.'

Morgan turns to look at the door, to see who is speaking. A shadow proceeds to move into the room then eventually moves into the light.

'Yes I do seem to be missing something,' Morgan says, looking at the gun that DC Foster is holding.

'DC Foster, I wondered when you might make an appearance,' Camilla says. 'We have of course been expecting you.'

'Have we?' Morgan exclaims, utterly confused by the turn in events.

Foster chuckles, 'poor Morgan, it seems you're always the last to work it out.'

Morgan glares at Foster who has moved further into the centre of the tiny cottage to stand next to Reece Browne.

'You can put that down now Reece, I'll take over from here,' Foster instructs as he places a hand on the shaft of the gun that Reece is holding and pushes it gently downwards before taking hold of it.

'What the hell is going on here,' Morgan shouts, exasperated.

'I hope you didn't think that myself or the Browne's had anything to do with poor Bobby and Janes deaths,' Camilla says smoothly.

'So what was the plan then, how did you think you were going to stop all of this from coming out?' Morgan asks, biting on his lower lip.

'The plan was for Mr Chalnor to go on an unexpected vacation, you found the fisherman's cottage where he stayed,' Camilla explains. 'We had no intention of harming Bobby or Jane. We thought if the course trainer disappeared that the course would simply be cancelled.'

'But you encouraged us to solve the mystery of what happened to the Bawdsey Boys?' Morgan says.

'I wasn't expecting the bodies of those three young men to be found. It seemed the right thing to do, to find out what happened to them,' Camilla explains.

'You mean you wanted to find out if Oswald Turner was responsible for their deaths,' Morgan snaps.

'I grew up believing that Oswald Turner was my father, I wanted to know what sort of man he was,' Camilla says softly.

Morgan nodded thoughtfully, 'so if you and the Browne's did not kill Bobby and Jane then someone else must've done.'

'Yeah, that's right, someone else did,' Foster interjects, a sly smile forming.

'Can someone please explain to me what on earth is going on here,' Morgan snaps.

'Gladly mate, I told you already that I was here to put the record straight about my grandad getting the blame for Oswald Turners death. My family were ostracised, they had to move to London to get away from the evil gossips. They wouldn't even serve my grandma in the local shops, they all thought grandad had gone on the run because he was a killer.'

'So it was you who killed Jane and Bobby?' Morgan says. 'But why?'

'Revenge my dear boy, for all that my family was put through. It was all because of that man Turner,' Foster spits, pointing the gun at Camilla. 'And now the last of Oswald's bastards will be eradicated.

~ Thirty Five ~

Morgan looks at Camilla who in turn looks at Reece and Cedric. For the first time since Morgan met the elderly councillor, he can see fear in her eyes. He can tell from the expression on her face that this is not what she planned, whatever it was she had intended, this was not part of it.

'I know what you're thinking and your wrong,' Morgan says slowly, licking his lips, wishing yet again that his team were with him.

'Am I? Are you sure about that?' Foster sneers, tilting his head to one side.

'Look at them, the three of them side by side, can't you see it?' Morgan says, pointing at Camilla, Reece and Cedric.

'See what?' Foster snaps, growing tired of the conversation.

'Oswald Turner wasn't Camilla's father, Cedric Browne is,' Morgan explains.

Foster stares at them all in turn, his hand still holding the gun that is pointed towards Camilla. 'What are you talking about? Oswald Turner was in love with Nell Fulcher, we all know that from his diary.'

'He was in love with her but that doesn't mean it was reciprocated. I also believed for a very long time that Oswald Turner was my father but I was wrong,' Camilla says quietly, turning to look at Cedric Browne.

'Surely she wasn't in love with him, the gardener with a limp,' Foster laughs, staring at Cedric Browne.

'I believe she was fond of Cedric but my mother was only really interested in her work.'

'She was fond of me,' Cedric says gently, 'that's something then.' Cedric sits back down into the chair and closes his eyes, a smile forming as he recollects the only woman that he has ever loved.

'Give me the gun Foster, it's over,' says a voice from the doorway.

As PC Smith steps into the cottage, Morgan catches sight of a shadow moving past the sitting room window towards the front door.

In a split second, everything changes. The sound of footsteps outside the door tells Foster that it is over. The police detective glares at Morgan, then hands the gun to Smith, who places it onto the small table next to the one that Reece Browne was holding earlier. Then someone else walks into the small cottage, someone who Morgan has not seen for what feels like a very long time.

'Fallow!' Morgan says, his heart almost stopping when he sees him. 'Thank god you're ok.'

'I'm ok, thank you for asking,' Fallow replies with his usual detachedness.

'Where have you been?' Morgan asks, almost forgetting that Foster is still there and is now being handcuffed by the ever-efficient PC Smith.

'The old icehouse, it's a bit further down the estate,' Smith explains. 'I found him and was just getting him out when Reece turned up and locked us both in.'

'I see, so kidnapping was part of the plan to stop your grandfathers secret from coming out,' Morgan says sternly, looking at Reece. 'Was Camilla in on this as well?'

Reece looks at the elderly woman, 'I wouldn't call it kidnapping exactly, just keeping people safe until the danger had passed.'

'What about Bobby Chalnor and Jane Stokes? You didn't keep them safe,' Morgan snaps.

'That was very unfortunate, up until then the plan went well, with me bumping into Bobby on the beach and promising to show him Shingle Street. The old fisherman's cottage came in very handy.'

'What went wrong?' Morgan asks.

Reece smiles tight lipped, 'DC Max Foster is what went wrong.'

Morgan nods, 'and what about Jane?'

'Jane was with me that night,' Reece says, glaring at Foster. 'He must've killed her on her way back to the Hall.'

'How did you get out of the icehouse?' Camilla asks PC Smith.

'Ah well, with me being a local lad and all that, I know all the secrets of this place. My great-uncle worked on a farm near here before the war, he used to tell my dad all sorts of tales whilst they sat in front of the fire in the winter. One of them was about all the secret passageways in the Hall. There's one that leads from the icehouse to the old scullery,' Smith explains.

'And one that leads from the cupboard in my bedroom down to an old boat house,' Foster interjects.

'What about the gun used to kill Bobby? How did you get hold of the one that Oswald Turner used to kill the Bawdsey Boys?' Morgan asks,

'Ah yes then gun, I thought that would be a nice touch. I noticed it when I was in the gardener's cottage with Fallow, asking about that dumb task Bobby Chalnor set.'

Morgan nods thoughtfully, 'The gun that Mr Browne took from Oswald Turner that night on the beach.' The detective turns to look at the elderly man who is staring out of the window into the darkness. He does not need a response, the silence is enough to affirm his thoughts. Morgan turns to look at Foster again whose smug smile is visible even in the dim light of the lamp whose candle is already burning down to its wick. He opens his mouth to say something, wanting to rid Foster of his arrogance when he hears more footsteps on the path outside the front door. The door opens wider and in walks DCI Tom Cook accompanied by Harry, the pathologist's assistant.

Morgan has never felt so relieved to see familiar faces. 'You two took your time didn't you, it's all been solved now.'

'I can see that, well let's get you all back to the Hall and then I'm taking you home,' Cook instructs, taking hold of Morgans arm to help him walk.

As they step out into the darkness, Morgan glances back at the cottage. Through the sitting room window, he sees PC Smith gently holding onto Camilla's arm as she tries to awaken her father. Then the two of them turn around and move out of sight as they head towards the front door, with Reece and Fallow following closely behind them.

In the sitting room, Cedric Browne's eyes remain closed, his face peaceful with a smile on his lips in remembrance of the woman that he loved and of the newly found knowledge of his daughter.

'When did you realise that Cedric Browne was your father?' Morgan casually asks Camilla as they walk back towards the Hall.

'I knew that my father was here at the Hall in 1940 and I had always assumed it to be Oswald as my mother wrote about him in her diary. She also mentioned a very kind gardener who sat with her on the veranda in the evenings and talked to her about all sorts of things that they were both interested in. I'm sorry to say that I never considered my mother would have preferred a simple gardener to the dashing Canadian. Our prejudices can lead us to make all sorts of presumptions. I only realised the truth when I came for the planning site visit and met Reece and Cedric. The family resemblance is rather strong. When I came back again to visit them afterwards and told them about Janes plan to find out what happened to Oswald Turner, Reece told me what his grandfather had done. I couldn't allow that particular secret to come out.'

'But you did want to find out what happened to the Bawdsey Boys?'

'Yes I did, especially after they were found.'

'I'm glad that you got to know your father a little, even if it wasn't for very long,' Morgan says uncharacteristically sympathetically.

'Yes, it was certainly not something I was expecting to happen and of course I now know that I have more relatives. How different things would have been though if I hadn't come here for that parish meeting, for one thing, Bobby Chalnor and Jane Stokes might still be alive.'

'You know that we're going to have to charge you and Reece, don't you?'

'Of course detective, I wouldn't expect any less of you.'

Morgan takes one last look at Bawdsey Hall, remembering all the people that he has met and how much he has learnt about them and himself. One thing is certain, his time here has changed him and it will always be a part of his life that he will never forget.

~ Thirty Six ~

The journey back to Deben Quay is a slow one as DCI Tom Cook commandeers the narrow country lanes as carefully as he can to avoid causing Morgan more in pain. The injured foot that is now so swollen that a shoe can no longer fit on it. The ever-resourceful Fallow, after packing up his belongings in his room at Bawdsey Hall, lent Morgan his favourite slippers to ease the discomfort a little until a more suitable alternative can be found.

The traffic in Deben Quay is light and the trio find themselves outside Fallows flat just before midnight. Cook says goodnight to Fallow, who eagerly trips up the stairs to his flat without looking back, then steers the car in the direction of Hemley Hospital so that Morgan can get his foot examined.

Even at this late hour the hospital car park is busy but Cook manages to find a space close to the emergency centre then assists Morgan into the waiting room where he books in him with the duty nurse.

'I hope this doesn't take long,' Morgan grumbles.

Cook chuckles, 'I know you're keen to get home but you need to get that foot looked at.'

Morgan grimaces when he sees the long queue of people awaiting treatment. He knows Cook is right, even if he is not going to admit it.

'You might as well fill me in on what's been happening while we're waiting,' Cook says, putting his feet up on the chair opposite.

'Where do I start? So much has happened,' Morgan says wistfully, thinking of Jane Stokes, Bobby Chalnor and of course Oswald Turner and the Bawdsey Boys. He is not even sure he can tell his friend what has happened, his mind still has not quite got around it all.

'What about the training course? Am I right in thinking that the task set for the course was a real mystery? That Jane Stokes and Bobby Chalnor thought they'd use the course to find out what happened to their grandfather?'

'It would seem so, they knew that he died at Shingle Street but suspected there was more to the story. It also transpires that Camilla Fields knew about the purpose of the task all along. From what I can gather Camilla initially didn't want the truth to come out but it all got out of hand and she then decided that she didn't want to be part of it anymore. The gardener Reece definitely didn't want the truth coming out to protect his grandfather Cedric Browne,' Morgan explains, stretching out his leg a little to ease the pain in his foot.

'Did they really think that it would come out? They couldn't have known that the landslip was going to uncover the pillbox or that you would find Oswald's diary?' Cook says, looking at Morgan.

'That was an odd coincidence for sure.'

'Talking about coincidences, it's really strange that DC Max Foster was there as well, especially given his grandfather was one of the Bawdsey Boys.'

'That was not a coincidence, he knew Bobby Chalnor had got a job at Bawdsey Hall and that he wanted to find out what had happened to his grandfather.'

'And Foster thought he would get his own back because of what happened to his family?'

'It would seem so. It's understandable really given what they all went through. I can also see why people thought the disappearance of the three lads looked suspicious, especially when Oswald Turner died that night on the beach just after they had laid the landmines there.'

'Have you found out yet what happened to Fallow?'

Morgan nods his head, 'Camilla filled me in on the walk back to the Hall. Cedric Browne told his grandson that he'd sent a letter to Oswald Turner in August 1940, telling him to keep away from Nell Fulcher otherwise he would make sure he did. Of course Cedric had no idea what was about to happen that night on the beach. Cedric felt certain that Oswald would have tucked the letter safely away somewhere and the only place he hadn't searched was Oswald's diary.'

'And Fallow had the diary.'

'It turns out that there's a passageway from the old pantry to the icehouse. Reece knew of course, he knows everything about the estate. It wouldn't have been difficult for him to lure Fallow into that part of the house.'

Cook ponders on it all for a moment then turns to look at Morgan. 'What about that rumour of the German invasion? How does it fit into all of this?'

'Nellie Fulcher set that one up when she found out what happened to Oswald Turner. She must've known that Oswald was meeting the three lads that night and what was going to happen to them. She wanted to keep their work a secret, even if it meant that three innocent men were murdered.'

'Makes you wonder if Nellie Fulcher might have been a double spy,' Cook mumbles, screwing up his forehead, trying to make sense of it all.

'I did wonder that though she died in occupied France not long after Camilla was born. It must have been hard for Camilla, not knowing either of her parents.'

'I guess so, though a lot of people lost their parents in the war.'

'Well that's what she was told anyway. She didn't know that her real father was Cedric Browne until she visited Bawdsey Hall,' Morgan explains, looking at the clock on the waiting room wall that reveals it is just past midnight. Morgans attention is diverted from the clock by a movement on the electronic information board at the far end of the waiting room. He watches as his name and an examination room number appears on the screen. 'That's me then, thank goodness it wasn't too long to wait.'

'Well you're bound to get lucky occasionally,' Cook teases before picking up a magazine from a nearby table to keep himself occupied while he waits for Morgan's check-up.

Two hours and one x-ray later, Morgan is duly returned to the waiting room in a wheelchair. He quickly locates Cook, who has fallen asleep in the same chair that he left him in.

'C'mon then, I'm ready to go home,' Morgan says, leaning forward to gently shake Cook's shoulder.

'Detective Inspector Morgan,' a voice booms from the other side of the room.

Morgan looks around to see the portly pathologist marching across the waiting room. 'Dr Bootle, what are you doing here?'

'Not checking up on you, if that's what you're asking. I was taking another look at the three cadavers from the pillbox, along with Dr Dunning who brought some of his students with him.'

'How is Clive?' Morgan asks.

'Not too bad, still not able to do any field work yet of course but he can teach, which is his main passion it seems.'

Morgan smiles, knowing that something positive has come out of this whole mess gives him some closure at least.

'Have you had the chance to look at Jane Stokes yet?'

'I haven't done the PM yet but I can tell you that she was strangled,' Dr Bootle informs.

'Ah Morgan, you're back,' Cook exclaims, finally waking up. 'I'd better get you back to your wife then, she's probably forgotten she has a husband by now.'

Morgan rolls his eyes theatrically, glad to slip back into their usual banter. He takes one last look at the waiting room, which is now much quieter than when he arrived. Morgan has always disliked hospitals but somehow he always seems to come back here. The weary detective takes one last deep breath, taking in the clinical aroma that always remind him of the difficult times that have happened here in this hospital, then he climbs out of the wheelchair and limps off towards the door towards the car park without looking back.

~ Thirty Seven ~

Celia Morgan has just drifted off to sleep in the bed that she shares with her husband, when the sound of a key being turned in the lock awakens her. The last few days have been atrocious, not knowing what her husband is going through or being able to be there to support him. Even worse, was the not knowing whether or not Morgan was even safe.

DCI Tom Cook, who Celia has known for almost as long as her husband, had sent her a text to let her know that they were on their way to the hospital to get Morgan's foot checked out. Cook had warned Celia that they could be some time, so she went to bed, not expecting her husband to return until the morning.

Celia throws back the duvet, locates her slippers and trots downstairs to find her husband standing in the living room wearing a pair of Fallows fluffy slippers.

'Well that's rather unexpected,' Celia laughs.

'I think they're rather fetching,' Morgan replies, a large grin spreading across his face.

'Perhaps I can get you a pair for Christmas then,' Celia muses as she takes hold of Morgans bag and carry's it into the kitchen before placing it next to the washing machine. 'Do you need help getting upstairs?'

'Yes please,' Morgan says cheekily. It is amazing how a break from home life has made him appreciate his wife so much more than before he left for Bawdsey Hall. 'Where's Bailey?'

'You know we had that rule about not having dogs on the bed?'

'Yes,' Morgan says slowly, knowing full well where the conversation is going.

'We don't have that rule anymore,' Celia says brightly. 'C'mon, I'm sure Bailey will be pleased to see you, once he wakes up that is.'

Morgan watches his wife trip back upstairs again then looks around the home that he feels as if he has not seen for weeks. The stress of the last few days has affected him deeply and not only is he very glad to be home but he is also appreciative that he has made it home at all. Morgan thinks back to all the people he met whilst at Bawdsey Hall and the complexity of their lives that led to the deaths of so many people. Morgan takes in the familiar surroundings of his home once more then steels himself against the pain in his foot that is about to worsen as he gingerly climbs one step at a time up the stairs to be reunited with his family.

Information Sources

'A Guide to Second World War Archaeology in Suffolk, Guide 3: Orford to Felixstowe'; Robert Liddiard and David Sims. Barnwell Print Ltd, 2014.

'Oral History – Aldeburgh Voices; Ronnie Ashford. WWW.aldeburghoralhisotry.weebly.com

WWW.shinglestreet1940.co.uk; Gary Ashford. Last updated March 2018.

'The A to Z of Curious Suffolk – A Talk by Sarah Doig'. Little Waldingfield History Society: www.waldingfieldhistorysociety.wordpress.com.

'Shingle Street: Flame, Chemical and Psychological Warfare in 1940 and the Nazi Invasion That Never Was'; James Hayward. LTM Publishing. 1994.

'The Bodies on the Beach: Sealion, Shingle Street and the Burning Sea Myth of 1940'; James Hayward. CD41 Publishing, 2001.

'Wartime sea of fire mystery solved'; Mariam Ghaemi. East Anglian Daily Times. 5 July 2010

'New claim about Shingle Street'. Ipswich Star. 13 September 2002.

'Dead Nazis at Shingle Street? Still bunkum'; Steve Russell. East Anglian Daily Times. 31 January 2016.

'What did happen at Shingle Street'; Linda Kendall. WWW.BBC.co.uk.

'What really happened on the East Anglian Coastline in summer 1940?'; Lee James. WWW.BBC.co.uk. 21 February 2004.

Authors Note

The legend of Shingle Street and the alleged failed German invasion in August 1940, is well known both within and outside of Suffolk. It has been the subject of much debate, both at the time and more recently as documents that were previously embargoed as official secrets have been released.

It does seem possible from eye-witness accounts and from the tales passed on through familial generations, that something occurred around the area of Shingle Street, one Saturday night in late August 1940. One such account detailed that soldiers were summoned from a dance at Aldeburgh village hall to attend an incident that was happening further down the coast, which reportedly involved the sea being on fire and there being a large number of casualties on the beach at Shingle Street. There was also a report by the occupier of a house in Shingle Street, of finding boxes of burnt German soldier uniforms after he broke into a bunker in his garden and that the uniforms were promptly removed by the Government.

One theory as to the source of the rumour of the failed German invasion at Shingle Street, is that it did indeed occur and that the British Government wanted to keep it a secret as it could have further damaged the British public's already low morale at that time. Another possibility is that the rumour related to a friendly fire incident and it is well known there were a number of these during the war, including one that involved a group of barges that resulted in numerous casualties suffering burns. It is also possible that the rumour was started as 'black propaganda' to deter the Germans from invading the vulnerable British coastline. Tests were conducted in 1940 on the use of fire at sea and although these were mainly considered to be a failure, the myth of their destructive power was allegedly leaked by the Directorate of Military Intelligence in July 1940 and then again in August 1940. There were also other tests that were undertaken in the Suffolk coastal region during the Second World War, such as a Canadian Pipe mine tested in June 1941 near Westleton, not far from Shingle Street.

For clarification, the location of this book is based on the small hamlet of Bawdsey and in particular Bawdsey Manor, which had an important and well documented role during the Second World War that included radar development. The Bawdsey Radar Facebook group posted that on 6 May 1941, three members of personnel were killed at Bawdsey from an attack by German bombers. Amongst those who were killed was a member of the Royal Canadian Air Force.

About The Author

J. D.Missen was born and raised in a small seaside town in Suffolk - the type of place that is overrun with tourists in the summer months and in the winter, an anticipatory quiet descends. She still lives in the town, with her two children and several rescued pets.

Julie was first inspired to write after studying First World War poetry at school and has had poems published in several anthologies as well as publishing her own poetry book 'Love, Death and Madness'. This passion for writing also developed into writing fiction and she quickly settled into the crime fiction and psychological thriller genres though she also has an interest in history, particularly modern and local history. J.D.Missen published her debut novel 'Confessions from a Fractured Mind' in 2024, along with the Detective Inspector Morgan Mystery's 'Secrets From A Misty River' and 'The Evil Within Us All'. She has also written two children's books; 'The Little Mole' and 'The Little Spider'.